Sigrid Undset

THE SNAKE PIT

Sigrid Undset was born to Norwegian parents in Denmark in 1882. Between 1920 and 1922, she published her magnificent and widely acclaimed trilogy of fourteenth-century Norway, *Kristin Lavransdatter* (composed of *The Bridal Wreath*, *The Mistress of Husaby*, and *The Cross*). And between 1925 and 1927, she published the four volumes of *The Master of Hestviken* (composed of *The Axe*, *The Snake Pit*, *In the Wilderness*, and *The Son Avenger*). Ms. Undset, the author of numerous other novels, essays, short stories, and tales for young readers, was awarded the Nobel Prize for Literature in 1928. During the Second World War, she worked with the Norwegian underground before having to flee to Sweden and then to the United States. After the war, she returned to Norway, where she died in 1949.

ALSO BY Sigrid Undset

Kristin Lavransdatter

The Bridal Wreath (VOLUME I)
The Mistress of Husaby (VOLUME II)
The Cross (VOLUME III)

The Master of Hestviken

The Axe (VOLUME I)
The Snake Pit (VOLUME II)
In the Wilderness (VOLUME III)
The Son Avenger (VOLUME IV)

THE SNAKE PIT

THE SNAKE PIT

THE SNAKE PIT

THE MASTER OF HESTVIKEN, VOLUME II

SIGRID UNDSET

VINTAGE BOOKS

A DIVISION OF RANDOM HOUSE, INC.

NEW YORK

VINTAGE BOOKS EDITION

Copyright © 1929 by Alfred A. Knopf, Inc.
Renewal Copyright 1957 by Alfred A. Knopf, Inc.

Translated from the Norwegian by Arthur G. Chater

Library of Congress Cataloging-in-Publication Data
Undset, Sigrid, 1982 – 1949.
[Olav Audunssøn i Hestviken. I. English]
The snake pit / Sigrid Undset.
p. cm. — (The master of Hestviken / Sigrid Undset ; v. 2)
Originally published in Norwegian as part 2 of Olav Audunssøn i
Hestviken (2 v.).

ISBN-10: 0-679-75554-3

ISBN-13: 978-0-679-75554-8

1. Norway—History—1030 –1397—Fiction.
2. Middle Ages—History—Fiction.
I. Title. II. Series: Undset, Sigrid, 1882 – 1949.
Master of Hestviken ; v. 2.
PT8950.U5061613   1994
839.8'2372—dc20   94-16660
CIP

Manufactured in the United States of America

150120837

THE SNAKE PIT

ESTVIKEN had been a seat of chieftains in old time. Traces of many great boat-sheds could still be seen by the water-side, and rotting logs strewed the slope over which the Hestvik men had drawn their longships in spring and autumn. They showed like the remains of an old roller-way, reaching from high-water mark up to the little plain between the crags.

Then Christian faith and morals came to Norway; Saint Olav forbade his subjects to go a-viking. Men were to believe, whether they liked it or no, that God will not suffer a man to rob his even Christian, even though he be of strange race. The Hestvik men sailed on merchant voyages, and from of old shipbuilding had been carried on at Hestviken. Even Olav Ribbung, while he was in his best years, kept a shipwright at his manor, and when, after the Birchlegs [1] had burned Hestviken, he rebuilt both the manor farm on the high ground and the houses by the shore, he set up the boat-house and the two sheds and the workshop as they stood to this day down by the hithe.

A couple of hours' rowing southward from the Thingstead, Haugsvik, brings one to a lofty crag; this great dull-red rock, which falls abruptly to the fiord and is bare of trees to near its summit, is called the Bull. Behind the point Hestviken runs up into the land; it is a small and rather narrow creek. On its northern side the Bull Crag falls sheer into the sea, and below it is deep, dark water. Upon the neck of the Bull grow sparse and wind-bent firs, but they thicken farther up the height—the promontory is like a foot thrust out into the sea from the low ridge, which extends on the whole northern side of the inlet and of Hestviksdal or Kverndal, as it is also called,[2] eastward into the heart of the dis-

[1] The Birchlegs (see note to *The Axe*, p. 4) were the adherents of the pretender Sverre, who became King of Norway in 1184. The Ribbungs were a remnant of the Church party, opposed to Sverre and the Birchlegs.
[2] Kverndal: Mill-dale.

trict. Inland along the valley the ridge falls steeply to the water-course—a little stream runs through Kverndal and comes out into the sea at the head of the creek. Here trees and grass and flowers grow luxuriantly among cliffs and screes, and the ridge itself is thickly wooded with spruce; but as it descends to the level ground this passes into foliage, with many oaks even, belonging to Hest-viken.

On the south side of the creek the rocks are rounded off into the fiord, much lower and less steep; juniper bushes combed flat by the wind and thickets of brier grow in the crevices of the rock, and here and there are short stretches of dry turf. But then the hill rises in a sheer cliff, dark grey and almost bare, facing north; and underneath this crag, which is called the Horse,[3] lies the manor, fairly high up and turned toward the north. The path from the hithe up to the houses runs along the edge of the manor fields on the fiord side and is fairly steep. Farther inland there is deep and good soil on the slopes, and fields and meadows suffer less from drought than in most other places on the Oslo Fiord, as many runnels trickle down from the Horse Crag, and higher up, the valley is somewhat moist. But almost all the plough-land of Hestviken lies on the south side of the valley and faces north.

The manor farm of Hestviken was built so that the houses stood in two rows enclosing a long and narrow courtyard, in which the bare rock cropped out everywhere like a ridge through the midst of it. Between this rock and the Horse Crag there was a hollow, marshy from the water trickling down the cliff, and the buildings on that side of the courtyard had therefore sunk and become damp; the logs of the lowest courses on the side facing the rock had rotted, so that the houses were draughty and the damp came in both above and below, but in summer nettles and weeds grew in the hollow, almost to the height of the turf roof. It was the stables, byres, and a few sheds that stood here.

Toward the sea, on the north side of the courtyard, lay the dwelling-houses, the cook-house, and the storehouses. Looking up the fiord the view was shut in by the Bull; but from the western end of the courtyard one could look across the creek to Hudr-heimsland and southward a great way down Folden.[4] And in

[3] *Hesten. Hestviken* may be translated "Horse-wick."
[4] The Oslo Fiord.

former days the lords of Hestviken, when there was war in the land, had been wont to keep a watch on the hill above the Bull; the turf hut was still there in which the watchmen had lived when they relieved one another on the lookout.

At the end of the courtyard, toward the meadows and Kverndal and a good way from the other houses, stood the barn, all that was left of the old manor. It was immense and strongly built, of heavy timber. The other houses were small and without embellishment, of somewhat light logs bonded together. It had been no easy matter for Olav Ribbung to rebuild his manor after the fire—his losses had been great, as his warehouses were crammed full of goods at the time of the burning, and in those days it was often difficult for landlords to get in what their tenants owed them. But it was the tradition of the neighbourhood that the old houses at Hestviken had been large and splendid. There had been a hall, built of upright staves with a shingle roof like a church; two rows of carven pillars supported the roof internally, and the hall was richly decorated besides with wood-carving and painting. And for high festivals they had blue hangings and a tapestry that was spread under the roof; it was of red woollen stuff embroidered with fair images. Of this tapestry two pieces still remained—one that had been given to the church and one that was in the manor; this latter piece was so long that it stretched over both sides and the end wall of the new living-room, and yet a part of the tapestry was said to be lost—so one could imagine the difference in size between the old hall and Olav Ribbung's house. Apart from this no more was left of the old glories than a carven plank, which people said one of Olav's house-carls had torn out to defend himself with as he ran from the burning hall. In the new house this plank was one of the doorposts of the bedchamber.

Olav Audunsson knew it again the moment he stepped into his own house, which he had not seen since he was a child of seven years. Never had he thought of this carving or known that he remembered it—but the moment his eye fell upon it, recognition came like a gust of wind that passes over the surface of a lake and darkens it: 'twas the doorpost of his childhood. The image of a man was carven upon it surrounded by snakes; they filled the whole surface with their windings and twistings, coiling about the man's limbs and body, while one bit him to the heart. A harp lay trampled under his feet—it was surely Gunnar Gjukesson in the snake pit.[5]

This doorpost was the only ornament of the hall, which was otherwise no different from the hearth-room of an ordinary farmstead; an oblong rectangular house, divided off by a wooden partition near the east end, so as to make two little rooms beyond the hall: the bed-closet at the far end and an antechamber by the door leading to the courtyard; for safety's sake the entrance was placed as far as possible from the sea. At the other end, farthest from the door, were two box-beds with a raised floor between them, and along both side-walls ran benches packed with earth. Of movable furniture there was none but a few three-legged stools—not so much as a side-table by the antechamber door or a backed chair or settle. The top of a long table hung on the north wall, but it could not have been taken down and used many times since Olav Ribbung's death.

The bed within the closet was intended for the master and mistress. But Olav Audunsson bade his old kinsman Olav Ingolfsson use this resting-place in which he had slept hitherto; he himself would take the bed on the south of the hall, where he had slept as a child.

He had no desire to move into the bed-closet. At the sight of the doorway leading to the pitch-dark room, ghosts of his childish loathing of this black hole arose within him. There his great-grandfather had slept, with his mad son, and when the fit came upon Foulbeard, they bound him and he lay roaring and howling and tossing in his bonds on the floor in the darkness. The child had been—not so badly frightened; in any case it was a kind of calm and composed horror, for he had been a witness of Foulbeard's attacks as far back as he could remember, and the madman had never harmed anyone; that he might do some hurt upon himself was all they had to fear. But of his own free will the boy never went near the closet—and indeed there was always a terrible stench within; a breath of pestilential air met him whenever he approached the doorway. His father and Aasa, the old serving-woman, did their best to clean up the madman's lodging, but it

---

[5] This is Gunnar of the *Völsunga Saga*, the husband of Brynhild. Gunnar was thrown into the snake pit by Atle (Attila); his sister Gudrun, Sigurd's widow and Atle's wife, secretly sent him a harp, and by his playing he charmed all the snakes save one, which bit him to the heart.

was difficult, so dark was it within. They changed the straw of the bed when they could come at it and strewed fresh mould on the floor so often that from time to time old Olav had to have it dug and carried out again, as the floor of the closet grew into hills and mountains. But all this availed but little.

And now Olav Audunsson remembered them so vividly—the two old men who used to appear at the door of the closet. When the madman had had a fit and struggled till he was faint and calm again, his father led him outside to sun him if the weather suited.

First the great-grandfather entered—a giant in stature, with long thick hair and a beard that fell over his chest; there was still as much black as white in it. He helped his son out, putting an arm about his neck and bending him, lest he should strike his face against the frame of the door. The madman had not the wit to turn aside from anything, but went straight on.

Torgils Foulbeard seemed a small man, for he was shrunken and bent. His whole head was overgrown with hair; the beard reached up to the eyes. All this tangle of his was matted with filth, grey and yellow of every dirty shade; from the midst of it shone the great eyes, pale greyish-green like sea-water, bloodshot in the whites, with an uncanny stare, and the nose small, straight and finely shaped, but red; it had been frostbitten one winter night when he had slipped out unknown to his father. But when old Olav had taken his son to the bath-house, cleansed him with lye and sand, and combed his hair, the whole shaggy head of Torgils shone silvery white and soft as a great tuft of bog-cotton. Torgils looked much older than his father.

Old Olav fed him as though he had been a child. Sometimes he had to shake and beat Torgils to make him open his mouth; at other times the trouble was that he would not shut it again, but let the food run out upon his beard. His father could get him to take meat and solid food by stuffing mouthfuls between Torgils's teeth and then thrusting his face close to his son's and chewing with empty jaws, up and down with all his force—then it might be that the madman mimicked him and chewed too.

Aasa sighed when she saw it. It was her charge to be like a foster-mother to young Olav, and he slept in her bed. But Aasa was more minded to herd Foulbeard and tend him, she as well as the great-grandfather. Koll, the old house-carl, was the only one who had care of the boy Olav.—Other than these four had not been dwelling at the manor, that Olav could remember. There were some who came and worked on the farm and down by the waterside.—Like enough the decline of Hestviken had already begun in those years. And after Olav Ingolfsson took over the conduct of the place, it had gone steadily downhill.

Now, farming had never been the main thing at Hestiviken; but neither Olav Ribbung in the last years of his life, nor Olav Ingolfsson had made such use of the sea as had been the custom here from old time. Then it came about that the rightful owner was outlawed, and the larger craft that still belonged to the place were seized by the King's officers. Olav Ingolfsson had never succeeded in providing new boats, nor yet in restoring the herds of cattle and making good the number of horses.

Olav guessed that the heritage that had fallen to him on the death of his father, Audun Ingolfsson, was so great that he would have been a very rich man at that time; but he himself had not known this and Steinfinn had never made any inquiries on his behalf. And even before his outlawry the estate had greatly shrunk. Now he owned no more than his ancestral manor and some farm-lands in the surrounding district, with others over in Hudrheim, across the fiord. He had sold the udal estate in Elvesyssel that had come to him from his grandmother, when he had to make atonement and pay weregild for the slaying of Einar Kolbeinsson; but there was still so much money owing to him by the monks of Dragsmark, who had bought most of the land, that he could again fit out ships and resume the trading by water.

And at that time there were not so many franklins in the country round the Oslo Fiord who possessed their udal estates whole and undivided. A great part of their property had come into the hands of the great landlords, or into those of the King or the Church. So Olav Audunsson of Hestviken might nevertheless be reckoned a man of substance and leading in his native district—and as such he was honoured as was meet, when at last he returned to his ancestral home.

Folk judged that he had shown himself generous when he took over his property from the aged man who had been his guardian and had acquitted himself so ill of his trust. But none had heard Olav complain of this, and he showed his namesake filial respect. And when certain men tried to find out what Olav himself thought, and asked how he had found his affairs situated, Olav replied very soberly: "Not well." But it could not have turned out otherwise—with the doom that had fallen on himself—and even before that the work of this place must have been more than Olav Ingolfsson could accomplish, crippled as he was. One of Olav Half-priest's legs had been broken, so that it was quite stiff and the foot was turned outward; he was very lame and could not move without a staff, and his stiff and straddling leg made it difficult for him to sit a horse or travel in a boat.

Olav Ingolfsson was a good deal more than threescore winters and he looked older yet—he seemed old as the hills. He was tall and thin and bent; his face was narrow and well-featured, with a fine curved nose—the younger Olav had a feeling that his namesake was not unlike his own father, so far as he remembered him. But Olav Ingolfsson was bald as a stone, with red and bleary eyes; the skin hung in shrivelled puckers under his eyes, on his shrunken cheeks, and below his chin. To cure the pain in his lame leg he used dogskin and catskin and many kinds of unguents. Whether from this or other causes, there was always a peculiar smell about the old man—as of mice—and the closet where he slept smelt of mice.

He was a son of Olav Ribbung's twin brother, Ingolf Alavsson, priest of St. Halvard's Church at Oslo. When the order came that the priests of Norway were to live in celibacy, Ingolf Priest sent his wife home to Tveit, the estate in Soleyar which she had brought him as her dowry; and all the children followed their mother, save the youngest son, Olav; he was himself set apart for the priesthood and newly ordained deacon when the accident befell him that made him a cripple. But he had lived in chastity all his days, and folk thought he had such great insight into many things that some held him to be more learned and pious than their parish priest. It was above all when folk were troubled by the walking dead and by goblins on sea and land, or when they had some sickness that was thought to be the work of witchcraft or evil spirits, that they sought counsel of Olav Half-priest, for he had more understanding of such things than all men else.

Olav Audunsson took to his namesake at once—in the first place because he was his nearest kinsman and the first man of his father's race whom he had met. It was strange to be here and to know that this was his ancestral manor and these surroundings his native soil; here he was destined to live the rest of his life—and he would have grown up here, but that his lot had been so markedly unlike that of other young men. But fate had cast him far from his home while he was yet a child, and since then he had been homeless and rootless as a log adrift in the sea.

Now he had come back to the place from which he had sprung. In a way he felt at home with many things, both indoors and out; but for all that it was very different from what he seemed to remember. The mill in Hestvikdal was familiar, but all that lay on the other side of the creek—the Bull, the wooded ridge—was as though he had never seen it, nor could he remember the marshy valley along the stream, a waste full of foliage trees. He could never have known what the country was like to the north of the creek—perhaps he had believed it settled and tilled like the shores of Lake Mjösen. But from Hestviken not a single human dwelling was to be seen.

The houses of the manor he remembered much bigger than they were. And the little strip of beach hemmed in by rocks, which had seemed to him a whole stretch of country with many distinctive marks—a great bluish rock on which he used to lie, some bushes in which he could hide—now he saw that the little strip of sand was scarcely fifty of a grown man's paces in length. He looked in vain for a hollow in the meadow above the manor, where he had been wont to sit and sun himself—it might have been a little pit east of the barn, which was now overgrown with osiers and alders. In a crack of the rock in the courtyard he had once found a curious snow-white ring—it must have been a vertebra of some bird or fish, from which the points were broken off, he now thought. But at that time he had taken it for a rare treasure, had preserved it carefully and often searched in the crevices of the rock to see if he could find others like it. It was almost like remembering old dreams—the scenes of the past floated before him in fragments—and at times he recalled a forgotten feeling of eeriness, as though after bad dreams he remembered no more than the dread.

So he snatched at everything that might help him to overcome this sense of insecurity, of dreams and shadows, and make him feel that Hestviken was his, and that when he walked over the fields here he had his own ancestral soil under his feet—the Bull, the woods and hills on both sides of the valley, all was *his* land.

And he was glad to think that now he was dwelling under the same roof as a kinsman, his own grandfather's cousin, who had known all the men and women of his race since the days of his great-grandfather's, Olav Ribbung's manhood. When he sat in the evening drinking with his namesake and the old man told him of their bygone kinsmen, Olav had a sense of fellowship with his father's stock which he had never known when he was in Denmark among his mother's kindred.

And he was drawn to the old man by the belief that Olav Priest's son was so pious and learned. During these weeks, while he was awaiting the time when he could go northward and fetch Ingunn, he felt in a way as though he were settling his account with God.

He himself was fully aware that it would not be easy for him to show perfect serenity and a glad countenance when he came to Berg to conclude the atonement with Haftor and receive Ingunn as his wife at the hands of the Steinfinnssons. But it could not be otherwise—and to get her was what he himself wished, in spite of all—and so he would surely be man enough to put a good face on it. But he could not defend himself against the insistence of childish memories—the certain knowledge that they belonged to each other and should always be together. That anything could come between them had been so far from their thoughts that it had never moved their hearts to either joy or wonder—they had taken it for granted that it should be as it had been determined for them. Until that summer when, locked in an embrace, they had fallen out of childhood and innocence, frightened, but at the same time giddy with rapture at the new sweetness they had found in each other—whether it were right or wrong that they abandoned themselves to it. Even when he awoke to a fear and defiance of all who would meddle with their destiny, he had been full sure that at last they two would win their cause. These memories would come suddenly upon Olav, and the pain of them was like the stab of a knife. That dream was now to take its course—but not the course he had imagined. And remembering himself as he was then was like remembering some other man he had known—a boy of such infinite simplicity that he both pitied and despised him, and envied him excruciatingly—a child he had been, with no suspicion of deceit, either in himself or in others. But he knew that for this anguish of the soul there was but one remedy—

he would have to hide his wound so that no one, she least of all, might see that he bore a secret hurt.

These thoughts might assail him while he sat conversing with the other Olav, and he would break off in the midst of his talk. The old man scarcely noticed it, but talked on and on, and the young man stared before him with a face hard and close—till old Olav asked him some question, and young Olav became aware that he had not heard a word of what the other had been saying.

But he made ready to shoulder the burden he had to bear—without wincing, should it be God's will to chasten him sorely in the coming years. For in a way the memory of that ski journey he had made with another and of the night at the sæter was ever present to him—except that he did not seem to see *himself* as the murderer. Rather was it as though he had witnessed a settling of scores between two strangers. But it *was* he, he knew that in a strange, indifferent way, and the sin was *his* sin. The slaying in itself could hardly be any mortal sin: he had not enticed the other into an ambush, the lad himself had planned this journey, and he had fallen sword in hand—and even a thrall had had the right to avenge his wife's honour in old days, he had heard; 'twas a man's right and duty by the law of God and men.

It was what came after—

And he had a feeling that he was offering God a makeshift in squaring his shoulders and making ready to bear the burden of Ingunn's misfortune. Never would he let anyone see it if it became too heavy. And he would live piously and in the fear of God from now on—so far as that was in the power of a man who had an unshriven sin on his conscience. He would act justly by his neighbour, be charitable to the poor, protect the forlorn and defenceless, honour the house of God and his parish priest and render such payments as were due, say his daily prayers devoutly and with reflection and repeat the Miserere often, pondering the words well. He knew that he had received far too little instruction in the Christian faith during his youth; Brother Vegard had done his best, but he came to Frettastein only once or twice a year and stayed there but a week, and there was none else who so much as made inquiry whether the children said their prayers every day. And the good instruction he had received while with Bishop Torfinn had fared as in the parable—so many tares had been sown among the wheat during the years he spent abroad that the wheat, just as it was beginning to sprout, was choked by the weeds. For the first time something like remorse for the slaying of Einar Kolbeinsson dawned upon Olav Audunsson: he had regretted it because it was an ill reward to Bishop Torfinn for his kindness and because, as his affairs were then situated, it was the most unlucky chance that could befall him—ay, and then he knew that he *ought* to repent it, because it *was* sin, even if he could not see why it was so sinful. Now he began to divine that a deeper meaning and a deeper wisdom underlay our Lord's commandment "Thou shalt not kill" than merely that which he had been told—God desires not the death of any sinner. Behind the commandment lay also a care for the slayer—the slayer also exposed his soul to many kinds of evil powers, which now found occasion for sudden assaults.

Therefore it might well be of service to him to dwell with so pious a man as Olav Half-priest; his kinsman could surely afford him useful guidance in many things. Such as the penitential psalms —he had learned a number of them of Asbjörn All-fat and Arnvid in his days at Hamar, but now he had forgotten the most part.

Olav invited his neighbours to a home-coming feast and told them that the wife he was to bring home was the daughter of Steinfinn Toresson, his foster-sister, to whom he had been betrothed when both were of tender age. So soon as he had looked about him at home and seen how his affairs stood he would ride back to the Upplands and fetch his wife. But as to the wedding he said not a word, whether it had already been drunk or was still to come; nor did he ask any of his neighbours to accompany him, though it was impossible for his kinsman to make the journey. Folk were quick to remark that the young Master of Hestviken was one who kept his own counsel and knew full well how far he would give an account of himself—not much was to be got out of him by asking questions.

Olav had thought long and deeply whether he should mention that there was a child. Perhaps it might make the matter easier if he spoke of this beforehand. But he could not bring himself to it. And then he thought that after all it might be dead. It had been born quick—but death came easily to young children, he had heard it said. Or they might hit upon some means—put it out to foster-parents on the way, perhaps. That Ingunn should give him

13

out as the child's father, as he had told her in his first bewilderment and desperation, he now saw to be madness. He could not
understand how he had come to conceive such a thought—bringing a bastard into the race. Had it but been a daughter, they could
have put her in a convent, and no man would have suffered any
great wrong by his letting her pass as his; but Ingunn had had a
man-child— Oh, he had been witless at the time, from grief and
anger. But he felt bound to accept the child, if the mother wished
to have it with her. It must now fall out as fate would have it;
useless to take up an evil before it was there.

Nevertheless he crept one day up to the little room that was
above the closet and the anteroom. The thought occurred to him
that the child and its foster-mother might live there, if Ingunn
wished to have her son in the house. Olav Ribbung's daughters
had slept in this loft with their serving-maids; but it was an age
since the young women had lodged there. The dust and cobwebs
of at least twenty years had collected there undisturbed, and the
mice scrambled out of the bedstead when he went to see what
might be stowed away there. Some old looms stood against the
wall, and trestles for a table, and then there was a chest, carven
with armorial bearings, which showed him that it had been his
mother's. He unlocked it: within lay spindles, spools, and combs
and a little casket. In the casket was a book and a child's swathe of
white linen—a christening-robe, Olav guessed, no doubt the same
that had been wrapped round him when he was lifted out of the
baptismal font. He lingered, sitting on his haunches and twisting
its embroidered border between two fingers.

He took the book down with him and showed it to Olav Half-
priest. But although the old man had always let it be thought that
he could read and write as well as any priest—and much better
than Sira Benedikt, their parish priest—there was in any case not
much that he could make out of Cecilia Björnsdatter's psalter.
In the evening Olav sat and looked at it: little images were drawn
within the capital letters, and the margins were adorned with
twining foliage in red and green. When he went to bed he buried
the book under the pillow, and there he let it lie.

A few days before he was to set out for the north there came
a poor woman to Hestviken who wished to speak with the master.
Olav went out to her. She bore an empty wallet on her shoulder,

so he guessed her errand. But first she greeted Olav with tears in her voice—tears of joy, she said; 'twas such a glad thing to see the rightful master stand at his own door at last, "and a fair and lordly man have you grown, Olav Audunsson—ay, Cecilia ought to have seen her son now—and they speak well of you among the neighbours, Olav. So methought I must come hither and see you—and I was among the first who saw you in this world, for I served at Skildbreid at that time and I was with Margret, my mistress, when she came to help your mother—I gave her a hand when she swathed you—"

"Then you knew my mother?" asked Olav when the woman had to pause for want of breath.

"You know, we saw her at church sometimes, when first Audun had brought her hither. But that winter she grew so sickly that she never went abroad—'twas too cold, the house she lived in, her handmaid said, and at last she had to move into the great room, where the old men were, for the sake of the warmth. It was right ill with Torgils that winter and spring. I mind me he raved most foully the night you were born, and the fit was upon him a whole week—Cecilia was in such fear of him, she lay trembling in her bed, and Audun himself could not comfort her. 'Twas that, I ween, that broke her, that and the cold. Audun carried her up to the loft-room when the weather was warmer; he saw she was not fit to dwell in the house with the madman—but she died straight. You must have been a month old then—"

The woman's name was Gudrid, she told him, and she lived in the cot that maybe Olav had seen when he rode east to the church town—to the north of the bogs, just before the road turns off toward Rynjul. In her first marriage she had had a little farm in the Saana district—with a good and worthy husband, but she had had no child by him. Then he died, and his brother moved to the farm with his wife; and as she could not be agreed with them, she married this Björn, with whom she was now. This was the most foolish counsel she could have taken. Nay, he was no poor man at that time; when they put together their goods, they might have had an easy lot. He was a widower and had only one daughter, and so they deemed that all might turn out well: she was minded to take a husband again, and she greatly desired to have children. And that wish alone was granted, of all she had looked for—eight children, and five of them lived. But the very first winter they were married Björn chanced to slay a man and had to pay fines, and there was soon an end of their prosperity. Now Björn was mostly out in the fiord, hunting seal and porpoise and sea-fowl, or fishing for Tore of Hvitastein—and she herself sat in the cot with all her little children and the stepdaughter, who was shrewish and ungodly—

Olav listened patiently to the woman's torrent of words, and at last he bade her follow him to the storehouse. He had laid in all that was needed for his home-coming feast, and he filled Gudrid's sack abundantly—"and if you are in straits this winter, you must come hither and tell us, foster-mother!"

"God bless you, Olav Audunsson—but you are like your mother when you smile! She had so gentle a smile, Cecilia, and she was always good to poor folk—"

At long last the old wife departed.

There was no one in the hall when Olav entered. And he stood awhile musing. With one foot on the edge of the hearth, and his hands clasped about his knee, he stared into the little heap of burned wood in which there was still a gleam—it hissed and crackled with crisp little sounds, and a faint breath came from the dying embers.

"Mother," he thought, and recalled the little he had heard of her. She had been young—and fair, they said; she had been reared as became one of noble birth in the rich nunnery, where she was the playmate of a King's daughter. And from the Queen's court she had been removed to this lonely manor, far from all she knew. In these poor and rustic rooms she had borne him under her heart, starved with the cold and left alone with two aged men—the madman, of whom she was afraid, and the master himself, who misliked his grandson's marriage.—It was hateful.

He smote his thigh hard with the palm of his hand. Intolerable it must be to be born a woman, to have so little say in one's own destiny. He seemed to pity *all* women—his own mother in silk and fine linen, this beggar woman Gudrid, Ingunn—it availed one as little as the other to meet force by force. Ingunn—a wave of desire and longing rose within him—he thought of her slender white neck: poor thing, she had learned perforce to bend her proud young head. First for his sake; and now she had been brought full low. But he would take her head upon his breast, softly and tenderly he would caress that poor, weak neck. *Never* should she hear a word from him of her misfortune; never should she see a sign, in word or in deed, that he bore her resentment.—At that moment he did not feel that there was any resentment in his soul toward the defenceless creature who would soon be in his power —his only wish was to protect her and do well by her.

Later in the day Olav saddled his horse and rode eastward to the church town. He was not sure what he wanted there, but his mind was in a turmoil that day. And when he came there, he tied his horse to the fence and walked across the graveyard up to the church.

He laid his sword and hat on the bench that ran along the wall, but chanced to sweep them to the floor with the skirt of his mantle. The echo within the stone walls made him ill at ease. And the light was unpleasantly pale and strange, for the walls had just been whitewashed—pictures were to be painted on them this summer.

Audun and Cecilia lay at the top of the nave on the left, between the Lady chapel and the apse. As Olav knelt by their tomb and said his prayers as softly as he could, his eye was caught by an image that the master painter had newly finished on the pier of the chancel arch. It was of a tall, slender, and graceful woman with bandaged eyes and a broken reed in her hand—her mien and bearing, nay, the very colour of her dark garment, were also unspeakably mournful. Olav had often seen this image in the churches, but had never remembered to ask what was its significance. But never had the woman looked so melancholy or so beautiful as here.

Bishop Torfinn's words about the motherless children suddenly occurred to his mind. For the first time he thought he was almost glad he had not required of Ingunn that she should part with her child. At that moment he felt able to think of this infant with a kind of compassion. Since she had borne it, he must find means to rear it.

When he came out of the church, he saw that the priest, Sira Benedikt Bessesson, was standing by his horse. Olav greeted him courteously, and the priest returned his greeting blithely. From the little he had seen of his parish priest Olav liked him uncommonly well. The priest had a fine and dignified presence—thickset, broad-shouldered, and well-knit. His face was wreathed about with reddish-brown hair and beard, and it was a broad face, but shapeful, with bold features, much freckled; he had large, clear eyes, sparkling with life. Olav judged him to be a pious, discerning man of cheerful disposition—and he liked the priest for having a strong, fine, and flexible voice, whether in speech or song.

At first they talked of the gelding. Olav had got him in Skaane —he was seven years old, big and strong-legged and handsome, white and dapple-grey over the quarters. He always groomed and curry-combed the horse himself, making him smooth and glossy, for he was very fond of the animal and he liked to hear that the priest could see what he was worth. Then Sira Benedikt closely examined the bridle, which was of red leather. Olav concealed a smile—the priest practised much tanning and dyeing of leather, and such work was his joy and delight. This was one of the faults Olav Half-priest had to find with Sira Benedikt—he thought this work altogether unseemly for a priest, since it made him soil his consecrated hands with the worst impurities. To this Sira Benedikt replied that he did not believe such impurities to be unseemly in God's eyes, since the priest's hands were as clean as before, when he had washed them. Our Lord Himself had done in like manner and honoured the work thereby, when He took axe and chisel in the same blessed hands that created and redeemed mankind, and wrought the logs in the workshop of his holy fosterfather—He surely would not deem His poor servant disgraced by following a noble and ingenious craft.

The priest invited Olav to accompany him home, and Olav accepted with thanks. Another thing at which Olav Ingolfsson turned up his nose was the smell in the priest's yard, like that of the dyers' booths in the town. But the house was clean and fair within; his living-room was far finer than that of Hestviken. Three well-favoured young maidens brought in butter, white bread, and ale, greeted the guest with comely grace and went straight out again. They were daughters of the priest's nephew; the eldest undertook the duties of his household, and at this time she had her sisters on a visit.

The ale was excellent, and the men sat a good while talking of this and that. Olav like Sira Benedikt better and better. Then their talk fell upon Olav Ingolfsson, and the priest praised the young man for having shown such loving-kindness toward one

who had misgoverned his affairs so ill. Olav answered that it was
his own outlawry that was chiefly to blame for the neglected
state of Hestviken; the old man had doubtless done his best, seeing
that he was a cripple and ailing. But indeed he held old Olav to be
a remarkably wise and holy man.

"That addle-pate?" said the priest.

Olav said nothing.

The priest went on: "Holiness, I trow, he had good cause to
seek—to judge by the fellows he resorted to in his youth, his holiness cannot have been much to boast of. And were he wise, he
would think and speak more of Christ and Mary Virgin, and less
of witchcraft and spectres and mermen and water-wraiths—would
pray, rather than practise these sorceries and incantations of his—I
marvel whether much of what he deals with be not downright
heresy. But he came out of school a half-taught priestling—and
the half he had learned was learned wrong. It may be diverting to
listen to his tales some evening or other—but you seem to be a
man of sense, Olav Audunsson, you surely do not believe all his
preaching—?"

Ah, thought Olav, now he knew it. And in fact he thought he
had already suspected how it was. Aloud he said with something
like a smile:

"There would seem to be no very warm friendship between
you and my kinsman?"

The priest replied: "I have never liked him—but that is not
merely because he was foster-brother of him who wronged me
and mine most grievously. And none of us bore hatred to the
other men of Hestviken—they were brave and honourable, all but
he. You may see that yourself, Olav—I have liked you since I saw
you for the first time, and I was minded that you should see I wish
you well, and I think myself that the old enmity between us of
Eiken and you of Hestviken should now be buried and forgotten.
Not that we ever counted Olav Ribbung and his other sons our
enemies—but we kept out of each other's way as much as we
could, as you may well suppose."

Olav busied himself with wiping off some ale he had spilt on
his jerkin; he did not look up as he asked:

"I know not what you mean, Sira Benedikt. I am but newly
come home and am strange to these parts—I have never heard
aught of this enmity between your kindred and mine."

Sira Benedikt seemed greatly surprised, and a little embarrassed as well. "I thought surely Olav Half-priest had spoken to you of this?"

Olav shook his head.

"Then 'tis better I tell you myself." The priest sat in thought awhile, jogging the little dipper that floated in the ale-bowl and making it sail round.

"Did you look at those fair children of mine, the little maids that came in here, Olav?"

"Indeed they were fair. And were it not that I have a young bride waiting for me in the Upplands, I had used my eyes better while your kinswomen were here, Sira!" said Olav with a little smile.

"If I guess your meaning aright," replied the priest, and he too smiled, but with a troubled look, "you cannot be aware that they are your own kinswomen, and near of kin too?"

Olav turned his eyes upon the priest and waited.

"You are second cousins. Torgils Foulbeard was the father of their father. He ruined my sister—"

Involuntarily Olav's face was convulsed with horror. Sira Benedikt saw it, guessed the young man's thought, and said:

"Nay, 'twas before God took his wits from Torgils, or the Evil One, whom he had followed so faithfully, while sin and lust tempted him. Ay, God knows I am not an impartial man when I speak of Olav Half-priest; he and Torgils were foster-brothers, and Olav backed the other through thick and thin. Olav Ribbung would compel Torgils to marry Astrid; he was an honourable, resolute, and loyal man—and when Torgils left her to her shame with his bastard son, while he himself kept to his leman in Oslo and would marry her, Olav Ribbung commanded his son to come hither. Ingolf, your grandfather, and Olav's daughters, and Ivar Staal, his son-in-law, all said they would not sit at meat with Torgils nor speak to him while he held fast to his purpose. But Torgils was living with the priest, the father of Olav Ingolfsson— the more shame to them that they received him; one was a priest and the other was to be one.

"Ay, and the end was that my father and brothers accepted fines and made atonement with the Hestvik men when we saw that neither Olav Ribbung nor Ingolf could do aught to shake Torgils or force him to make amends for Astrid's misfortune.

20

'Twas the better and more Christian way—that is true. But had I
been of an age to bear arms, I know full sure I would not have
rested till I had laid Torgils low—I had done it even if I had been
a priest, ordained to the service of God. I have hated that man so
that—God sees my heart, and He knows it. But He knows too, I
ween, that the hardest thing He can require of a man is that he
shall not avenge his kinswoman's honour with the sword.—I was
ten years old when it happened. Astrid had been to me as a
mother; she was the eldest of our family, and I was the youngest.
I shared a bed with her that summer: she wept and wept; I know
not how it was she did not weep herself to death. I tell you, Olav,
the man who can forgive such a thing from his heart, him I would
call a holy man."

The priest sat in silence. Olav, still as a rock, waited for him to
say more. But at last he thought he must say something.

"What became of her, your sister?" he asked in a low voice.
"Did she die?"

" 'Tis eight winters since she died," said the priest. "She lived
to be an old woman. She was married some years after, to Kaare
Jonsson of Roaldstad, north in Skeidis parish, and she had a good
life with him. Father was too hard on her and could not bear the
sight of her child; had it been another man's—but that a daughter
of his should swell the flock of Torgils's concubines— But Kaare
was good to them both; it was he too who brought about the good
marriage for his stepson, with the daughter and heir of Hestbæk.
And when disaster fell upon Olav of Hestviken and he began to
feel the lack of kinsmen, he sent word to Astrid—if she would let
him have the child, Arne, he would make the boy heir to his
father's name and goods. Kaare answered that the lad no longer
needed the support of his father's kindred, and both he and Astrid
loved Arne Torgilsson far too dearly to send him out to Hestviken
to inherit the fortunes of the Hestvik men. So Olav fetched home
Aasa, who had served there at one time, and the son that she had
had by Torgils; but he was not long in life—

"But these are all old matters, and I deem that we should now
forget our enmity and you young ones should claim kinship and
meet in charity. I believe that Arne of Hestbæk and you would
like each other. You must go thither with me one day, Olav, and
greet the kinsfolk you have in this part of the land."

Olav said he would do so more than gladly. But then he asked:

"That word you spoke of the Hestvik men's fortunes—what meant you by that?"

The priest looked as though the question troubled him.

"You know that your great-grandfather was not blest in his kindred. That was the time when he sat there in Hestviken with the madman—his other children he had lost, all but Borgny, who was in a convent, and he had no true-born heir to follow him other than the little lad Audun, your father—and him Ingolf's widow had taken with her, when she went home to the place she had come from, south in Elvesyssel. So it may well have seemed to Kaare and Astrid that the race would not prosper after him."

Olav said pensively: "'Tis true for all that, Sira Benedikt, favoured of fortune they were not, from all that my kinsman has told me of them."

"They were brave men and loyal, Olav, and that is worth more than good fortune."

"Not Torgils," said Olav. "I knew not this thing of him. I knew naught else but that he had been witless all his days—old Olav has never spoken his name."

"Bitterly as I have hated him," said Sira Benedikt, "I will yet tell you the truth of him—he was a brave man—and with men he kept faith. And all say that no goodlier youth has been seen within the memory of man in the country about Folden. Ay, 'tis strange I should have liked you so well, when first I saw you, for you bear great resemblance to Torgils. But then Arne too is like his father, and his daughters—methought perchance you had seen it, when all three came in—they might well be your sisters. You all have the same abrupt little noses and the white skin—and the same fair hair, pale as thistledown; nay, so handsome as he was you are not—though I hated him, I must say with the rest, a fairer man have I never seen. So there may well be truth in what they report of him, that he had no need to run after women or to allure them with wooing arts and false words. They followed him of themselves—as though bewitched if he did but fix those strange blue-green eyes of his upon them. Ay, you have the same light eyes, you too, Olav—"

Olav had to laugh at this—and he laughed on, trying to laugh off his sense of oppressive discomfort.

"Nay, Sira Benedikt—I cannot be very like my kinsman Torgils

—in the eyes at least. For *I* have never marked that I could charm women—"

"You are like him, Olav, though you be not so handsome—and you have the same light eyes, both you and these little maids of mine. But the evil power of bewitching folk dwells not in the eyes of any of you, God be praised. And this prating of misfortune that is thought to pursue certain houses and kindreds—it may have been so in heathen times, I am ready to believe that. But you are surely wise enough now to lay your life and destiny in the hands of God Almighty and not to believe such things.—God be gracious to you, my Olav—I wish you happiness and blessing in your marriage, and that your race may be called fortune's favourites from now on!"

The priest drank to him. Olav drank, but could not bring himself to say anything. But now Sira Benedikt fetched in the three daughters of Arne—Signe, Una, and Torgunn—and Olav greeted his kinswomen with kisses. They were so fair and debonair that Olav warmed little by little and stayed a good while in cheerful converse with them. To his home-coming feast at Hestviken they thought they could not come, for it would be just at the time when they were to go to a great wedding near their own home. But late in the autumn they would return to the priest's house and stay with him awhile, and then they promised to visit him and pay their respects to his wife.

Olav was profoundly troubled in his mind as he rode homeward. That he should have been impelled to visit the church today—and that he should have met Sira Benedikt and learned this of his grandfather's brother and the priest's sister, this seemed so singular to Olav that he could scarce believe it to be pure chance.

For though it was true that only the Bishop could give him absolution for the slaying of Teit, yet he could confess it to Sira Benedikt first. And with a sort of terror Olav felt how unspeakably he longed to do so.

He knew that if he knelt at Sira Benedikt's knee and laid it bare to him that he was a murderer, and how it had come about that he was one—then he would find himself in the presence of a servant of God who was not merely a spiritual father. Sira Benedikt would understand him as a father understands the son of his body.

He had loved Bishop Torfinn because that monk from Tautra had suffered him to approach a world of riches and beauty and wisdom, which before he had only known as something distant and strange. The Christian faith had been to him a power like the King and the law of the land—he knew that it was to govern his life, and he bowed to it, without reluctance, with reverence and with the recognition that a man must be loyal to all these things if he was to be able to meet his equals and look them freely in the face without shame. In Bishop Torfinn he had seen the man who could take him by the hand and lead him on to all that gave happiness and self-knowledge to serve and to love. What manner of man he would have been had it been his lot to follow the lord Torfinn for a longer space, he could not tell. To Olav the Bishop remained an advocate from the eternal heights—and he himself was as a child, who had only understood a little of that to which the other opened his eyes, before his own conduct forced him to fly from his good instructor.

Of Arnvid he was fond, but their tempers were so unlike that he had felt Arnvid's piety as merely a part of what he did not understand in his friend. Arnvid was reserved, Olav felt, though he was far from being a taciturn man—but Arnvid's loquacity seemed a part of his readiness to help. Time and again Olav remembered that it was always himself who had received and Arnvid who had given—but such a man was Arnvid Finnsson that Olav could not feel humiliated by it; he might have accepted even more of the other, and still they would have been close friends. Arnvid knew him through and through, thought Olav, and yet was fond of him —*he* did not know Arnvid, but yet was fond of him.

It had diverted him greatly to listen to Olav Half-priest's talk of spiritual things. But all that the old man talked of, angels and devils, pixies and sprites and fairies and holy men and women, seemed as it were to belong to another side of life than that in which he himself contended with his difficulties. The Lady Sancta Maria herself became almost as a king's daughter in a fairy tale, the fairest rose of paradise—but it seemed very far from his part of the world, this paradise, when old Olav talked of it.

Sira Benedikt was the first man he had met in whom he had recognized something of himself—a man who had fought the fight in which he himself was engaged. And Sira Benedikt had won, had become a God-fearing man, strong and steadfast in the faith.

24

And Olav felt longing and hope pulsing in his veins. All he needed was to take heart. Pray for strength, as Brother Vegard had said, without the reservation: O God, grant not my prayer too quickly.

He lay awake most of that night. It came over him that now he understood one thing: a conflict had been waged in the whole of creation since the dawn of the ages between God and His enemy, and all that had life, soul, or spirit took part in the fight in one host or the other, whether they knew it or not—angels and spirits, men here on earth and on the farther side of death. And it was most commonly by a man's own cowardice that the Devil could entice him into his service—because the man was afraid God might demand too much of him—command him to utter a truth that was hard to force through his lips, or to abandon a cherished delight without which he believed himself not strong enough to live: gain or welfare, wantonness or the respect of others. Then came the old Father of lies and caught that man's soul with his old master lie—that he demanded less of his servants and rewarded them better—so long as it lasted. But now Olav himself had to choose whether he would serve in one army or in the other.

It was thick weather, mild and grey, when he came out next morning. The mist shed tiny drops of water over him, which fell gratefully on his face and refreshed his lips after the sleepless night.

He went out on the high ground west of the manor, where the hill sloped in a rounded curve toward the open fiord, with stretches of bare rock and flowery crevices. It was already his habit to turn his steps thither every morning and to stand and watch the weather. He was beginning to be familiar with the voice of the fiord. Today the sea was calm. A light swell lapped the smooth sides of the Bull, breaking through the mist with little gleams of white, where the spray was thrown high into the air when the slightest breeze blew on the shore. There was a trickling of water among the rocks down on the beach, a lapping of the wreath of seaweed just beneath him, where the smooth rock slid down into the sea; a breath of good salt water came up to him.

Olav stood motionless, gazing out and listening to the faint sound of the fiord. Now and again the fog thickened so that he could scarcely see it.

He had seen long ago that he had committed a sinister folly in not proclaiming the slaying straightway at the first house he came to. Had he done *that*, 'twas not even certain that he would have been condemned to make amends—Teit's life might have been found forfeit, if Ingunn's kinsmen had been willing to witness that he, Olav, had an older right to the woman. He had now thought so long this way and that, that he scarce remembered what had been in his mind, when he chose to remain silent and wipe out all traces of the deed—but he must have fooled himself into the belief that so the shame might be kept hid. No man must learn that he had rid himself of Teit Hallsson, since thus he thought no man would learn that Ingunn had been disgraced by Teit. Now it seemed to him incomprehensible that he could have thought anything so totally fatuous.

But now he was caught in his own snares. Never would the Bishop give him absolution for a manslaughter on other terms than that he should publicly acknowledge the deed, that justice might be done. But now it had become a secret murder and dastard's work, and never could it be anything else.

Behind him he had his manor, his lands along Kverndal, the forest on the ridges north and south of Hestviken—his property extended far inland into the mist. The sheds, the quay, his boats he could glimpse down in the creek; the smell came up to him of nets and tar and fish offal and salt water and wood soaked by the sea. And far away in the north Ingunn waited; God knew how she fared now. To take her out of her misfortune, bring her hither to a place of refuge, that was the first duty that lay upon him.

No. The burden he had been mad enough to fasten upon himself he would have to bear henceforward. He could not lay it down now. Perchance he would have to drag it on till he saw the gates of death open before him. And he might die—a sudden death— But that too he must venture. His case was not such that he could turn about and retrace his steps to the point where he had gone astray. He could only go on.

It was with such thoughts that he journeyed northward. Arrived at Berg, he learned from the mouth of Arnvid that Ingunn had tried to slay herself. Six weeks later he came home to Hestviken for the second time, bringing his wife with him.

. . .

The sea lay glittering white in the sunshine beneath the burning hot cliff of the Bull when at noonday Olav led Ingunn ashore at the Hestvik hithe. It was the day after Lavransmass.[6]

The water gurgled under the boat's side and smacked against the piles of the quay; the air was heavy with smells—salt water, sweating tar, rotten bait, and fish offal, but now and again there was a breath of flowery scent, sweet and warm and fleeting—Olav caught it and wondered, for it was so familiar. Memories were called forth by it, but he knew not what it was that had this scent.—All at once Vikings' Bay and Hövdinggaard came vividly before him—that world which had wholly vanished from his memory since he fled from it to serve the Earl. At once he knew the smell—'twas lime trees. That fine moist breath as of honey and pollen and mead—there must be flowering lime trees somewhere in the neighbourhood.

The scent grew stronger as they walked up the slope. Olav could not understand it; he had never seen limes at Hestviken. But when he came up to the courtyard, he saw them growing on the steep cliff behind the cattle-sheds. They were firmly rooted in the crevices, clung flat against the face of the rock and let their branches sweep downward. The dark-green heart-shaped leaves lay one over another like the shingles on a church roof, covering the golden bunches of blossom—Olav could glimpse them underneath. They were fading and turning brown, and their scent was somewhat sickly and past, but there was a faint, soft buzz of bees and a swarm of flies about them.

"Nay, Olav, what is it that smells so sweet?" Ingunn asked in wonder.

"It is lime. You have never seen limes before, I ween—they grow not in the Upplands."

"Ay, but they do. I mind me now—there is a lime tree in the garden of the preaching friars at Hamar. But I cannot see the trees."

Olav pointed up at the cliff. "They are not like the trees that are planted on level ground, the limes that grow here."

He recalled the mighty lime that stood in the castle court at Hövdinggaard—its waxen, honey-dewed flowers hung in the midst of the foliage as though under a tent of leaves. When the lime flowered at Hövdinggaard he had always had a longing— and it

[6] St. Laurence's Day, August 10.

was not Frettastein or Heidmark or any of the places where his destiny had been set moving, but the half-forgotten home of his childhood that came to his mind. It must have been the scent of the lime blossom that he recognized—though he did not seem to have known that there were limes at Hestviken.

Toward sundown he wandered up Kverndal, to look at the cornfields on that side. The smell of lime blossom was so heavy and strong—Olav moved his feet languidly; the sweet fragrance seemed to weigh upon him. He felt quite weak with happiness. And now he saw that limes grew all over the ridge on the north side as well.

The sun had left the valley; the dew was falling as he turned homeward. He passed through an enclosure of alders and thought he remembered that there had been a meadow here, where they cut grass; but now it was overgrown with alders. There was a rustling and crashing of leaves and bushes as the cows burst their way through the thicket. They were strange beasts, the Hestvik cattle—long-haired, deep-bellied, with misshapen legs and curiously twisted horns, big heads and mournful eyes. Most of them had but three teats, or some other malformation of the udder. Olav patted their cheeks and spoke kindly to them as he passed through his herd of melancholy beasts.

Ingunn came out on the path behind the barn, tall and slender as a wand in her blue habit, with the linen coif waving about her. Quietly, as though hesitating, she advanced along the path by the edge of the field. Meadowsweet and setwall, which had almost shed its blossoms, reached to her waist and almost met around her. She had gone out to meet him.

When he came up to her he took her hand and led her as they walked homeward. Their guests were to come next day, but this night they two and the old man in the closet were the only ones in the house.

2

THE fine weather lasted over the late summer. In the middle of the day the bare rocks glowed with heat; the vapour rose from them, and the sea glittered and the spray dashed white beneath the crags, in the places where it was never at rest.

Olav was up early in the mornings, but he did not go out on the rocks now. He would stand leaning over the fence round the northernmost cornfield, where the path from the waterside came up. From there he could see down to the creek and up the valley, almost the whole of his home fields. But toward Folden and southward the view was shut in by a crag that jutted out and gave shelter to the last strip of arable land in Hestviken—of the fiord he had only a glimpse northward past the smooth skull of the Bull and its shaggy wooded neck. Over on the other side lay Hudrheim in the morning sun—a low ridge of waste, with sparse fir trees; the higher ground was tilled, with great farms; he had been over there one day, but from here nothing could be seen of any dwellings.

In the cornfield the rock cropped out in so many places that the pale carpet of stubble seemed riddled with it—here and there a ribbon of soil between two brown rocks. But they often had good corn here—it was manured with fish offal from the quayside—and it ripened early. In the crevices of the rock grew a flowering grass that Olav had never seen before; when he came hither in the early summer it blossomed with fair purple stars, but now the grass itself was blood-red and rust-red in all its fringed blades and bristled with seed-bolls that looked like herons' heads with long beaks.

The work of the farm was what Olav understood best. He saw that there were tasks enough before him—the old meadows to be cleared of scrub, the herds to be brought up to their number, the houses to be repaired. He had hired Björn, Gudrid's husband, to fish and hunt seals for him in the fiord during the coming half-year. Of such things he had no experience, but he intended to go out with Björn this winter, to gain a knowledge of the pursuits on which the ancient prosperity of Hestviken had most depended. Björn also advised him to take up again, next summer, the salt-pans on the creek south of the Horse Crag.

But behind his thoughts, which were busy with the work of the day and the work of the future, a deep, happy calm dwelt in Olav's mind. His day flowed over him now like a stream of nothing but good hours. And since he knew that the dangerous memories lay sunk beneath this stream, and that it was only by virtue of a kind of strength that he was able to let them lie there in peace and not think about them, he felt at the same time proud that he was now happy and safe.

29

He knew, in a clear and cool fashion, that the old disasters might return and afflict them. But he took the good days while they were there.

So he stood, morning after morning, gazing and thinking of this and that, while this dreamlike feeling of happiness surged beneath his thoughts. His fair face looked hard and angry at times, and the black pupils of his eyes grew small as pin-points. When he might expect Ingunn to be up, he went back to the house. He greeted his wife with a nod and the shadow of a smile when they met, and watched the little blush of joy that appeared on her healthy face and the calm, meek happiness that beamed in her looks and bearing.

Ingunn was so fair now, never had she been fairer. She was a little fuller than of old, and her skin was shining white; her eyes seemed larger and a deeper blue under the white coif of the wedded woman.

She moved in a gentle, subdued way—her manner had become quiet and simple; she was meek with all, but almost humble toward her husband. But all could see that she was happy, and all who had met Olav's wife liked her.

Olav still slept but little at night. Hour after hour he lay awake without stirring, unless he moved the arm on which she lay, when it was numb. She reposed so confidingly against him in her sleep, and he breathed in the sweet hay-scent of her hair. Her whole being exhaled health, warmth, and youth—and in the pitch-darkness it seemed to Olav that the smell of old folk dwelt in the corners, overcome and driven out. He lay thus and felt the time go by, not longing for sleep to come—it was so good to lie like this and simply be aware of her presence; now at last they were safely together. He passed his hand over her shoulder and arm—it was cool and soft as silk; the coverlet had slipped down. He drew it up, bending over her with caresses, and she replied from her drowsiness with little sleepy words of endearment, like a bird twittering on its nightly perch.

But his heart was wakeful and easily scared—it started like a bird that flies up. He noticed this himself, and was on his guard lest others should see it.

One morning he stood by the fence, looking at his cows, which had been let into the stubble-field; the big bull was there. It was the only really handsome animal in his herd, massive and sturdy, black as coal, but with a pale buff stripe down its back. As he stood and watched the bull striding along, slow and heavy, he thought all at once that the pale stripe on the dark back wriggled like a snake, and for a moment it made his flesh creep. It was only for a brief instant, then he collected himself. But after that he was never quite so fond of the bull as he had been, and this feeling clung to him so long as the bull was in his possession.

While the summer weather lasted, Olav was in the habit of going down to the beach daily during the midday rest. He swam out till he could see the houses of the manor above the rocks—lay floating on his back and then swam again. Usually Björn bathed with him.

One day, when they had come out of the water and were letting the wind dry them, Olav chanced to look at Björn's feet. They were large, but high in the instep, with strongly curved soles—the sure sign of gentle birth. He had heard it said that it could be seen at once by a man's feet if a drop of blood from the old thralls' stock were mingled with his. Björn's face and limbs were tanned brown as the bark of a tree, but his body was white as milk and his hair was very fair, but much grizzled.

The question slipped out of Olav's mouth: "Are you akin to us Hestvik men, Björn?"

"No," said Björn curtly. "The devil! Know you not who are your own kindred, man?"

Olav was rather embarrassed and said: "I grew up far from my own people. There may be branches of which one has scarce heard."

"You thought maybe I was one of these wild shoots that have grown up after that Foulbeard," said Björn gruffly. "Nay, I am true-begotten, and so were my forefathers for seven generations. I have never heard that there were bastards in our stock!"

Olav bit his lip. He was angry—but then he had himself provoked the man. So he said nothing.

"But there is one fault in us," Björn went on; " 'tis as though the axe leaps up of itself in our hands when we are goaded—if you will call that a fault. And short is the joy that comes of a stroke—unless the hand that strikes have gold within its reach."

Olav was silent.

Björn laughed and said: "I slew my neighbour, when we fell out over some thongs. What think you of that, Master Olav?"

"Methinks they must have been costly thongs. Were they so wonderful?"

"I had borrowed them of Gunnar to carry in my hay. What think you of that?"

"I think you to be such that I cannot believe it your custom to reward folk thus for a service," said Olav; "so I think there must have been something rare and strange about those thongs nevertheless."

"Gunnar must have thought I thought so," replied Björn, "for he charged me with cutting off a piece of them."

Olav nodded.

Björn asked, bending down to tie his shoe: "What would you have done in my place, Olav Audunsson?"

" 'Tis not easy for me to say—" said Olav. He was struggling to get the pin of his brooch through his shirt.

"Nay, for none would think of charging a man of your condition with stealing a wretched piece of thong," said Björn. "But you held not your hand either, Olav, when your honour was at stake."

Olav was about to put on his kirtle, but he let his arm drop with it.

"What mean you—?"

"I mean—when word came hither, how you had served your brother-in-law for seeking to deny you the maid you were promised and giving you foul words withal—methought I could have a mind to do you a friendly office when you came home some day. But for that I had not taken service so near the haunts where once I owned a farm myself—though 'twas not a great one—"

Olav was putting on his belt. He unfastened the dagger that hung to it: a good weapon with a blade forged by a foreign armourer and a plate of silver with a hook to hold it to the belt. He handed it to Björn:

"Will you accept this as a token of friendship, Björn?"

"No. Have you never heard, Olav, that a knife is not a gift between friends?—it cuts friendship asunder. But you must do me this friendly office—you will cease giving to the wife who is here ever and anon."

Olav blushed—he looked very young for the moment. To hide

his embarrassment he said lightly, as he leaped onto the rock and began to walk up:

"I wist not that they knew so much hereabout of what has been between the Kolbeinssons and me."

Björn had given him a start with what he said about being quick of hand when honour was at stake. The slaying of Einar Kolbeinsson had been far from his mind, it weighed so little on his spirit, except as the cause of the difficulties from which he was now free. So it had not occurred to him that Björn was alluding to *that*—

Olav had taken to Björn when he came and offered him his service, and he continued to like him. But he saw that the man had an ill report in the neighbourhood. His wife, Gudrid, came down to Hestviken at all times; Björn showed little joy at meeting her, and he seldom went home. Olav soon found out that she was the most arrant gossip, who preferred to roam from house to house mumping with her wallet rather than look to her home. Nor were they so poverty-stricken over at Rundmyr as she pretended; Björn took better care of his own than Gudrid gave him word for, he sent home both meat and fish and a little meal, and they had cow and goat. But now Olav had once called the woman foster-mother, so she never went from him without a gift. Now he was sorry he had put himself in this difficulty—he guessed it must be intolerable for Björn, when the man was to be chief of the serving-men at the manor, and his wife came and accepted alms in this way.

A desire had come upon Olav to associate with older men. Without his knowing it he had felt the want of someone who might have cared to teach him and be a guide as he grew up. He was now very courteous and respectful toward all old men among his equals, and helpful to the aged poor, received old men's advice patiently, and followed it too, when he saw that it was beneficial. Moreover Olav was himself a man of few words when he came among strangers—but old folk could usually succeed in keeping the talk going, without his having to say much for his part or to listen the whole time. So they thought very well of the young Master of Hestviken.

Nor was he ill liked among those of his own age, though they thought it could scarce be said that Olav Audunsson brought mirth and gladness with him, and some mistook his quiet and silent man-

33

ner for pride. But others deemed that the man was only somewhat heavy of disposition and not too keen-witted. That Olav and his wife were uncommonly fair to look upon and knew well how to demean themselves among folk, all were agreed.

One Saturday afternoon, about the time when the work ceased, Olav and Björn with both the house-carls were coming up from the waterside when they saw a company ride out of the little wood in Kverndal and go up the slope toward the manor. There were two men and three young maids whose flaxen hair floated freely down to their saddles; their gowns were red and blue. It was a fair sight on the meadow, which was still fresh and green with the after-grass—and Olav was glad when he recognized the daughters of Arne.

He took them in his arms and kissed them with a merry greeting as he helped them from their horses, and then he led them forward to his wife, who stood at the door and received her guests in her quiet and gentle way.

They had not been to the home-coming feast, and during the holy-days the two younger were to go home to their father; so the priest had sent them hither that they might bring greetings and gifts to the wife of their kinsman. The priest's house-carl accompanied the maids, and as they rode past Skikkjustad, the son of that house came and offered to join them; he had spoken with Olav the week before about a bargain.

Olav went over to the loft-room, changed his sea-clothes, tidied himself, and put on his Sunday garments. He was glad to have these young kinswomen in the neighbourhood, so Ingunn would be less lonely. He had heard a rumour that Sira Benedikt and Paal of Skikkjustad were thinking of a marriage between Signe and Baard Paalsson, and it looked as though the two young people were not disposed to gainsay the matter either; indeed, it might be a comfort to them at Hestviken too if this bargain were made.

Outside, the weather was still and cold; the pale, clear air was a sure presage of frost at night. It was cold indoors too—much wood was thrown on the hearth, and after the household had been fed, the young people were minded to play in the courtyard awhile, till darkness came on, to warm themselves. But Ingunn would not take part in the game. She sat with her cloak wrapped about her and looked as though she felt the cold; she was so quiet that something seemed to have depressed her spirits. Seeing it, Olav left the dance and seated himself by his wife—and soon after, it grew so dark that they all came into the house. It then appeared that the three sisters knew many games, riddles, and jests that were fitted for indoors, and they had sweet voices when they sang—in everything they were courtly and well-bred maidens. But Ingunn remained in ill humour, and Olav was not able to enjoy himself fully, for he could not guess what ailed his wife.

Olav put his arm about Torunn and led her to Ingunn. Torunn was not yet thirteen, a fair and merry child. But not even she could thaw the mistress of the house.

In the evening Olav accompanied his guests on the way. It was fine weather; the full moon shone brightly in the clear sky, but the frost fog was beginning to creep in from the fiord, blotting out the shadows. Olav walked, leading Torunn's horse.

"Your wife likes us not, Olav," said the little maid.

"Can you think that?" said Olav with a laugh. "Not like you! I know not what it is that has gone against Ingunn tonight."

Ingunn was in bed when Olav came home, and when he lay down beside her, he found that she was weeping. He stroked her and bade her say why she was so sorrowful. At long last he got her to come out with it—she felt so mortally unwell; it must come from her having eaten some shellfish when she was down by the waterside that morning. Olav told her not to do such things—she could speak to him or to Björn if she had a mind to such food, and they would find her some shellfish that was good to eat. Then he asked if she did not think his kinswomen were pleasant and comely maids.

Ingunn answered yes, "and merry indeed were these daughters of Arne," she said in a tone of disapproval. "And you sported right wantonly with them, Olav—utterly unlike you. I can guess that *you* like them."

"Yes," said Olav, and his voice was filled with gladness at the thought of the mirthful evening. 'Twould be a great comfort to them both that he had these blithe and courtly young kinswomen so near at hand, he said again.

Olav could hear that she was breathing heavily. After a while she whispered:

"Were we not as sisters to you, Tora and I, in your boyhood?—
but never do I mind me that you romped and jested so wantonly
with us."

"Oh, maybe 'twas not unknown," replied Olav. "But I was under another man's roof," he added quietly. "Had I grown up
among my own kindred and in my own home, I trow I had been
less grave and silent as a boy."

Soon after, he heard that she was weeping again. And now her
sobs took such hold that he had to get water for her. On lighting
a splinter of wood he saw her face so red and swollen that he
feared she had eaten something downright poisonous. He threw
on some clothes, dashed out, and fetched fresh milk, which he
forced her to drink, and then at last she began to mend and fell
asleep.

One day just before Hallowmas Olav was at the manse together with certain other franklins; they had come to have letters drawn up by the priest. Olav had—not exactly fallen out—
with another man, named Stein; but yet the two had exchanged
words somewhat sharply once or twice.

As they were about to ride home again, some of the men went
out to look at Apalhvit, the horse Olav Audunsson was riding.
They praised the horse highly and remarked how well groomed
he was. And they teased Stein, who also had a white horse, but his
was ill kept and rusty yellow, and it was easy to see that he had
been roughly handled by his rider.

Stein said: "It has been Olav's calling to break and tend horses—
'tis but meet that a knight's horse should be well groomed. But
wait till you have known a few years of husbandry; then you will
have forgotten all your courtly ways. And then you will own the
truth of the old saying that white horses and too fair wives are
not for country folk, for they have no time to watch them."

" 'Twill surely never go so hard with me that I have not the
means to keep two white horses," said Olav proudly. "Will you
sell me the horse, Stein?"

Stein named a price, and at once Olav held out his hand and
bade the others witness the bargain. It was settled on the spot how
and when Olav should pay over the purchase money. Stein took
the saddle off his horse and went into the house to borrow a halter
of Sira Benedikt. The other men shook their heads, saying that
this time Olav had made a bad bargain.

"Oh well—" Olav shrugged his shoulders and gave a little laugh. "But I care not always to be so thrifty as to split a louse into four."

He put his saddle on the horse he had bought and let Apalhvit trot behind. The other men stood and watched him; one or two of them gave a little sneering laugh. The first trial of strength between horse and rider came at the bend of the road. It looked as though Olav would be well warmed ere he reached home.

Ingunn sat sewing alone in the hearth-room when she heard the beat of hoofs on the rocky floor of the courtyard. She went to the outer door and looked at her husband in surprise: in the rarefied autumn sunlight he was holding in a strange and restive horse; his face was fiery red and both he and the horse were bespattered with the foam that covered the bridle, while the horse champed and pranced till the stony ground rang again, and would not stand still. Olav greeted her and the house-carl, who came up, with a laugh.

"I will tell you all when I come in," said Olav; he leaped from the saddle and stayed by the house-carl who was to lead the new horse to the stable.

"What is it?" she asked in wonder when he came in. He stopped just inside the door—looking like a drunken man.

"Is the old man at home?" asked Olav.

"No, he went down to the sea—shall I send Tore for him?"

Olav laughed and closed the door behind him. Then he came forward, lifted his wife as one takes a child in one's arms, and squeezed her till she gasped.

"Olav—" she cried in terror. "What has come over you?"

"Oh, naught else but that you are too fair a wife," he muttered with the same drunken laugh, and pressed his heated face against hers till she thought he would break her neck.

Late in the afternoon Olav betook himself to the mill, and Ingunn went into the cook-house; she had a pan of cheese standing by the fire, below the bake-stone.

The lid could not have been fitted on tightly, so much ash had got in. And it smelt ill—had doubtless stood too long, but it would not curdle sooner. Ingunn could never get her cheeses to work in the right way: the cheeses she had made the week before had gone soft again and run over onto the shelf where she had put them to dry.

Her mouth twitched as she stood kneading the sticky, evil-smelling cheese in the pan, with slow and clumsy hands. She was no skilful housewife—all work was to her heavy and difficult, and accidents were always happening. Each new misfortune made her so utterly despondent—when would it strike Olav that his wife was incapable besides her other faults? At the end of a day like this, when everything she put her hand to had gone wrong, she felt bruised all over, as though from a number of falls.

He had not been drunken after all, Olav. At first she had sought comfort in the thought that he must have partaken more freely than was his wont of that ale of which their priest made such boast. But he had been quite sober. And her heart fluttered fitfully as she pondered—what could have come over Olav to make him so utterly unlike himself? Never had he been aught but kind and affectionate and tender in his love. At times she would fain have had him—not quite so calm and sober-minded.

The thought weighed heavily upon her: true enough, he was calm in his bearing, master of himself—as long as might be. But she had seen occasions when he lost his self-control. But even in that night of madness when the boy came to her and said he had slain Einar, she had felt his love for her as a safeguard. His rage she had seen *once*—when it was turned against herself; once she herself had lain cowering, mortally afraid, face to face with his white-hot anger. It was a thing she could not bear to think of—and she had not thought of it, till now. But now she recalled it, with such stifling vividness— But *now* she could not have done anything to make him angry?

She had felt so easy in these four months they had been married. Unconsciously she reckoned her marriage from the hour when her kinsmen in the presence of witnesses had given her into the hands of Olav Audunsson. He had been so good to her that the memory of all the terrible things that had befallen her on the eve of that event was now but as the shadow of a horrible dream. And she had been obliged to acknowledge the truth of what he said—Hestviken was far away; it had been easier than she could ever have imagined to forget what had happened there in the north. But at the same time she had striven to show him that she was grateful and loved him—unspeakably.—Surely, then, *she* could not have done anything to cause him to be so—strange—just now, when he came home. But then she was seized with terror at the thought of *what* might have caused it—

And yet that was foolish—for he had shown no sign of wrath; it had all been caresses, in a way, the whole of it. Only wild ones—and then he had played with her, roughly, mad with an ungovernable merriment that had scared her, for she was not used to seeing Olav thus. But perhaps that was no proof that anything out of the common had befallen him—perhaps it was the way with all men, that such a fit came over them now and again. It had been Teit's way—

Teit—she felt a kind of sagging at the heart—it had been just like Teit. Her memory of him had grown distant and unreal like all the rest that sank below the horizon as she moved farther and farther away from it with Olav. Now it had again come nigh her, alive and threatening, the memory that she had been Teit's—

She uttered a scream and started, trembling all over, as Olav suddenly appeared just behind her—she had not noticed his coming.

He had stood in the doorway for a while watching her, the tall and slender young wife bending over the board, narrow-shouldered and lithe, working slowly and awkwardly with her long, thin-fingered hands in the mess of cheese. He could not see her face beneath the coif, but he had a feeling that she was in low spirits.

He was ashamed of himself for the way he had behaved to her when he came home before. 'Twas far from seemly for a man to show his wife such conduct. He was afraid she might feel insulted.

"Have I frightened you?" Olav spoke in his usual voice, calmly, with a shade of tender solicitude. He placed himself beside her, a little awkwardly—took a pinch of the curds she was now kneading into balls, and ate it.

"I never did this work until I came hither," she said in excuse. "Dalla would never let me. Maybe I have not pressed out the whey enough."

"You will learn it, I doubt not," her husband comforted her. "We have time enough, Ingunn.—I was so vexed over that matter of the horse—but the man Stein provoked me to it." He looked down with embarrassment, turned red and laughed with annoy-

ance. "You know 'tis not like me—to make a fool's bargain. I was
so glad when you came out to meet me—" he looked at her as
though begging forgiveness.

She bent yet deeper over her work, and her cheeks flushed
darkly.

"She is not yet fit for much," thought her husband. "The unwonted labour tires her."—If only the old man in the closet would
keep quiet tonight. His poor frame was rent by rheumatic pains,
so that he often wailed aloud for hours at night, and the young
people got little rest.

Olav Ingolfsson had broken down completely as soon as his
young kinsman had relieved him of the duties of master. He had
worn himself out at Hestviken, though there was but little to show
for it. Now he abandoned himself wholly to the afflictions of old
age. The two young people were kind to him. Olav felt it as a
support—without being clear in what way he needed support—
that after years of waiting he was living under the same roof as a
man of his father's kindred. And he was glad that Ingunn was so
kind and thoughtful in her manner toward the feeble old man. He
had been a little disappointed that she seemed to like neither the
daughters of Arne nor their father, whom they had since met.
Olav himself had a great liking for this cousin of his father's. Arne
of Hestbæk was a man of some fifty years, white-haired, but handsome and of good presence; the family likeness between him and
Olav Audunsson was striking. Arne Torgilsson received Olav very
open-heartedly and bade him be his guest at Yule. And for this
Olav had a right good mind; but Ingunn did not seem so set on
going.

But he was glad that in any case she seemed to take to Olav
Ingolfsson, though the old man gave no little trouble. He was
often restless at night—and then he befouled the place with all the
simples and unguents he prepared for himself—and the old dog,
who lay in his bed at night and was to draw out the pain from
his sick leg, was uncleanly, thievish, and cross-tempered. But Ingunn patiently assisted the old man, spoke to him gently as a
daughter, and was kind to his dog.

Both the young people found it diverting to listen to old Olav's
talk in the evenings. There was no end to what he knew of men
and families and their seats in all the country around Folden. Of

the warfare that followed Sverre Priest's coming to Norway he could tell them many tales learned from his father; but in King Skule's cause Olav Half-priest had fought himself. Olav Audunsson's great-grandfather, Olav Olavsson of Hestviken, had followed Sigurd Ribbung to the last, and then he had fought *against* Skule. But when the Duke was proclaimed King at the Öre Thing, Olav Ribbung mustered men about him and marched northward with his three sons to offer him his support; and his brother, Ingolf the priest, gave his son leave to accompany his cousins: "We were then in our fifteenth year, Torgils and I—but we gave a good account of ourselves. The scar I bear on my back was gotten at Laaka. They made such sport of me, the Vaarbelgs,[7] for getting hurt *there*—but we had come into a deep cleft with a stream between landslides and had the Birchlegs above us both behind and before—there were Torgils and I and three other lads—there were so many young lads among our party. One of them we called Surt, for he had the reddest hair I have seen on any man.[8] It chanced, as we followed Gudine Geig into the Eastern Dales, that we lay one night at a little farm and woke to find the house afire. 'You have lain with your shockhead against the bare wall, you devil,' said Gudine. 'Yes, and then you blew on it,' said Surt—he-he-he, his words were less decent than I will repeat for Ingunn's sake; we lay all over the floor, Surt just behind Gudine. The penthouse was all ablaze, but out we came and hacked our way through. They had an ill habit of setting fire to houses, the Birchlegs—'twas a jest with us that there were so many sons of bathhouse carls and bake-house wives among them. But now you are to hear how we fared, Torgils and I, at Laaka—nay, first let me tell you a little of this Gudine Geig—"

Olav noticed that it vexed Ingunn when the old man questioned her impatiently whether she would not soon have news for them. Now she and Olav had been married five months—

[7] *Vaarbelger* was the name given to the followers of Skule by their enemies, the Birchlegs. Various explanations of the name have been suggested, the most probable being "hides taken in springtime" (*vaar*, spring, and *belg*, hide), the hides being almost valueless during the spring months. Duke Skule was proclaimed King in 1239. In the following year he was victorious over the Birchlegs at Laaka, but the Vaarbelgs were afterwards defeated by King Haakon at Oslo. Skule fell at Trondhiem in May 1240.

[8] *Surt* is the Norwegian name for a ferruginous earth used as a dye.

"We do what we can, kinsman," said Olav with a little laugh.

But the old man was angry and told him not to jest lightly with the matter, but rather to make vows and pray God to grant them an heir betimes. Olav laughed and thought there was no such haste. In his own mind he deemed it hard enough for Ingunn, even now when she was in full health, to cope with the affairs of the household and keep her three serving-women to their work.

But Olav Ingolfsson complained: he believed he had not long to live. Now he had known four generations of the family, great-grandfather, grandfather, father, and son—"I would fain greet a son of yours, Olav, before I quit this world."

"Oh, you will live sure enough to greet both my son and my grandson," Olav consoled him. But the old man was despondent:

"Olav Torgilsson, who was the first man of our race here in Hestviken, was married to Tora Ingolfsdatter ten years before they had children—and he fell before his sons saw the light. That was his punishment, to my mind, for having married her against his father's will. Ingolf of Hestviken and Torgils of Dyfrin had been enemies, but Olav Torgilsson said he would not forgo this good marriage because the two old men had quarrelled once in a drinking-bout. Tora was the heiress here, for Ingolf was the last man of the old Hestvik line, who are said to have dwelt in this spot since there were men in Norway. And Torgils Fivil was the last of the barons' line at Dyfrin. Sverre gave the manor and Tor-gils's young widow to one of his own men—he had been thrice married, Torgils Fivil. He had been given the name in his youth from his flaxen hair and the fine, white skin that has ever been an inheritance in our kin.[9]

"So you may see, our ancestor had cause enough for vengeance upon Sverre—his manor, his father, and three brothers. And the winter that his wife perceived there was a hope that the race would survive them was the same winter when the country folk here around Folden rose to take vengeance for Magnus, their crowned King, and strike down that Sverre, who had no right to the kingdom and sought to upset all our ancient rights and bring in new customs, which we liked not. Men of the Vik and of the Upplands, of Ranrike and Elvesyssel, wellnigh the whole people of Norway were with us. Olav Torgilsson was among the

[9] *Fivil*: bog-cotton.

nobles who were foremost in counsel and boldest in fight from the very first.

"You know how we fared at Oslo that time. The Devil helps his own, and he bore up Sverre Priest till he had him well housed within the gates of hell, 'tis my belief. Olav Torgilsson fell there on the ice; but some men from these parts rescued the body and carried him home. So many men had fallen above Olav there around the standard that the Birchlegs had not despoiled him, and home he came, axe in hand; they could not loosen the dead man's grip of the weapon. But when the widow came up and took hold of it, he let go—the arm dropped, and Tora was left with the axe, and at the same moment the child quickened within her—'twas as though the unborn babe had struck out with his clenched fist, she told the sons she bore that spring. From the time they were big enough to understand, she spoke of this early and late, that they had vowed to avenge their father while they were yet in the womb. That axe was the one you have now, 'Kin-fetch.' Tora gave it that name; of old it was called 'Wrathful Iron.' It came to Olav, since he was the elder of the twins, when she sent the boys to a man named Benedikt, who was said to be a son of King Magnus Erlingsson. His was the first company in which these brothers took part.

"I can well call to mind my grandmother, Tora Ingolfsdatter. She was a large-hearted woman, of great judgment, feared God, and was charitable toward the poor. While she was mistress here—and she had a long life; your great-grandfather and my father obeyed her to her dying day—there was great fishery here in Hestviken. Grandmother sent her ships along the whole coast, as far as the border by the Gauta River and down to Denmark—you can guess, she spied out news of what was brewing against the race of Sverre. Tora always had scent of all such plans that were afoot, and all who were minded to oppose the Birchlegs found good backing with the widow of Olav Torgilsson. Tora had loved her husband with marvellous devotion. Olav Torgillson was a little fair-skinned man, but full of strength, and handsome—somewhat lacking in chastity, but so they were, the men of King Magnus's time.

"Grandmother herself can never have been fair of face. At the time I remember her she was so tall and so portly that she had to go sideways and bend double to get through the door here in the new house. She was half a head taller than her sons, and they were big men. But fair she was not: she had a nose so big and so crooked that I know not to what I can liken it, and eyes like gulls' eggs, and her chins hung down upon her chest and her breasts upon her stomach.

"First she sent her sons to Filippus, the Bagler King,[1] but soon she grew very dissatisfied with him, deeming him lacking in energy, lazy, and a lover of peace. When therefore this Benedikt came forward in the Marches, she bade the lads go to him. His company was for the most part a rabble of vagabonds of every kind—my father always said that this Benedikt was of little worth as a leader. He was rash and heedless and somewhat foolish— sometimes a coward and sometimes overbold. But Olav held staunchly to him, always, for he firmly believed that Benedikt was King Magnus's son, though he did not come up to his father. Now, it befell Bene that at the first he had but this herd of rogues that they called the ragged host, but soon more and more good franklins took up his cause, since no more likely leader could be found at the time. But then they were minded to rule Bene and not let themselves be ruled by their claimant to the crown. And when, after a time, Sigurd Ribbung came forward and gained the support of the nobles, the old Bagler leaders, the chiefs of the ragged host took Bene with them and went over to Sigurd, and Benedikt had to content himself with being one of Sigurd Ribbung's petty chieftains. But Olav Olavsson always bore in mind that Benedikt was the lord to whom he had first sworn fealty, and served and honoured him accordingly. Olav was a loyal man.

"Tora made good marriages for her sons—for Olav, Astrid Helgesdatter of Mork; they were very young, some sixteen years both of them, and they had a goodly life together and loved each other with true affection. Their sons were Ingolf, your grandfather, he was the eldest; then there was the Helge who fell at Nidaros with King Skule, and Torgils, he was the youngest of the sons; he and I were of equal age. The daughters of Olav and Astrid were Halldis, who was married to Ivar Staal of Aas in Hudrheim, and Borgny, the nun—a lovable, holy woman. She died the year after you were born.

[1] The Baglers (or "crozier men") were the party of the Church and the old nobility, opposed to Sverre and his followers, the Birchlegs.

"Father was older when he married, for he wished to be a priest. It was the Bishop himself, Nikulaus Arnesson, who ordained him, and he loved my father very dearly, for Father was exceeding pious and learned and wrote books more fairly than any priest in the diocese. My mother, Bergljot of Tveit, was merry, fond of feasting and show, so she and Father were ill matched and did not agree well together, though they had many children—five of us lived to grow up. She was somewhat greedy of money, my mother —Father was so generous that he robbed his own larder behind Mother's back to give alms. But it chanced unluckily that the townsmen got word of this and laughed at it—you know, it looks ill if a priest be not master in his own house. I remember one day Mother was angry over something—she took two sheets of a book Father had just finished writing and threw them on the fire, but then he beat her. Father was a big, strong, valiant man and he had fought bravely against the Birchlegs, but toward his even Christians he was the most gentle and peaceful of men—but with Mother there was ever some dissension. Between our house at Oslo and the sea there was a piece—one could not call it ground; 'twas but beach and weeds and bare rock. The townspeople had been wont to use a path across it to shorten the way. Mother wished to close this path—Father deemed it unseemly for a priest to wrangle over such a small matter. But there were quarrels without end on account of this right of way—between Father and Mother and between us and our neighbours.

"When the order came that the priests of Norway were to live in celibacy like those of other Christian lands, Father bade my mother go home to Tveit, to enjoy the manor and a great part of his estate. But she and her kinsmen and my brothers and sisters were very wroth, for they thought in their hearts that Father was more glad than sorry to be forced to break up their married life. I know full well that my father had always held the marriage of priests to be an evil custom, and that was also the opinion of Bishop Nikulaus—but 'twas the usage when my father was a young man, and then he had to do as his mother willed. My brothers and sisters and my mother then went upcountry, and I have not seen much of them since: Kaare, my brother, got Tveit, and Erlend got Aasheim; now both the manors are divided among many children. I stayed with Father; I had always been intended for the priesthood—and Father and I lived happily together and looked on Halvard's Church as our true home. I was ordained subdeacon three years after King Skule's fall. Grandmother Tora died soon after.

"But it was of your great-grandfather Olav Ribbung and his kin that I was to tell you. Ingolf, you know, was married to Ragna Hallkelsdatter from Kaaretorp—'twas Tora who had busied herself to secure this good marriage for her grandson, as soon as he was grown; Audun, your father, was already some two years old when we kinsmen set out to follow King Skule and the Vaarbelgs. When Torgils turned mad, Ingolf and Ragna had an uneasy life at Hestviken, and afterwards they lived mostly at Kaaretorp. But one Yule, when they were here, Ingolf wished to accompany Halldis, his sister, and her husband across the fiord to Aas and to stay with them awhile. They ran upon a rock, and all who were in the boat were drowned.

"Olav Ribbung bore this disaster so well that my father used to say he had never seen a man bear adversity so nobly—he always named his brother as a pattern of firmness and strength—those twin brothers loved each other so dearly.—Ay, 'twas his son and daughter and son-in-law who were lost. Olav merely said that he thanked God his mother and Astrid, his wife, had died before these disasters had fallen upon his children. He dwelt on there with the madman, and there were no others of his offspring left but Borgny, the nun, and Audun, a little lad. Ingolf's widow married again in Elvesyssel, and Olav gave his consent that Audun should be brought up by his mother and stepfather. Olav Ribbung then adopted the son that Torgils had gotten by a serving wench here at Hestviken, but the boy lived no long time.

" 'Twas the third year I was lame from my broken leg, when Ingolf and the others were lost. And I bore it ill—I thought it unbearably hard to be a cripple, young as I was, and that I could never be a priest. Then father always held up Olav Ribbung to me as an example.—But I know that Olav took it sorely to heart that Audun would not marry again after your mother's death and would not bide at home in Hestviken—and the race bade fair to die out.

"But now there is good hope, I ween, that it will thrive again, with such young and sound and goodly folk as you and your wife. And you may be well assured that I yearn to take a son of yours in my arms. Four generations have I known—five, if I may reckon our ancestress among them—gladly would I see the first man of the sixth ere I die. 'Tis not given to many men to know their own kindred through six generations. And I would deem it a reasonable thing, my Ingunn, if your husband too should conceive a great longing for the same—his departed kinsmen have possessed this manor of Hestviken since there were men in Norway. Do you hear that, young woman?" he said, laughing to himself.

Olav saw how red she turned.—But it was not the modest blush of happy longing; it was the hot glow of shame that mantled her face. Her eyes grew dark and troubled. In charity he took his glance from her.

3

INGUNN came out into the balcony and stood gazing at the falling snow. High up against the pale clouds the great wet flakes looked grey as they whirled in the air, but when they settled they seemed pure white, a gleaming white mass against the obliterated white heights toward Kverndalen.

When she looked up for a while into the driving flurry, she felt as though she herself were being sucked up, to hover in the air for an instant; then she sank down and all grew dark. She tried this again and again. The unbearable giddiness that came over her all at once was somehow turned to gentle rapture as she felt herself borne upward; but when the drop came she could not see that she was falling—nothing but grey and black streaks that whirled around.

There was such a strange hush that the very sea-mews were silent—she had seen how they settled in such weather, in cracks of the rock and on the great stones of the beach. Now and again they moved a little, but without uttering a note. When first she came here she had thought these great white birds with their wide stretch of wing were fairer than anything she had seen—even their curious screams made her strangely happy at heart. She had been brought to a new land, far from the region where she had suffered intolerably. In summer, when she came out in the morning and heard the regular pounding of the sea at the foot of the rock on which she stood, saw the wide and bright expanse of the fiord and the bare shore on the other side, and the circling white sea-mews screamed hoarsely, unreal as wraiths—it had made her so light at heart: the world was so great and so wide; what had befallen her somewhere in a spot far, far away could not possibly be so great a matter—it must surely be forgotten in time.

But as autumn drew on out here by the fiord she was alarmed by its being never still. The unceasing murmur and booming of the waves, the cries of the sea-birds, the sweep of the storm over the wooded ridge—all this made her dizzy. If she had but to cross the yard, the wind seemed to rush in at her ears and fill her whole head with noise. And rain and fog drifted in from the sea and took away her courage. She thought of the autumn at home—the ground hard with black frost, the air bright and clear, so that the blows of an axe or the baying of a dog could be heard from farm to farm; there the sun made its way through the morning mist and thawed the rime to dew in the course of the day. And she longed to listen to a stillness around her.

It was as though she had sunk lower and lower as the days and the year grew shorter and darker. Now she was at the bottom—midwinter was past, the year was climbing again. And she felt utterly powerless at the thought that now she was to take the uphill road. Soon the sun would rise higher and higher—the time was near at hand when day by day it would be manifest that brighter and longer days were drawing on—the springtime. But to her it was as though she faced a lofty mountain up which she was to climb—with the burden she now knew full surely that she bore—and it made her sick and giddy to think of it.

Still, still was the air, though the snow whirled so madly—the flakes drifted hither and thither, but at last they fell straight down. The sea was dark as iron, when she had a glimpse of it, and the surf-beat on the beach sounded faint and monotonous in the mild, snowy air.

All was covered now—the road down to the wharf was blotted out. The footprints of the maids who had gone to the byre, her own tracks across the yard, were snowed under. And all the white was turning grey and slowly fading as the first shades of dusk came on.

The door of the bath-house burst open, and in the cloud of white steam that poured out she caught a glimpse of the men's bodies, dark against the snow. They ran up toward the barn, where they had left their clothes, rolling in the drifts as they went, with shouts and laughter. She recognized Olav and Björn, who came first; they closed and wrestled, ducking each other in the snow.

She lifted up the platter of pickled fish and threw her cloak over it. It was so heavy that she had to carry it in both arms; she could not steady herself or see beyond her feet and was afraid of slipping on the snow-covered rocks. The dusk had deepened and the flickering snow made her yet more giddy.

Olav came into the house and took his place in the high seat at the end of the room. He was hungry and tired—settled down in ease at the thought that it was Saturday and the eve of a holy-day, and that three women were busied about him, bringing in food.

The fire on the hearth glowed red, with little low flames playing over the burned-out logs, but through the dim light of the room the man in the master's seat was conscious of the new comfort that had been brought in. The table was always set up now on the raised floor along the end wall; there were cushions in the high seat, and a piece of tapestry had been hung over the logs of the wall behind it. By the side of this the axe Kin-fetch hung in its old place, together with Olav's two-handed sword and his shield with the wolf's head and the three blue lilies. A blue woven curtain had been hung about the southern bed, where the master and mistress slept.

A faint light showed within the closet—the old man was reciting his evening prayers in a half-singing voice. Sira Benedikt might say what he would, thought Olav—his kinsman was a man of no little learning: he said his hours as well as any priest. When the old man had finished, Olav Audunsson called to him: would he not come in and sup?

The old man answered that he would rather have a little ale and groats brought to him in bed. Ingunn hastily filled a bowl with the food and carried it in to him. At the same moment the housecarls appeared at the door—Björn with a bundle of wood, which he flung on the floor. He made up the fire, threw open the outer door and raised the smoke-vent, so that snowflakes drifted down to the hearth with a hiss. Ingunn stayed with the old man till the wood had caught and the worst of the smoke had cleared away. Then Björn closed the door and the smoke-vent.

49

Ingunn came in and stood at her table. She made a cross with
her knife on the loaf before cutting it up. The five men on the
bench ate in silence, long and heartily. Ingunn sat on the edge of
the bed and picked at a little fish and bread, enjoying it, for the
salmon was good and well pickled. The ale was of the Yule brewing and might have been better, but she had had such dirty grain
for the malt, mixed with all manner of weeds.

She glanced over at her husband. His hair was dark with wet;
the eyebrows and stubbly beard stood out with a golden gleam
against his face, which was red and weatherbeaten this evening.
He seemed to have a good appetite.

The three serving-maids sat on the bench below the bed, facing
the hearth, and ate their supper. Herdis, the youngest of them,
whispered and giggled as she ate; that child was always full of
laughter and games. She was showing the other maids a new horn
spoon that she had been given; the laughter spurted out of her as
she did so—then she gave a terrified look at the mistress and struggled to keep quiet, but the girl was all squeaks and gurgles.

The house-folk went out soon after the meal was ended. The
men had been on the water from early morning, and the road
from Hestviken to the church was so long that they could not lie
late abed on the morrow, when the going was as heavy as it was
now.

Olav went in to his kinsman—the old man always needed a hand
with one thing or another before he lay down to rest. Olav Ingolfsson was specially inclined to talk toward bedtime and wished
to hear all about the fishing and the day's work on the farm. And
every answer he received of the younger Olav put him in mind
of something that had to be told.

Igunn was sitting on a low stool before the hearth, combing
her hair, when Olav came back into the room. She was half undressed—sitting in a white, short-sleeved linen shift and a narrow,
sleeveless under-kirtle of russet homespun. Her thick dark-yellow
hair hung like a mantle about her slender, slightly stooping form,
and through it gleamed her delicate white arms.

Olav came up behind her, filled his hands with her loosened
hair, and buried his face in it—it smelt so good.

"You have the fairest hair of all women, Ingunn!" He forced
her head back and looked down into her upturned face. "But
you have fallen away since Yule, my sweet one! You must not

work beyond your powers, I will not have it! And then you must eat more, else you will grow so thin, ere Lent comes and we must fast, that there will be nothing left of you!"

He struggled out of his jerkin and shirt and sat down on the edge of the hearth to warm his back. The sight of the man's naked chest, the play of the muscles under the milk-white skin, as he bent down to pull off his boots, affected the young wife painfully. His sound health made her feel her own weakness all the more.

Olav scratched himself on the shoulder-blades—a few little drops of blood trickled, red as wine, down his smooth skin. "He is such a rough fellow, Björn, when he bathes one," laughed Olav.

Then he bent over the bitch that lay with her litter on a sack by the hearth, and picked up one of the puppies. It squealed as he held it to the light—its eyes were only just opened. The mother gave a low growl. Olav had bought the dog but a little while before and had paid so much that his neighbours had again shaken their heads at his grand ways. But it was a special breed of dog, with hanging ears, soft as silk, and a short coat—keen-scented, excellent sporting dogs. Olav handled the puppies with satisfaction: it looked as if they would take after their mother, all five of them. He laughingly laid one in his wife's lap, amused at the dog, which now growled more threateningly, but dared not fly at him.

The tiny, round-bellied creature, still soft of bone, crawled and scrambled, trying to lick Ingunn's hands. It was so weak and jointless—all at once she felt unwell, a lump came into her throat.

"Let its mother have it back," she begged feebly.

Olav looked at her, stopped laughing, and laid the puppy back beside the bitch.

Torre was past and the month of Gjö came and froze the fiord— the ice stretched far to the south of Jölund.[2] The days began to lengthen and grow lighter. The frost fog crept up the fiord from farther out where there was open sea, and when clear days succeeded, with blue sky and sunshine, the whole world glistened with rime. Olav and Björn went out hunting together.

Ingunn's only thought was how long yet would she be able to conceal it. Her tears burst forth—an impotent despair she knew

[2] Torre and Gjö were the names of two of the old Scandinavian months, the former beginning with the next new moon after the "Yule moon." Gjö would usually include the latter part of February and most of March.

that now indeed she had no need of concealment: was she not Olav's wife in Hestviken, where she was to bear him a child in the old manor that had been the seat of his kin from time out of mind? And yet she would fain have crept underground and hidden herself.

She saw that Olav had guessed how it was with her. Still she kept going and could not bring herself to utter a word of it. She kept the fast like the others, though her chest was drawn with hunger so that it gave her pain. She noticed that Olav stole a glance at her more and more often, with something of wonder and covert anxiety in his looks. Afterwards he would remain silent a long while. Her heart was filled with dread when she saw him thus, brooding and wondering about her. But she did not get herself to say anything.

Then there came a Sunday; they had just come home from church and were alone in the room for a moment. Olav seated himself on the bench; as she was hurrying past he caught her by the wrist and held her.

"Ingunn mine—you must do a kindness to Olav Ingolfsson and tell him of it. I believe he will scarce live through the spring. You know how eagerly he awaits it!"

Igunn bowed her head; her face was red as fire.

"Yes," she whispered obediently.

Then her husband drew her to him and would set her on his knee.

"How is it with you?" he asked in a low voice. "You are so unhappy, Ingunn? Does he plague you so ill, this little guest of yours? Or are you afraid?"

"Afraid!" For an instant the young wife seemed to flare up, like her old headstrong self of former days. "You must surely know how it is— Never have you been anything but good to me—and now I must think day after day that I am not *worth* it!"

"Be silent!" He squeezed her hand hard. Ingunn saw Olav's face shut up. When he spoke again, his voice was forced, though he made an effort to speak calmly and gently:

"Think not of that, Ingunn, which we do much better to forget. 'Twere foolish indeed of us to awaken memories that—that— And you know full well that I love you so dearly that I could never have the heart to be aught but good to you."

"Oh, I should be worth still less, if I could forget—!"

She sank on her knees before him, hid her head in her husband's arms, and kissed his hand. Olav quickly withdrew it, leaped up, and raised his wife to her feet. Ingunn bent backward in his arms, looked into his eyes, and said in a kind of defiance:

"You are fond of me—ay, God knows I see it—but I believe, Olav, that had I offered to treat you as of old—with an overweening, fanciful humour, claiming to have my own way in all things —I scarce believe you would have suffered it in me, or loved me so much, after what I have done to you—"

"Oh, be quiet now!" He let her go.

"I often wish you had treated me harshly, as you threatened that time—"

"That you do not wish," he said with the cold little smile she knew so well from old days.

But then he drew her passionately to him, hid her head on his breast.

"Do not weep," he begged.

"I am not weeping." Olav raised her face and looked into it— he felt strangely ill at ease. He would much rather she had wept.

In the time that followed, a kind of paralysing dread crept over Olav again and again. He had a feeling that all had been in vain. In vain the payments he had made to buy peace for himself and her, in vain that he had sunk his own bitterness to the bottom of his soul and quenched it with all the old streams of his love: his life with her was a dear old habit of his childhood; when he took her in his arms, he recalled the first rapture of his life. Never had he let her see that he remembered her—weakness, he called it now. And now he was at his wit's end, recognizing that against the sense of shame that gnawed at her heart he could do nothing.

And when he saw her in this state, he himself could not avoid the thought—it was not her *first* child.

During their first months together at Hestviken he had been so pleased with her quiet bearing, knowing it was happiness that made her so meek and gentle a wife. But now it hurt him. For she had spoken the truth—had she been as in old days, when she would have her own way and always expected him to give in to her—he would not have brooked that of her *now*.

Then he straightened himself, as though shouldering his burden anew. At home he always appeared calm and contented, he had a cheerful answer when anyone spoke to him, and put a good face on the prospect of the old stock sending out fresh shoots. He was affectionate toward his wife and tried to console himself: Ingunn had never been strong, and this sickliness must prey heavily on her meagre powers. No doubt her melancholy would pass off when she grew well again.

Old Olav Ingolfsson had failed greatly during the spring, and Olav Audunsson tended him as well as he could. He often lay at night in the closet with his kinsman; at any moment the old man might require help of one kind or another. A little oil-lamp burned all night long, and the younger Olav lay on the floor in a leather bag. When old Olav could not sleep he would babble by the hour together, and now it was always of their kin: how possessions and prosperity had come into the hands of the Hestvik men, and how they had been lost again.

One night, as they lay talking of such things, young Olav asked his namesake about Foulbeard. All he knew of this man was but scraps—and these scraps were scarcely more agreeable, he thought, than what he himself remembered of the madman.

Old Olav said: "I have not told you much of him before—but maybe you ought to have knowledge of this too, since you are now to be the head of our line. Is your wife asleep?" he asked. " 'Twere better she did not hear this.

"It was truly spoken of him that he acted cruelly and faithlessly toward—many women. And many spoke ill of me, because I was always in company with Torgils, I who was intended for the priesthood. But Torgils I have loved more dearly than any man on earth—and never have I been able to understand his evil life, for I never saw that he sought the company of women or paid court to young maids, when we were at feasts and merrymakings. And when the talk fell upon women and loose living, as you know will often happen among idle young men in hall, Torgils would sit in silence with a little scornful smile—and never have I heard him use immodest or lecherous speech. He was rather sparing of words and grave in all his dealings, a bold, manly, and valorous man. I never knew him have any friends, save me—but we had been as foster-brothers from childhood. I grieved at his evil living—but I could never bring myself to say a word about it to my cousin. Father reproved him often with hard words—he was so fond of Torgils, he too: he would remind him of the day that awaits us all, when we must answer to our Lord for all our deeds —'It had been better for you, Torgils,' my father often said, 'if you had been sunk in the fiord with a millstone about your neck, as the inhuman wretches did to God's beloved Saint Halvard when he sought to protect a poor, simple woman—but you do outrage to such poor and simple ones.' Torgils never said a word in return. There was something secret about Torgils: I never saw him go up to a woman, sit down by her, and talk to her but I noticed that she was uneasy so soon as he looked at her—he must have had an evil power in his eyes. He had a kind of power over men too. For when King Skule's cause was lost, Torgils lent assistance to the Bishop—and afterwards he was made captain of the Bishop's men. But more than once the Bishop was minded to turn him away on account of the ugly rumours. When the matter of Astrid Bessesdatter and Herdis of Stein came out, the Bishop threatened him with excommunication and outlawry and with expulsion from the town—but nothing came of it.

"It was at Yule, seven years after King Skule's fall, that Torgils had been at home in Hestviken, and in Lent Besse and his sons and Olav, my uncle, came to Oslo, and it was agreed that Torgils should marry Astrid as soon as might be after the fast. That was the only time Torgils spoke to me of such matters—he said he would stay here and not go home to his wife; but Besse and his children were such good folk that there was no way out, he must take Astrid. But I guessed that he had taken a dislike to her. Never have I been able to understand how a man can have the heart to bring ruin upon such a young child, when he did not even like her better than that. But Torgils replied that he could not help turning against them always—God be merciful to his soul.

"He met Herdis Karlsdatter just after, and then he did not go home to his own betrothal feast. Olav was beside himself with shame and anger over his son's behaviour, but Torgils said he would rather fly the country than let himself be pressed into taking a wife whom he could not bear to set eyes on. When the rumours got abroad about Torgils and Herdis, it was yet worse; they both begged and threatened him, Uncle Olav and Father and the Bishop, but Torgils heeded them not at all. Astrid Bessesdatter was not surpassingly fair, but she was young, red and white —Herdis Karlsdatter was fat and yellow of skin, thirteen years older than Torgils, and eight children had she borne, so no one could understand it, but folk thought that Torgils had been bewitched. I myself thought it must be the Devil—that he had now got Torgils wholly into his power, after he had treated the young maid, Astrid, so heartlessly. I told him this, but then his face turned so white and strange that I was sheer afraid, and he answered me: 'I think you are right, kinsman. But now it is too late.' And all my prayers and persuasion were as though I had preached to stocks and stones. Some days after came the news that Jon of Stein, Herdis's husband, was dead."

Olav Audunsson started up in his sleeping-bag—stared at the old man in horror, but said nothing. Olav Ingolfsson was silent for a moment, then he said in a low voice, as though it irked him:

"He was on his way home from a gathering, had been absent for the night, and two of his own faithful men were with him—he fell right down by the roadside and died at once. Jon was old and weak—God knows I surely think neither Herdis nor Torgils had a hand in this. But you may well suppose that much was said when it was rumoured that Torgils would marry the widow. Olav Ribbung said he wished the sons of Besse had cut down Torgils before this happened, and he declared that so long as Astrid was left unmarried with Torgils's son, he would not suffer Torgils to offend her kinsmen yet worse by marrying any other. But if it were true that his son had ended by loving a married woman, he would himself pray God to smite Torgils with the hardest of punishments if he did not turn from his sinful life, do penance, and put away his leman. And ere he would let Torgils marry her, his father would bind him as a madman.

"Not long after, Herdis died suddenly. I was with Torgils when the news came. But I cannot tell you how Torgils looked—first his eyes grew so big that I have never seen the like, then they shrank in again and the whole man shrivelled and faded. But he said nothing, and in the days that followed he went about and performed his duty as though nothing had happened—but I felt that something was brewing, and when I was not at church I did not move from his side, day or night. I noticed too that he wished me to be with him—but when he slept I know not; he lay down in his clothes and neither washed nor shaved himself, and he began to be strange in his manner and unlike himself to look at.

"Herdis was buried in the church at Aker. That day week the

Bishop sent Torgils up to Aker, and I went with him. It was the
eve of a holy-day and the tenant of the nuns' farm offered us
baths; then I got him to shave off his foul yellow stubble, and I
cut his hair. 'Ay, now I am ready,' said Torgils—and an uncanny
feeling came over me, for he smiled so queerly—and I saw that
his face was ravaged and wasted, and skin and hair were yet paler
than before, but his eyes had grown so big, and they too had paled
till they were of the colour of milk and water. He was handsome,
for all that—but he little resembled a living man as he sat motionless on the bench, with a fixed stare.

"At last I lay down on the bed awhile, and then I fell asleep.
But I was awakened by a knocking at the door, three blows, and
I started up.

"Torgils had risen and moved as a man walks in his sleep. 'I am
sent for—'

"I rushed up and took hold of him—God knows what I thought
at that moment—but he pushed me aside, and again there was a
knocking at the door.

" 'Let me go,' said Torgils. 'I must go out.'

"I was a tall man, much taller than Torgils, and very strong I
was in my youth, though never so strong as Torgils—he was thickset and small of limb like you and had immense bodily strength.
I threw my arms around him and tried to hold him, but he gave
me a look, and I knew that he was beyond human aid.

" 'It is Herdis,' he said, and again there were three blows on
the door. 'Let me go, Olav. Never did I promise the others aught,
but her I have promised to follow, living or dead.'

"Then he flung me from him, so that I fell on the floor, and he
went out; but I got on my feet, grasped my axe, and ran after
him. God forgive me, had I taken my book or the crucifix in my
hand, it had gone better, but I took no time to think. I was young
—more of a warrior yet than a priest at heart, maybe; I put more
trust in the sharp steel when it came to the push.

"When I came out into the yard I saw them by the castle gate.
'Twas moonlight, but open weather with driving clouds and the
ground was dark, for we had no snow lying in the lowlands that
year. But it was just light enough for me to see them before me
out in the field as I came through the gate—the dead woman went
first, and she was like a shred of mist, scarce touching the ground,
and after her ran Torgils, and I followed. At that moment the

moon peeped out and I saw that Herdis stopped, and I guessed her purpose—so I called to her: 'If he promised to follow you, he must—but he has not promised to *go before* you.'

"But to bid her begone in the Lord's name and let go her prey—that did not cross my mind. And as we were near the church a gleam of moonlight shone on the stone wall. The dead woman glided in by the churchyard gate and Torgils ran after her, and I leaped—I was through the gate in time to see Herdis standing by the wall of the church and reaching out an arm for Torgils. I swung my axe with all my force and threw it, so that it flew over the head of Torgils and rang on the stone wall. Torgils fell flat down, but in an instant they were upon me from behind and flung me to the ground so hard that my right leg was broken in three places—the thigh, the kneecap, and the ankle.

"After that I knew no more till folk came to mass in the morning and found us. Torgils was then as you remember him—his wits were gone, and he was more helpless than a suckling, only that he could go about. If he came near edged tools he roared like a beast and fell down, foaming at the mouth—and he had been the boldest wielder of his weapons that I have known. I have been told that his hair turned white in the very first winter.

"I lay in bed year after year with my broken leg, and in the first years the splinters of bone worked out of the wounds, and the matter ran out and stank so that I could not bear myself—and many a time I besought God, with floods of tears, to be allowed to die, for my torments seemed intolerable. But Father was with me and helped me and bade me bear it as befitted a man and a Christian. And at last my leg was healed—but Torgils knew me not when I came hither—'twas five winters after. And Olav Ribbung bade me keep away, for he could not brook seeing his nephew dragging himself about as a wreck—I went on crutches at that time—when his own son had been the cause of it."

Olav lay awake long after the old man had fallen asleep. Favourites of fortune they had not been, the men of his race. But they had endured one thing and another—

The broken man there, asleep in his bed. His other namesake, the great-grandfather, whom he remembered living here with his grisly mad son—Olav felt warmed by a fellow-feeling with them. The aged woman, Tora, Ingolf the priest: loyal they had been, to a lost cause, to dead and doomed ones who were their own flesh and blood.

He thought of the Steinfinnssons—such, no doubt, were the favourites of fortune. Carefree, reckless folk—to them misfortune was as a poison they had swallowed. They held out till they had thrown it up again—but then they died. And tonight he saw it, fully and clearly—Ingunn too was of that sort—she too had been stricken by misfortune as by a mortal sickness; she would never hold up her head again. But it was his fortune to be so moulded that he could endure, even without happiness. His forefathers had not abandoned a lost cause—they had raised the old standard so long as there was a shred left of it. In his heart he never knew whether he regretted or not that he had accepted Earl Alf's offer and taken his discharge from the service of his lord—but he had accepted it for the sake of the woman who had been given into his hands while both were yet little children. And he would protect her and love her, as he had protected her when a boy and loved her since first he knew he was a man—and if he got no happiness with her, since she could never be aught but a sick and useless wife, that made no difference, he now realized—he would love her and protect her to her last hour.

But in broad daylight he knit his brows when he recalled his thoughts of the night. One has so many queer fancies when one cannot sleep. And she had been happy and well in the summer—fair as never before. She was utterly disheartened now—but then she had never been any great one at bearing trouble, poor girl. After the child was born she would surely be both happy and well.

For an instant it crossed his mind: "Can it be that she is thinking of the child she bore last year?" She had never mentioned it, and so he had not been willing to do so either. He knew no more than that it had been alive when they left the Upplands the summer before.

4

INGUNN was thinking of Eirik now—night and day. This too had grown pale and unreal to her in the first happy days—that she had had a little son who slept in her arm, sucked her breast, and lay against her, small and soft and warm, and she breathed the sourish milky scent of him as she flooded him with her tears in the blind, dark nights. And she had parted from him, as though tearing herself in two, before she faced the final horror and the outer darkness.

But all these horrors lay sunk beneath the horizon of her fevered nights of darkness and tumult, when she was tossed high and drawn down into the abyss by waves of dizzy swooning. When she came back into the light of day, Olav was there and took her to him. When she was made happy, it was as though the hapless being of her memory were not herself. Weeks passed without her thinking once of the child; as though she wondered, vaguely and almost indifferently: "Is he still alive?" And she would not have been greatly moved, she thought, if she had heard that he was dead. But then it might chance that an uneasy thought stirred within her: "How *is* he, is Eirik *well*—or is he ill-treated among strangers?" And from among the pale and distant memories of last year's misery, one shot out and came to life—the little, persistent scream that nothing could quiet but her breast. The truth smote her with a cruel stab: she was mother to a whimpering babe that had been flung out among strangers far away and perhaps at that moment was screaming himself hoarse and tired for his mother— But she thrust these thoughts from her with all her might. The foster-mother had a kind look, so perhaps she was more charitable than the mother who had brought the child into the world. No—she thrust the thought aside, away with it! And the memory of Eirik faded out again. And here she was at Hestviken, as Olav's wife, in all good fortune—and she felt her youth and beauty flourish anew. She bent her head, radiant with bashful joy, if her husband did but look at her.

But as the new child grew within her—from being a secret, wasting exhaustion which turned her giddy and sick with fear of the shadows it might conjure up to stand between Olav and her, it had become a burden that weighed on her and obstructed her whenever she would move. And meanwhile the most important thing about her now in the eyes of all was that she should bring new life into the old stock. Olav Ingolfsson talked of nothing else. Had she been queen of Norway and had the people's hopes of peace and prosperity for generations been centred on the expected child, the old man could not have regarded the coming event as more momentous. But the neighbours too, when they met the young mistress, let her know that they counted this glad tidings. Olav Audunsson, since he was seven years old, had been the only one on whom rested the hope of carrying on the Hestvik race, and ever since that time he had wandered far from the spot where his home was. After twenty years of roaming he had come back to the lands of his ancestors. When children began to grow up about him and his wife, something that had long been out of joint would be put right again.

Her own household also took their share in what awaited their mistress. They had liked Ingunn from the first, because she was so charming to look at, kind and well-intentioned, and they had pitied her a little for being so utterly unfitted for all the work of her house. And now they pitied her, seeing her sorry state. She turned pale as a corpse if she did but enter the cook-house when they were cooking seal-meat or sea-birds—she was not used to this oily smell in the food where she came from, she murmured. The maids laughed and pushed her out—"We will get through it without you, mistress!" She could not stand up to serve out the meat without the sweat bursting out on her face—the old dairy-woman gently pressed her into a seat on the bench and stuffed cushions behind her back—"Let me be carver today, Ingunn—you can scarce stand on your feet, poor child!" She laughed, seeing that the mistress was shaking with weariness. And they were fearful how it would go with her. She did not look as if she could bear much more. And it was over three months to her time, from what she herself said.

Olav was the only one who never showed sign of joy at the expected child; he never uttered a word about it—and his household marked that well. But Ingunn thought in her heart that, when once the boy came into the world, he would be no less wonderful in his father's eyes than in those of all the others. And the bitterness, at which she herself was terrified, welled up anew.

Not a spark of affection did she feel for the child she bore, but a yearning for Eirik and a grudge against this new babe, whom every good thing awaited and all were ready to caress when he came. And it seemed to her as though it were the fault of this child that Eirik was cast out into the darkness. When she felt that folk looked kindly upon her, took pains to clear her path and make things easy for her, the thought struck her: "When Eirik

was to be born I had to hide myself in corners; the eyes of all
stoned me with scorn and anger and sorrow and shame; Eirik
was hated by all before he was born—I hated him myself." As she
sat at her sewing she recalled how she had staggered from wall
to wall when the first pangs came upon her: Tora made up a
bundle of swaddling-cloths, the worst and oldest she had left over
from her own babes. And she, the mother, had thought they were
good enough and more, for this one. The maid sitting with her
looked in astonishment at her mistress—Ingunn tore impatiently
at the fine woollen swathing she was sewing, and threw it from
her.

Now he was a year old, a little more. Ingunn sat out of doors
the first summer evenings, watching the little child, Björn's and
Gudrid's youngest, as he stumped about, fell and picked himself
up, stumped on and tumbled again in the soft green grass of the
yard. She did not hear a word of all Gudrid's chatter. My Eirik—
barefoot, poorly clad like this one here, with his poor foster-
parents.

Old Olav died a week before the Selje-men's Mass,[3] and Olav
Audunsson made a goodly funeral feast for him. Among the
ladies who came out to Hestviken to help Ingunn with the prep-
arations was Signe Arnesdatter, who was newly married and
mistress of Skikkjustad. Her younger sister Una was with her,
and when the guests were leaving, Olav persuaded Arne and the
priest to let Una stay behind, so that Ingunn might be spared all
toil and trouble at the end of her time.

Olav was somewhat vexed, for he could not help seeing that
Ingunn did not like the girl. And yet Una was deft and willing
to help, cheerful, and good to look at—small and delicately built,
nimble and quick as a wagtail, fair-haired and bright-eyed. Olav
himself had grown fond of his second cousins. He was slow to
make acquaintances, with his reserved and taciturn nature, but
there were not many folk he disliked. He took them as they were,
with their faults and their virtues, was glad to meet them as
acquaintances, but not unwilling to make friends with those he
liked, if only he were given time to thaw.

. . .

[3] July 8.

Olav Ingolfsson had got together a quantity of good timber, and in the previous autumn Olav Audunsson had already done a good deal to repair the most pressing damage in the houses of the manor. This summer he pulled down the byre and rebuilt it, for the old one was in such a state that the cows stood in a slough of mire in autumn, and in winter the snow drifted in so that the beasts could hardly have suffered more from cold if they had been out in the open.

One Saturday evening the household was assembled in the courtyard. It was fine, warm summer weather and the air was sweet with the scent of the first haycocks. And the fragrance of lime blossom was wafted down from the cliff behind the outhouses. The byre was set up again and the first beams of the roof were in place; the heavy roof-tree lay with one end on the ground and the other leaning against the gable as the men had left it when work ceased for the week.

Now the two young house-carls took a start and ran up the sloping beam, to see how high up they could go. Presently the other men joined in, even the master himself. The game went merrily, with laughter and shouts whenever one of the men had to jump off. Ingunn and Una were sitting against the wall of the house, when Olav called to the young maid:

"Come hither, Una—we will see how sure of foot you are!"

The girl excused herself with a laugh, but all the men crowded round her—she had laughed at them when they had to jump off halfway up the beam—no doubt she would be able to run right to the top, she would. At last they came and dragged her forcibly from the bench.

Laughing, she pushed the men aside, took a run and sprang a little way up, but then she had to jump down. Again she took a run and reached much higher this time—stood swaying for an instant, lithe and slender, waving her outstretched arms, while her little feet in the thin summer shoes, without soles or heels, clutched the beam like the claws of a little bird. But then she had to jump to one side, like a tomtit that cannot get a hold on a log wall. Olav stood below and caught her. Now the young maid had entered into the sport and ran up time after time, while Olav ran backwards below and received her laughing in his arms every time she had to jump down. Neither of them had an idea of anything, till Ingunn stood beside them, panting and white as snow beneath her freckles.

"Stop it now!" she whispered, catching at her breath.

"There is no danger, I tell you." Olav comforted her with a laugh. "Do you not see that I catch her—"

"I do see it." Olav looked at his wife in astonishment; she was on the point of tears, he could hear. Then she burst out, in mingled sobs and scornful laughter, with a toss of the head toward the girl: "Look at her—she is not so foolish but she has the wit to be ashamed."

Olav turned round to Una—she was red in the face and looked troubled. And slowly a flush rose in the man's cheeks. "Now I never heard—are you out of your senses, Ingunn?"

"I tell you," cried his wife, with bitterness in her voice, "she there, 'tis not for nothing she comes of Foulbeard's brood—and I trow there is more likeness between him and you than—"

"Hold your mouth," said Olav, revolted. " 'Tis *you* should have the wit to be ashamed—are *you* to say such things to me!"

He checked himself, seeing her wince as though he had struck her in the face. She seemed to collapse with wretchedness, and her husband took her by the arm.

"Come in with me now," he said, not unfriendly, and led her across the yard. She leaned against him with her eyes closed, so heavy that she could scarcely move her feet; he had almost to carry her. And within himself he was furious—"She makes herself out far more wretched than she is."

But when he had brought her to a seat on the bench and saw how miserable and unhappy she looked, he came up and stroked her check.

"Ingunn—have you clean lost your wits—can it displease you that I jest with my own kinswoman?"

She said nothing, and he went on:

"It looks ill and worse than ill—you must be able to see that yourself. Una has been here with us four weeks, has taken all the work she could from your shoulders—and you reward her thus! What do you suppose she thinks of this?"

"I care not," said Ingunn.

"But I care," answered Olav sharply. " 'Tis unwise of us too," he went on more gently, "to behave so that we challenge folk to speak ill of us. Surely you must see that yourself."

Olav went out and found Una in the cook-house; she was cleaning fish for supper. He went up and stood beside her—the man was so unhappy he did not know what he was to say.

Then she smiled and said: "Think no more of this, kinsman—she cannot help being unreasonable and ill-tempered now, poor woman. The worst is," she added, making the cat jump for a little fish, "that I cannot be of much use here, Olav, for I saw from the first day that she likes not my being here. So I believe it will be wiser if I go to Signe tomorrow."

Olav answered warmly: "To me it seems a great shame that she —that you should leave us in this wise. And what will you say to Signe and to Sira Benedikt about your not staying here?"

"You may be sure they have more wit than to make any matter of this."

"'Twill grieve Ingunn most of all," the man exclaimed dolefully, "when she comes to herself again—that she has offended our guest and kinswoman so abominably."

"Oh no, for then she will scarce remember it. Let not this vex you, Olav—" she dried her hands, laid them on his arms, and looked up at him with her bright, pale-grey eyes, which were so like his own.

"You are kind, Una," he said in a faltering voice, and he bent over her and kissed her on the lips.

He had always greeted the sisters with a kiss when they met or parted. But he realized with a faint, sweet tremor that this was not the kiss that belongs to courtesy between near kinsfolk who count themselves something more than cottagers. He let his lips dwell upon the fresh, cool, maidenly mouth, unwilling to let go, and he held her slender form to him and felt a subtle, fleeting pleasure in it.

"You are kind," he whispered again, and kissed her once more before reluctantly releasing her and going out.

"There can be no sin in it," he thought with a mocking smile. But he could not forget Una's fresh kiss. It had been—ay, it had been as it should be. But that was a small thing to trouble about. He had been *angry* with Ingunn—had never believed she could behave so odiously and ridiculously. But no doubt Una was right, there was little count to be taken of what she said or did at this time, poor creature.

But when he had accompanied Una to Skikkjustad next day

after mass—it was the feast of the Translation of Saint Olav [4]—and was riding homeward alone, his anger boiled up anew. Had she come to such a pass that she now suspected him of the worst, simply because she herself had sinned? No, now he remembered that she had shown his kinswomen ill will before, in the autumn, when there was naught amiss with her. She *was* jealous—even at Frettastein she had been quick to find faults and blemishes in other women—the few they met. And that was unseemly.

Olav was indignant with his wife. And then the fact that she should mention Torgils Foulbeard. All his childhood's vague aversion to the madman had turned to open hate and horror since he had heard the whole story of Torgils Olavsson. He had been a ravisher whom God struck down at the last, a disgrace to his kin. And *he* lived in folk's minds, while none remembered the other Olavssons who had lived and died in honour. Surely he might just as well be said to take after them—Olav was always ill at ease when he heard it hinted that he was so like Foulbeard. But he was annoyed with himself for feeling as it were a cold blast of ghostly terror at the back of his neck when such things were said.

His worst enemy could not accuse him of being mad after women. In all the years he had lived in outlawry he could scarcely recall having looked at a woman. When his uncle Barnim suggested that he ought to take the pretty miller's daughter and keep her as his leman, while he was at Hövdinggaard, he had sharply refused. Fair she was, and willing too, as he could see—but he had held himself to be a married man in a way, and he would keep his troth, even if his uncle teased him for it and laughingly reminded him of Ketillög.—This was a poor vendible girl he had fallen in with one night when he was in the town in company with other young men from the manor and they were all dead-drunk. In the morning, when he was sober again, he fell to talking with the girl, and after that he had conceived a sort of kindness for her—she was unlike others of her kind, sensible and quiet in her ways, preferring a man who did not care to play the fool and raise a riot in the inn. And then he had continued to look in on her when he was in the town on his uncle's business. Often he simply came in and sat with her, ate the food he had brought, and sent her for ale: he took pleasure in her quiet way of waiting upon him. But his

[4] August 3.

friendship for her had been no heavy sin—and no one in his right mind would assert that he had been unfaithful to Ingunn with *her*. He had often thought of her, however, in the first years that succeeded—hoped she had got into no trouble for helping him to get away to the Earl that time. He wished he could have known for certain that she had been able to hide from the others in the inn the money he gave her at parting, and whether she had carried out the plan she often spoke of: that she would turn her back on that inn and seek service with the nuns of St. Clara's convent. In truth she was far too good to be where she was.

It was the sense of this secret guilt that made him insecure—he felt defenceless against the Evil One, like a man who must go on fighting though crippled by a secret wound. His wife's prolonged ill health and her unreasonableness—and her being herself the cause that he was never allowed entirely to forget what *must* be forgotten—all this made him uneasy, wavering in his mind. And he felt a little thrill of pleasure as he remembered how good it had been to hold Una in his arms.

It angered him as he thought of Ingunn—it was her senseless behaviour to the kind, fair child that had been the cause of this.

But he would have to take it patiently—she had so little to comfort her now, Ingunn.

But the same evening Ingunn fell sick; it came so suddenly that before the ladies who were to help her could reach the place, it was over. None but Ingunn's own serving-women were with her when the child came—and they were all terrified and bewildered, they told Olav afterwards, with tears in their eyes. They thought the boy was alive when they lifted him up from the floor, but a moment later he was dead.

Never, thought Olav, had he seen a creature look so like a piece of broken, washed-out wreckage cast up on the beach as did Ingunn, lying there crouched against the wall. Her thick, dark-yellow hair lay tousled over the bed, and her dark-blue eyes, full of unfathomable distress, stared from her swollen, tear-stained face. Olav seated himself on the edge of the bed, took one of her clammy hands, and laid it on his knee, covering it with his own.

One of the weeping maids came in bearing a bundle, unwrapped

it, and showed Olav the corpse of his son. Olav looked for a few
moments at the little bluish body, and the mother burst into another harrowing fit of weeping. Quickly the man bent over her.
"Ingunn, Ingunn, do not grieve so!"

He himself was unable to feel any real grief over his son. In a
way he was fully aware how great was the loss—and his heart was
wrung when he reflected that the boy had died unbaptized. But
he had never had peace for rejoicing in the past months—had felt
nothing but a vague and faltering jealousy of what had gone before, anxiety for Ingunn, and a longing for the end of this cheer-
less time. But he had never realized that the end would be the
birth of a son in his house—a little boy whom he would bring up
to manhood.

The mother was not very sick, said the neighbours' wives when
they came and nursed her. But when the time came for her to be
helped to sit up in bed in the daytime, she had no strength. She
was drenched with sweat if she did but try to bind her hair and
put on her coif. And Sunday after Sunday went by without her
being strong enough to think of churching.

Ingunn lay on her bed, fully dressed, with her face turned to
the wall the whole day long. She was thinking that she herself
had been the cause of this child's death. She had received it with
loveless thoughts as it lay within her, groping for its mother's
heart-strings. And now it was dead. Had skilful women been with
her at its birth, it would surely have lived, the neighbours told
her. But she had always insisted, when they came to see her this
summer, that she did not expect it before St. Bartholomew's Day.[5]
For she had been afraid of these wise neighbours of hers—lest they
might find out and spread it abroad that Olav Audunsson's wife
had had a child before. And the morning she woke up and felt it
was coming, she had risen and kept on her feet as long as she was
able.— But Olav must never know this.

But at last it could be put off no longer—it was on the Sunday
after Michaelmas that Ingunn Steinfinnsdatter had to submit to be
led into church. Olav had learned that there were four other
women newly delivered who were to go in; one of them was the
daughter-in-law of one of the richest manors of the neighbour-

[5] August 24.

hood, and she had just brought an heir into the world; the church would surely be half full of her kinsfolk and friends alone, who would come to make offerings with her. Olav could scarce bring himself to think of Ingunn, kneeling before the church door, poor and empty-handed, while the others bowed to receive the lighted candles—as the psalm of David was sung over the women: "Who shall ascend into the hill of the Lord? or who shall stand in His holy place? He that hath clean hands and a pure heart . . . he shall receive the blessing from the Lord, and righteousness from the God of his salvation."—To Ingunn and him this would sound like a judgment.

Olav had been shy of going near Sira Benedikt since the day Ingunn drove Una Arnesdatter out of their house in such a shameful manner. But now he rode one day up to the priest's and begged him to be kind and bring consolation to Ingunn.

Sira Benedikt had ordered that all corpses of unbaptized infants should be buried on the outer side of the churchyard fence; they were not to be hidden under a heap of stones, like cattle that had died a natural death, or buried in waste places like evil-doers. He reproved people severely for believing in the ghosts of such children: dead infants could not appear, he said, for they were in a place which is called Limbus Puerorum, and they can never come out from thence, but they are well there; Saint Augustine, who is the most excellent of all Christian sages, writes that he would rather be one of these children than never have been born. But if folk have been scared out of their wits and senses in those places where the corpses of infants have been hidden away, it is because they themselves have such sins on their consciences that the Devil has power over them to lead them astray. For it is clear that the place where a mother has made away with her babe is wellnigh an altar or a church to the Devil and all his imps—they are fain to haunt it ever after.

The priest consented at once to accompany Olav home. Olav Ingolfsson had firmly believed in infant apparitions and thought indeed that he himself had once laid such a ghost. So Sira Benedikt was zealous to dissuade Ingunn from this heresy and give her consolation.

The woman sat, white and thin, with her hands folded in her lap, and listened to their parish priest discoursing of the Limbus Puerorum. It was written of this in a book—a monk in Ireland had been rapt in an ecstasy seven days and seven nights, and he had had a vision of hell and purgatory and heaven; he had also been in the place where are the unbaptized infants. It appears as a green valley, and the sky is always clouded as a sign that they can never attain the bliss of beholding God's countenance; but light is shed down between the clouds, in token that God's goodness dwells upon the children. And the children appeared to be happy and in good case. They do not feel the lack of heaven, for they know not that there is such a place, nor can they rejoice at being saved from the pains of hell, for they have never heard of it. They play there in the valley and splash water upon one another, for the place is passing rich in brooks and meres.

Olav interrupted: "Then meseems, Sira Benedikt, that many a man might be tempted to desire he had died an infant and unbaptized."

The priest replied: "It is so ordained, Olav, that in our baptism we are called to a great inheritance. And we must pay the price of being men."

"Are the parents suffered to come thither sometimes?" asked Ingunn in a low voice—"to have sight of their children and watch them at play?"

The priest shook his head:

"*They* must go their own way, up or down—but it will **never** take them over that valley."

"Then meseems God is cruel!" exclaimed the woman hotly.

"That is what we human creatures are so prone to say," replied the priest, "when He grants not our desires. Now, it was of great moment to you and your husband that this child should have grown to man's estate—he was born to take up a great inheritance and carry on the race. But if a woman bear a child whose only destiny is to be a testimony of her shame and whose only inheritance is his mother's milk—then her mother's heart is oftentimes not to be depended upon. It may be that she will hide herself and give birth to it in secret, destroy her child body and soul or put it out with strangers, well pleased if she neither hear nor see it more—"

Olav sprang up and caught his wife as she fell forward in a swoon. Kneeling on one knee, he supported her in his arms; the priest bent down and quickly loosened the linen coif that was tightly wound about her neck. With her white face hanging backward over her husband's arm, and the bare arch of her throat, she looked as one dead.

"Lay her down," said the priest. "Nay, nay, not upon the bed —on the bench, so that she may lie flat." He busied himself with the sick woman.

"She is not strong, your wife?" asked the priest as he was about to ride away. Olav stood holding his horse.

"No," he said. "She has ever been weak and frail—ay, for you know we are foster-brother and sister; I have known her from childhood."

5

EARLY in the following spring Duke Haakon made ready for an inroad upon Denmark; the Danish King was to be forced to make a reconciliation with his outlawed nobles upon such terms as they and the Norwegians should impose on him.

Olav Audunsson set out for Tunsberg; he was one of the subordinate leaders under Baron Tore Haakonsson. He was not altogether glad to be away from home this summer. He was now striking root at Hestviken: it was his ancestral seat and his native place —he had so long been homeless and an outlaw. As he proceeded with repairing the decay of his property, so that the source that had long been dried up began to flow again with riches, and as he himself acquired a grasp and a knowledge of the work ashore and afloat, he came to take pleasure in these labours on his own behalf. He would have liked Björn to stay behind as his steward, but Björn had no mind to it. In the end Björn accompanied Olav as his squire, and an older man named Leif was to take charge of Hestviken together with the mistress of the house.

He also felt some anxiety for Ingunn—about midsummer she would be brought to bed again. True, she had been in much better health than last time; she had managed her housekeeping and her share of the farm work the whole time—and now she had learned and was not nearly so helpless as she had been when they were newly married. But Olav was uneasy, just because he guessed that she awaited this child with impatient longing. If a disaster should befall it, she would be utterly struck down with sorrow. And he seemed to have a presentiment—that he should find a child in the house when he came home in the autumn, seemed to him well-nigh unimaginable.

As soon as he reached Tunsberg, Olav Audunsson found old acquaintances of his years of outlawry wherever he turned. Earl Alf's men had flocked to the son-in-law of their slain chief, begging Lord Tore to take them into his service. Also among the Danish outlaws and their men, of whom the town was full, he met many that he had known while he was with the Earl. And one day a vessel ran into the harbour with letters from the Danish lords at Konungahella; her captain, Asger Magnusson, was from Vikings' Bay and he and Olav had been friends when Olav was at Hövdinggaard; they were also kinsfolk, but very distant. In the evening he went up into the town with his Danish kinsman and took a good rouse—he was much better for it afterwards.

Lord Tore made Olav captain of a little sixteen-oared galley, and his ship, with three small war-vessels from the shipowners of the south-east of the Vik, was to sail under the orders of Asger Magnusson in the *Wivern*, which the Norwegians called *Yrmlingen*.[6] Feeling between the Danes and their allies was often barely friendly, for this time the greater part of the force was Norwegian. And now the Norwegians made no secret of what they intended by the expedition: King Eirik and Duke Haakon would claim the whole kingdom of Denmark in succession to their grandfather, the holy King Eirik Valdemarsson, and make the country tributary to the crown of Norway. But the Danes did not like to hear this; they jeered at it, saying that their lords, the Constable, Stig Andersson, and Count Jacob, had never bound themselves by promises to any king, and that the Norwegians would have reward enough for their aid when they helped themselves with both hands among the towns and castles of the Danish King. The Norwegians answered that when it came to dividing the spoil, the Danes were great tricksters who always knew how to get the best share for themselves. The Norwegians were the more numerous, but they were mostly peasants and seamen, less inured to war than the Danes. For nearly all of these had served for years under their outlawed chiefs, had grown hardy and resolute, and let the Devil take every law but those of the fighting trade. But in this matter Earl Alf's old band were a match for

[6] *Little Snake.*

the Danes and more than that. Olav and Asger had their hands
full keeping the peace among their men.

The war fleet lay off Hunehals, and the squadron to which
Asger's and Olav's small vessels belonged harried the northern
coasts of the Danish islands. To Vikings' Bay they did not come.
Olav had heard from Asger that the Danish King's men had
stormed Hövdinggaard, burned the manor, and pulled down the
stone hall; Sir Barnim Eriksson had fallen, sword in hand. So it
booted not to think of him any more, else Olav would have had
a mind to see his uncle again. Now he could only let say a mass
for the man and let it go. For that matter he felt even less bound
than before to his mother's land and kindred.

There was something light-minded and foolhardy about these
low, defenceless coasts that lay awash in the midst of the glittering
sea. Above the broad white beach the yellow sand-dunes sloped
up, and forest trees grew right out to the point: the trunks of
full-grown beeches and gnarled oaks stood just above the stormy
waves; turf and roots overhung the edge of the bluff like the
threads of a torn tissue. It looked as if the sea had seized and bitten
out great pieces of the naked bosom of the land. Olav thought it
ugly. Inland there were indeed fair tracts—great and lordly manors, rich soil, swine in the woodland, fat cattle in the meadows,
fine horses in the parks—nevertheless, he had never felt at home
here. His homeland, the coast of Norway, ring within ring of
rocky defences—shelves, skerries and holms, the inner channel,
and at last the bright rocks of the mainland, before the first streaks
of green soil stole down to the head of an inlet, as though spying
out. The great manors lay inland, built mostly on ground from
which one could see far afield and know what was coming.

He thought of his own home—the bay within the bare rocks,
the manor on the slope of the hill with the Horse Crag at its back.
Ingunn would be up again by now—maybe she was standing out
in the yard, fair and young and slender again, sunning the child.
For the first time he felt an intense desire for children in his home.
But the bright vision was far off and incredible.

He was back in the same life he had led when he was outlawed
from Norway. The very feeling of wearing a coat of mail again
was strangely good; under the weight of it his bodily forces
seemed gathered together—it was good to feel the coolness of it
when he was at rest, and how it shut in and saved up the heat of

the body when fighting; it was like a warning to husband his strength, not to waste himself without plan or object. The trials of strength, afloat in rough weather, or in a descent ashore—both one and the other demanded of a man that he should be prompt and vigilant, but at the same time reckless in his inmost will, not caring if he were conquered by the danger he was using all his powers to conquer. It was something of this sort that loomed within Olav, more as feelings than thoughts—and at times he felt a kind of repugnance as he recalled the two years he had lived upon the land as a married man. A vague pang at the heart, like a faint throbbing beneath a healed wound—was he wasting his manly strength as he toiled in his loose woollen working-clothes, powerless to determine what he would gain in the end by his trouble? And a kind of revulsion against the memories of his intimate life with the sickly woman—it was as though he surrendered his powerful youth and unbroken health in order that she might absorb vigour from his store, and in his heart he did not believe it would be of any use. Like swimming with a drowning companion hanging about one's neck—no choice but to save the other or go down with him, if one would deserve the name of man. But one might be pardoned a failing at the heart, at the thought that the end was certain—to be drawn under—though one would struggle to the last, because a man can do no less.

Had she been in good health, and had it seemed natural to him that they would have children to reap where he sowed and inherit all his gains, then he would have looked upon his lot with different feelings. And now and then, when he tried to persuade himself into the belief that Ingunn might be well again, and that, for all he knew, he had a healthy, squalling infant son or daughter in the cradle at home—he would long for his own house. But usually this longing was absent—he had a profound sense of wellbeing at having no one but himself, no other care but his duties as one among many subordinate captains in the army.

He liked this life among none but men. The women he saw ashore, old or aging women who were charged with the food, venal hussies who were to be found wherever men were, he did not count these. There were wet days and nights afloat, fighting when they forced a landing—this had not fallen to Olav's lot very often, nor was he altogether sorry for it: in all the years he had followed Earl Alf he had never been able to overcome his dislike

74

of useless cruelty—and the Danes were cruel when they harried
their own country. Indeed, they would scarce have been anything
else if they had harried another country. But down here they
were used to the game; these coasts had seen plunder and rape and
burning since there were men in Denmark. Olav felt himself a
stranger among his mother's people. It was true his heart had
been set upon warfare and fighting in his young days, but then
the struggle was to end in a decision: death or victory. At times
an image would rise before him—a hostile attack upon Hestviken;
he defended himself in this home on the rock, with its back to
the cliff, drove the enemy downhill into the sea, or fell on his own
lands.

· The Danes were different, softer and tougher. They let themselves be chased away—peasants into the depths of the forests,
lords overseas—but they came back, even as the waves of the sea
retire and come again. They lost and they won, and neither one
nor the other made much difference to their appetite or en-
joyment of life. And with a strangely buoyant patience they
bore the thought that things would never be otherwise—they expected to have to fight to all eternity, winning or losing along
the low, wet shores, without calling any victory or defeat the
last one.

Then they were quartered ashore for a time. The men were
closely packed in the houses of the town; the air was dense and
hot with rank smells, foul talk, ale and wine, belching, wrangling
and quarrelling. There was fighting every night in the streets and
yards—the captains had hard work to keep anything resembling
peace and discipline among their bands.

Rumours were ever in the air—of ships' crews that were re-
ported to have made descents and carried off great booty. At
Maastrand a body of Earl Alf's old men-at-arms had fought with
some German merchants and killed all their prisoners—in payment
of an old score of their dead lord's, it was said. The Danish King's
fleet had taken the Constable's fortress on Samsö, and Sir Stig
Andersson himself had fallen, folk said. Among the Norwegians
it was believed that Duke Haakon aimed at winning Denmark
for himself, and that it was over this he had quarrelled with his
brother the King; it was for this reason that King Eirik had sailed
home to Björgvin already in the early summer, and that the captains of the King's fleet, lords from the west country and some

few from Iceland, had wrought such destruction. But the Duke caused strict discipline to be kept in his army: he did not wish to see the total ruin of the land he intended for himself.

Olav thought that even if the great lords knew the truth or falsity of all these rumours, the rank and file of the army had little grasp of what was going on. And the lesser captains, like himself, were reckoned with the rank and file, not with the lords —whom the fighting men usually knew only by name; but the less they knew of them, the more inclined they were to talk about them. That he himself was related to many of the outlawed Danish nobles, he was too proud to mention, if they did not remember him. His own chief, Baron Tore, counted him as no more than a subordinate captain on the same footing as the masters of the ships of the country levies; he deemed Olav of Hestviken to be a brave man and a useful leader—but he had not distinguished himself in any way above the rest; he had had no opportunity of performing deeds that attracted attention.

One thing resulted from this life: when Olav recalled his secret dread that there was some connection between the load on his conscience and the fact that there had been so little joy in his life with Ingunn, this now seemed to him a very preposterous thought. Imperceptibly an idea of this sort had grown up in him during these two years. But these men among whom he was had robbed the peasants of their cattle, burned houses and castles, had not only reddened their weapons in fight, but often slain and maimed defenceless folk without just cause. Some had on them treasures that they were mightily afraid of showing—likely enough these things were stolen from churches. And though it was Duke Haakon's order that rape should be punished with death, it could hardly be thought that all the women and girls who drifted among the fighting men while the army was ashore had taken to this life entirely of their own free will.

His own settlement with that Icelander seemed an utterly unimportant affair. Surely no one believed that all these fellows here confessed every scrap to such priests as were to be found—it was impossible that the men could remember all or the priests find time to hear such scrupulous confessions. Many a man who cheerfully took *corpus Domini* before setting out certainly had heavy sins on his conscience which he had forgotten to confess. The wretched Teit had his deserts—Olav now thought himself strangely foolish to have seen signs in this and that: in the chance words of strangers, in dreams that had come to him, in the colour and markings of his beasts. He had believed at last he felt God's hand over him, seeking to make him turn aside from the path he followed. Here, among all these men, where he himself was of so little account, his own affairs were also lessened in his eyes: so many a brave man's death had he seen and heard of that it was unreasonable to think that the Lord God was so scrupulous over the slaying of Teit, or that He singled out him, Olav Audunsson, for chastisement, penance, and salvation, when there were great men enough who needed it much more—such as the Danish lords, for the way they treated their own countrymen. Even Ingunn's transgressions seemed to grow less—he heard and saw so much out here.

One day in late autumn he steered into the fiord. The sun was hot, between the rain-squalls that swept over the sea. There was a fresh breeze; the white spray shooting high under the Bull gave him a greeting from afar. Up at the manor they had recognized his little craft—Ingunn stood on the quay as he came alongside, her coif and cloak fluttering about her thin, stooping figure. And as soon as he saw her, the husband knew that all was as it had been:

The child had been stillborn, a boy again.

Two months after the new year Ingunn fell sick again—she had miscarried, and this time her life was in danger. Olav had to fetch the priest to her.

Sira Benedikt counselled husband and wife to live apart for a year and employ the time in penitence and good works; weak as Ingunn Steinfinnsdatter now was, the priest deemed it impossible that she could bear a living child.

Olav was willing enough to try this expedient. But Ingunn was clean beside herself with despair when he spoke of it to her.

"When I am dead," she said, "you must marry a young and healthy wife and have sons by her. I told you that I was broken down—but you would not let me go then. I have not long to live, Olav—give me leave to be with you the little time I have left!"

Olav stroked her face and smiled wearily. She often talked of his marrying again—but she could not bear him to look at another woman or to say two words to their neighbours' wives when he met them before the church door.

Sleeplessness troubled him this spring even worse than the other years. With a heart heavy with compassion he lay with his arm about the poor, ailing woman—but he felt her clinging love as an encumbrance. Even in her sleep she lay with her thin arms clasped about his neck and her head resting on his shoulder.

He was glad to get away from home when he set out for Tunsberg in the spring. The summer passed like the previous one. But whenever he thought of his home, Olav was sick at heart. It mattered not, he felt, that he had had so little joy in his life with her—the loss of Ingunn would mean the loss of half his life.

But she was well and cheerful when he came home late in the autumn, this time she was so certain that all would go well. But six weeks before Yule the boy was born, more than two months before his time.

Awhile before this happened it became known in the countryside that Lord Tore Haakonsson had had Björn Egilsson beheaded at Tunsberg. After the first campaign in Denmark he had entered the Baron's service—he would not go back to Hestviken any more. When the war fleet returned to Norway this autumn, Björn had been on board the ship that brought Lord Tore himself home, and while on shipboard he had fallen out with another man and cut him down. When the Baron ordered him to be seized and bound, he had defended himself, wounded two men to the death, and given several others lesser hurts.

Gudrid, Björn's wife, had died during the summer, and now Olav Audunsson thought he ought to help the orphans of the man he had liked so well. Torhild Björnsdatter had held aloof from all —she was cross and taciturn; Olav had rarely seen her and scarcely exchanged two words with the girl, so he did not rightly know how he was to put his offer to her.

But when Ingunn lay sick so near to Yule and there was no mistress at Hestviken to cope with all the work that was at hand —their numbers were increased during the fishing season, with the hunting of seals and auks—Olav considered whether he should speak to Torhild Björnsdatter and ask if she would move to Hestviken and keep house for him. She was said to be a capable and industrious woman—and the mismanagement had now reached such a pitch that any housekeeper at all must be able to do the work better than the mistress; Ingunn was of little use when she was well, and she had had scarcely a day's health in three years. The food was so wretched that Olav had had difficulty in getting house-carls this winter, and when strangers visited the house, he dreaded and was ashamed of what might be sent to table. Except the fresh fish and frozen meat in winter, there was hardly anything that did not smell and taste abominably. The stores in the larder lasted an unaccountably short time—until Olav discovered that many of the servants stole like magpies. Bought ale from town he always had to keep in the house, dear though it was, for Ingunn's brew had a bad name all along the fiord. Even the drink in the curd-tub was not merely sour, but rotten. He himself had hardly had a new garment made at home since he was married, and his everyday clothes looked like a beggar's rags—they were neither kept clean nor properly mended.

He had proposed to Ingunn more than once that they should take a housekeeper, but each time she had been in utter despair, weeping and begging him not to bring such a shame upon her. It was in vain he replied that sickness is every man's master; it could be no shame to her. He saw that if he was to speak to Torhild, he would have to do it without consulting his wife. The worst thing was about her children—she would have to bring the younger ones with her, and that was likely to lead to noise and disturbance, which Ingunn could not bear.

The six surviving offspring of Björn and Gudrid were known to all as "Torhild's children." Gudrid had been an unnatural mother—she shook off one child after another; her stepdaughter took it up, laid it in her lap, and fed it from a cow's horn. Gudrid cared for nothing but gadding about the neighbourhood. Torhild had been betrothed in early youth to a lad of substance and honour, but he was near akin to that Gunnar whom Björn had had the misfortune to slay, and so the marriage came to naught. Since then she had been drudging in their poor home, doing the work of a man and a woman together. Folk knew little about her, but the maiden was of the best repute. Nor was she ugly, but no one seemed able to conceive that Torhild Björnsdatter might change her condition. She was now no longer young—eight or nine and twenty winters old; the two eldest of her half-brothers were of an age to take service, but when this was spoken of, Torhild answered that she needed them at home.

One Sunday, not long after Ingunn fell sick, Olav saw Torhild Björnsdatter in church. She stood farthest back on the women's side and was completely shrouded in a long and ample black cloak, which she held closely about her. She had drawn the hood forward, and from time to time the man saw her face in profile, pale against the black woollen stuff. She was like her father: the forehead high and abrupt, the nose long, but finely curved, the mouth broad and colourless, but with lips tightly closed as though in mute patience; the chin was powerful and shapely. But her fair hair was faded and hung straggling about her forehead; her complexion seemed grey and turbid from smoke and soot that had eaten into the skin. She had large grey eyes, but they were red-rimmed and bloodshot, as though she had stood too long over the fire in the narrow, smoky cot. Her hands, which held the cloak together, even when she clasped them in prayer, were not large, and the fingers were long—but they were red and blue, covered with broken chilblains, ingrained with black, and the nails were worn. And though she was so well shrouded, it could be seen that the girl held herself very erect.

After mass Olav stayed outside the church talking with some other franklins, and it came about that he rode home alone—his people had gone on ahead.

He had reached the place where the forest gives way to open ground, with some great meres and a little croft on the edge of the largest of them. The bridle-path divides here just behind the outhouses, one path going to Rynjul and southward, and another down to Hestviken. As Olav was turning into the road for home, he saw Torhild Björnsdatter standing outside the hut; she had taken off the cloak and gave it back to the woman from whom she had borrowed it. As she caught sight of the horseman, she turned abruptly and crossed the frozen mere, as quickly as if she were flying from him. But Olav had seen why she kept the cloak so closely about her—without it she was in her bare shift, of coarse, undyed homespun. It was cut low at the neck, the sleeves reached to the elbows, and her arms were blue with cold, as were her naked ankles, which showed between the edge of the shift and the big, worn-out man's shoes she wore on her feet. She had bound a strip of homespun about her waist for a belt—again Olav could not help being surprised at her erect bearing.

She was dressed like working-women when they cut the corn on a summer's day. A memory flashed across Olav's mind—of blue sky, sunshine, and warmth over the fields, where the women bent to grasp the sheaves of ripe, sweet-smelling corn. He watched the summer-clad maid flying across the frozen mere toward the edge of the wood, where the spruces were grey with rime. How she must feel the cold!—she was bareheaded, her plait of hair hung thick and straight down her resolute, unbending back. All at once Olav felt an intense liking for her. He halted awhile on the path, watching the girl. Then he rode on a little way—turned his horse and set out across the mere.

The croft that Björn Egilsson had owned lay up the slope on the other side—an alder thicket almost hid it from travellers on the road. Olav saw that a good deal of clearing had been done since he had last had occasion to come here, two years ago. Some small patches must have been dug last autumn: some stones and roots were not yet cleared away. Farther up, the strips of stubble showed lighter than the rest of the rime-covered, swampy ground. The little byre that Björn had put up a few years before shone yellow with its fresh logs, but he had never got the dwelling-house built: they were still living in the round turf hut.

Torhild Björnsdatter came out on hearing the horseman. The children peeped behind her in the doorway. She stepped outside and stood erect, blushing slightly and glancing ungraciously at the man as he dismounted, and she guessed he had some business with her. Olav tied Apalhvit to a tree and covered him with his grey fur cloak. "You must let me come in, Torhild; there is a matter about which I would fain speak with you." He did not wish her to stand there in the cold; she was now barefooted.

Torhild turned and went in. She laid a worn sheepskin on the earthen bench, bade her guest be seated, and offered him a ladle of goat's milk from a bowl that stood behind him on the seat. The milk tasted and smelt strongly of smoke, but Olav was fasting and thought it good. The room was like a cave, with a narrow passage between the two benches of earth that filled it entirely. Torhild sat down opposite her guest; she had a two-year-old child on her lap; another girl, a little older, stood behind her with her arms about her neck. The two eldest boys lay by the fire near the door, listening to the talk between their sister and the stranger.

After they had spoken of other things for so long as was proper, Olav mentioned his business. She must have heard what a pass he had come to at home—how little likely it was that his wife would be fit for any work that winter. If Torhild would grant them a boon and help Ingunn and him in their difficulty, they would never be able to thank her enough. Olav spoke as one asking a favour, he liked her so cordially. Strong she looked, with her broad, straight shoulders, high, firm bosom, and powerful hips. *She* had never let herself be bent double by all her drudgery here between the cot and the little byre.

Torhild raised some objections, but Olav replied that it was clear she should have leave to bring all six children with her to Hestviken. He had not thought of offering to receive more than the two eldest—they could no doubt be of some service—and the two youngest, who could not be parted from their foster-mother. The middle ones they could surely find a home for in the neighbourhood. Her beasts—the cow, four goats, and three sheep—he would also receive; when the roads were fit for sledges they would send for the fodder she had stacked. And he would see to it that the fields here at Rundmyr were manured and sown in the spring.

The end of it was that Torhild took service with Olav and was to move to Hestviken as soon as she had made ready a few clothes for herself and the children. Olav promised to provide the stuff. He himself rode up with it next day; there was no need for her fellow servants to know how poor she had been.

He had thought of telling Ingunn of his agreement with Torhild the same evening. But when he came in to the sick woman, she lay in a doze, so faint and bloodless that she looked as though she could neither hear nor answer him. So he merely sat on the bedstead beside her. Her face was fearfully wasted; the eyelids lay like thin brown membranes over the sunken eyes, her skin was grey and flecked with brown over the cheek-bones—the dark streaks that had come with her second child had never gone away. Her white linen shift was fastened with a good brooch—her throat was wizened like a plucked fowl's. He remembered that Torhild's grey woollen shift had been held together with a pin of sharpened bone—but her throat was round as the stem of a tree, and her bosom was full and high. She was sound and strong, although her lot in life had been so heavy and toilsome. His own poor creature was well provided with all that was needed to make pleasant the lot of a young wife—and here she lay, for the fourth time in three years, childless and broken in health.—Olav stroked her cheek.

"Did I but know some means of helping you, Ingunn mine!"

He did not bring himself to tell his wife that he had hired a housekeeper until Torhild moved in with all her following of children and animals. Ingunn looked displeased, but all she said was:

"Ay, so it is, I ween; you must have one that can take charge of the house. I was never good for aught—and now it seems I can neither live nor die."

Ingunn lay sick a great part of the winter, and it looked as though she had spoken truly—she could neither live nor die. But then she began to mend, and by the first days of Lent she could sit up. Spring came early on the fiord that year.

It was expected that the levies would be called up again for the summer. The franklins were now heartily sick of the war with Denmark. No man believed that either the King or the Duke would reap anything by it in the end but the loss of their mother's inheritance, which indeed they *had* wrested from their cousin, the late King of Denmark,[7] before he was murdered.

That spring Sira Benedikt announced that he intended to repair to Nidaros for the Vigil of St. Olav. Many of the folk of his parish joined him for the sake of having good company on this pilgrimage, which every man and woman in Norway desired to make at least once in his life.—Olav leaped at the thought, seeing in it a hope and a remedy—Ingunn should take part in the journey. It seemed a very prodigy that she had been so well of late and ailed not at all—she must needs make use of this rare occasion.

At first Ingunn was by no means willing to go—if Olav could not go with her. But then the thought came to her that she would go home and see her sister and brothers—accompany the pilgrims only as far as Hammar. Olav was displeased with this; he wished her to make the pilgrimage, then perhaps she would be restored

[7] Erik Glipping.

to health at Saint Olav's shrine. If she was equal to travelling so far into Heidmark, then she could surely make the whole journey: they were to move slowly, for there were many sick people in the company. But when he saw how she longed to see her own family again, he gave his consent.

He accompanied her as far as Oslo and stayed in the town a few days, buying and selling. One morning Ingunn was sitting in the inn when Olav entered hastily. He searched in their leather bags, did not find what he wanted, and opened another bag. There he came upon some little garments—they might have fitted a child of four years. Unconsciously his eyes fell upon his wife—Ingunn's head was bent and her face was red as fire. Olav said nothing, packed the bag again, and went out.

6

HAAKON GAUTSSON had bought Berg after the death of Lady Magnhild Toresdatter. Now Tora Steinfinnsdatter had dwelt there as his widow for over a year. Ingunn guessed from her talk that she had had a good life with Haakon, but she lived well without him too. She was a very capable woman. Ingunn never ceased to marvel at her sister, who busied herself deftly, promptly, and shrewdly both indoors and out, although her bulk was prodigious. She still preserved her fair red and white complexion and her regularity of feature, but her cheeks and chin were grown to an immense size and her body was so unwieldy that she could scarcely sit on horseback; even her hands were so fat that the joints only showed as deep hollows—but Tora could make full use of them. Wealth and prosperity surrounded her, and her children were handsome and promising. She had had six, and all were alive and thriving.

On the third evening the sisters were sitting together in the balcony before going to rest. Ingunn sat in the doorway listening to the stillness—far away in the woods the cuckoo still called now and again, and the corncrake chirped in the fields. But she had now lived so long in a place where the very air seemed always to be full of voices, the soughing of the wind, the roar of the sea dashing against the rocks below: under this clear and silent vault the little sounds of birds seemed only to make the stillness more audible—to Ingunn it was as though she drank deep draughts of refreshment. The bay was so small and so dear; bright and smooth it lay, with dark reflections of the wooded headlands. The last banks of cloud had settled upon the distant hills—the day had been showery with gleams of sunshine, and a sweet scent came up to them from the hay spread out below.

Her longing would not be kept back—all at once, without thinking, Ingunn declared the purpose for which she had come. She had fought with herself these two days, now to speak out, now to hold back the question:

"Do you ever see aught of my Eirik?"

"He is well," said Tora, with some hesitation. "Hallveig says he is thriving and promises well. She comes hither every autumn, you know."

"Is it long since you saw him?" asked her sister.

"Haakon was so much against my going there," said Tora as before. "And since then I have put on so much flesh that I am little suited for such a journey. But you know that he is with honest folk, and Hallveig has naught but good news to tell of him. I have much upon my hands here at home—and little time to wander so far afield," she concluded, with some heat.

"When saw you him last?" Ingunn asked again.

"I was there in the spring after you left home; but then Haakon would not have me go thither any more; 'twas only keeping the gossip alive, he said," Tora replied impatiently. "He was a fine child," she added, more gently.

"Then that is three years ago?"

"Ay, ay."

The sisters were silent awhile.

Then Tora said: "Arnvid went to see him—many times—in the first years."

"Has he too given up, Arnvid? Has he too forgotten Eirik now?"

Tora said reluctantly: "You know—folk could never find out who was the father of your child."

Ingunn was silent, overcome. At last she whispered: "Did they believe then that Arnvid—!"

"Ay, 'twas foolish to make such a secret of the father, since the child could not be hid," said Tora curtly. "So they could but guess the worst—a near kinsman or a monk."

There was a little pause. Then Ingunn said impulsively:

"I had thought of riding up their tomorrow—if the weather suits."

"I think it unwise," said Tora sharply. "Ingunn, remember we have all had much to suffer for your misdeeds—"

"*You*—who have six. How think you it feels to have but a single one, and to be parted from him? I have longed and longed for Eirik all these years."

"It is too late now, sister," said Tora. "Now you must remember Olav—"

"I *do* remember Olav too. He has had four dead sons by me. He claimed his own, the child I deserted and betrayed—he claimed his mother; he has sucked at me without ceasing, he almost sucked the soul out of my body, and he sucked the life out of my children while they were yet unborn, the outcast brother. There was yet a little life in the first son I bore to Olav, they say, when he came into the world—he died before I could see him, unbaptized, nameless. You have seen all your children come living into the light of day, and grow and prosper. Three times have I felt the child quicken within me and grow still and die again. And I knew I had nothing to hope for, when the pains came upon me, but to be quit of the corpse that burdened me—"

After a long silence Tora said:

"You must do as seems good to you. If you think the sight of him will make it easier for you, then—"

She patted her sister's cheek as they went in to bed.

It was drawing near to midday when Ingunn halted her horse at a gate in the forest. She had refused to listen to all Tora's prayers, but had ridden off alone. No worse thing had befallen her but to mistake the road; first she had come to a little farm that lay high up the slope on the other side of a little river. The people who lived there were the nearest neighbours to Siljuaas, and two children from this croft had gone with her down the hillside to a place where she could cross the river.

She stayed awhile sitting in the saddle and looking out over the country. The forests rolled endlessly, wooded ridge behind ridge into the distant blue—toward the north-west there was a gleam of snow under the shining fine-weather clouds. Deep down and far away she saw a small stretch of the surface of Lake Mjösen glittering beneath the foot of wooded hills, and the land on the other side lay blue in the noontide heat, with its green patches of farms and crofts.—From Hestviken one could not see a scrap of cultivation beyond the fields of the manor itself.

Homesickness and yearning for her child united in a feeling of crying hunger within her. And she knew she had but this one little hour in which to assuage it, for once only. Then she must turn back again, bow her neck, and take up her burden of unhappiness.

It seemed to her that in the south, by the fiord, the sunshine was never so clear and deep as here under the blue sky. It was glorious to be up on a high ridge once more. Below and to the right of her she had the dark, steep wooded slope, up which she had toiled on foot, leading her horse. The roar of the stream at the bottom of the ravine came up to her, now louder, now softer. Right opposite, on the other side of the secluded little valley, lay the croft that she had come to first, high up under the brow of the hill, and between her and it the air quivered in a blue haze over the hillside.

Before her was the clearing. The houses stood on a little knoll of rock-strewn, tussocky turf—they were grey and low, not more than a couple of logs high. The little patches of corn lay for the most part at the foot of the knoll, toward the fence.

Ingunn dismounted, pulled up the stakes of the gate—and a group of grey-clad little children came in view on the knoll. Ingunn was unable to move—she was trembling all over. The children kept as still as stones for a few moments, watching her; then they whisked round and were gone—not a sound had she heard from them.

As she walked up the knoll, a woman appeared at the door of one of the little houses. She seemed rather scared at sight of the stranger—perhaps she took her for something other than human, this tall woman with the snow-white coif about her heated face, and the sky-blue, hooded mantle and silver brooch, leading a great sorrel horse by the bridle. Ingunn hastened to call out, greeting the woman by name.

They sat indoors for a while, talking, and then Hallveig went out to fetch Eirik. The children could not be far away, she thought—they were scared of the lynx; it was abroad and had been sitting on the fence that morning. But they were shy of the visitor, for lynxes were more common than strangers here.

Ingunn sat and looked about her in the tiny room. It was low under the gabled roof and darkened by smoke; tools and earthen pots lay all about, so that there was scarce room to turn. A baby was asleep in a hanging cradle, snoring soundly and regularly. And then she heard a fly buzzing somewhere with a high, sharp, piercing note, incessantly, as though caught in a cobweb.

Hallveig came back, dragging with her a very small boy who had nothing on but a grey woollen shirt. Behind them swarmed the whole flock of the woman's own children, peeping in at the door.

Eirik struggled to be free, but Hallveig pushed him forward and held him in front of the strange woman. Then he raised his head for an instant, glanced in wonder at this splendidly clad person—crept back behind his foster-mother and tried to hide.

His eyes were a yellowish brown, the colour of bog-water when the sun shines into it, and the long, black eyelashes were curled up at the end. But his hair was fair and curled about his face and neck in great glistening ringlets.

His mother stretched out her arms and drew him onto her lap. With a voluptuous thrill she felt the hard little head on her arm, the silky hair between her fingers. Ingunn pressed his face to hers —the child's cheek was round and soft and cool; she felt the little half-open lips against her skin. Eirik resisted with all his force, struggling to escape from his mother's impetuous embrace, but he did not utter a sound.

"It is I who am your mother, Eirik—do you hear, Eirik?—it is I who am your real mother." She laughed and wept at once.

Eirik looked up as if he did not understand a word of it. His foster-mother corrected him sharply, bidding him be good and sit still on his mother's knee. Then he stayed quietly in Ingunn's lap, but neither of the women could get him to open his mouth.

She kept her arm about him and his head against her shoulder, feeling the whole length of his body. She passed her other hand over his round, brown knees, stroked his firm calves and his dirty little feet. Once he plucked a little at his mother's hand with his grimy little fingers, playing with her rings.

Ingunn opened her bag and took out the gifts. The clothes were far too big for Eirik—he was very small for his age, said his foster-mother. That these fine shirts and little leather hose were for him seemed quite beyond Eirik's comprehension. Not even when his mother tried on him the red cap with the silver clasp did he show any sign of joy—he only wondered, in silence. Then Ingunn took out the loaves and gave Eirik one that he was to have for himself—a big round wheaten cake. Eirik seized it greedily, clutched it to his chest with both arms, and then ran out—to all his foster-brothers and sisters.

Ingunn went to the door—the boy was outside with the cake held tightly in his arms; he thrust out his stomach to support it and straddled with his bare brown legs. The other children stood round in a ring staring at him.

Hallveig produced food for her guest—cured fish, oaten bannocks, and a little cup of cream. The children outside were given the pan of milk from which the cream had been skimmed. When Ingunn looked out again, they were sitting round their food; Eirik was on his knees, breaking off big pieces of the cake and passing them round.

" 'Tis his free-handed way," said the foster-mother. "Tora gives me a cake for him every year when I go down to Berg, and Eirik always shares it and nigh forgets to eat any himself. 'Tis such things, and others too, that show the boy comes of gentle kindred."

Now that all the children were sitting in a ring in the sunshine, Ingunn saw that Eirik's fair hair was quite different from the coarse flaxen shocks of the others; Eirik's was curly and shining, all unkempt as it was, and it was not yellow, but more like the palest brown of a newly ripened hazelnut.

Ingunn had to set out for home about the hour of nones, to be sure of reaching Berg before evening. She had not been able to conquer Eirik's shyness of the strange woman, and she had scarce heard his voice, except when he spoke to the other children out of doors. It was so sweet, so sweet.

Now Eirik was to have a ride on her horse as far as the forest. Ingunn walked, leading the horse and supporting the child with one arm, while she smiled and smiled at him, trying to coax forth a smile on his pretty little round and sunburned face.

They had passed through the gate: here no one could see them.

She lifted the boy down, hugged him in her arms, kissed and kissed again his face and neck and shoulder, while he struggled, making himself long and heavy in her embrace. When he began to kick her as hard as he could, his mother took a firm hold of his smooth bare calves—feeling with painful joy how firm and strong his little body was. At last she sank into a crouching attitude, and as she wept and muttered wild endearments over the child, she strove to coax and force him to sit in her lap.

When she was obliged for a moment to loosen her grip of him, the boy managed to wriggle away from her. He darted like a hare across the little clearing, was lost among the bushes—then she heard the gate close.

Ingunn stood up—she wailed aloud with pain. Then she staggered forward, bent double by sobs, with drooping arms. She came to a hedge, saw Eirik running over the turf so fast that his heels nearly reached his neck.

The mother stood there, weeping and weeping, as she bent over the hedge. The withered, rust-red branches of spruce had been felled to fence in a little field, where the corn had just begun to shoot—still soft and pinched like some kind of new-born life, it appeared ever after to her inner vision, when she thought of her sorrow, though now she had no idea of what her tear-blinded eyes looked upon.

But at last she had to go back to her horse.

7

IN the course of the autumn Sira Benedikt Bessesson fell sick. And one day a message came for Olav of Hestviken—the priest would bid him farewell.

Sira Benedikt did not look like a dying man as he lay propped up by pillows. But the wrinkles, which had seemed few and shallow in his fleshy, weatherbeaten face, were deeper and there were more of them. Nevertheless he predicted his approaching departure with certainty. When Olav had seated himself on the edge of the bed, as the other bade him, the priest, as though absently, took the riding-gloves out of the franklin's hand, felt the leather, and held them critically to his nose and eyes—Olav could not help a little smile.

They talked for a while of one thing and another—of Arne Torgilsson and his daughters. Two of them were now married in the neighbourhood, but Olav had seldom met them or their husbands of late.

"Folk see less and less of you, Olav," said the priest; "and many wonder at it, that you always keep to yourself as you do."

Olav reminded him that he had been at sea the last few summers, and every winter his wife had been sick.

Again the priest spoke of his imminent dissolution, asking Olav to be diligent in prayers for his soul. Olav gave him his promise. "But you have surely little need to fear what may await you, Sira Benedikt," said he.

"I think there is none of us but needs must fear it," replied the priest. "And I have always lived negligently, in that I took little thought of the small daily sins—I spoke and acted as my humour prompted me and consoled myself with the thought that it was no great and deadly sin—thinking it could be no such great matter what I did from frailty and natural imperfection, though I well knew that in God's eyes all sin is more loathsome than sores. And you and I would not like to live with a man and take him in our arms if he were full of sores and scabs all over. Now I have every day partaken of the remedy that surely heals the leprosy of sin. But you know that even the surest remedy and the most precious ointment is slow to heal the sickness if every day a man shall scratch himself again and tear his skin anew. And so it is with us, when our Lord has washed away our sins with His blood and anointed us with His mercy, but we are careless to do the deeds to which we were anointed—thus we scratch ourselves as soon as He has healed us, and we must bide in purgatory, bound hand and foot, until we are cleansed from our scabs and taints."

Olav sat in silence, twisting his gloves.

"Too great love have I borne to mine own, I fear. I thank God I have never been the cause of sin in them or backed them in an unrighteous cause—to that I was never tempted, for they were honest folk. But I ween I have been over-zealous sometimes for their advancement and wealth—it is written in my testament that it is to be given back.—And I have been headstrong with my enemies and my kinsmen's enemies—hasty and ready to believe evil of every man I liked not."

"Nevertheless we others must have worse than ill to fear," said Olav, trying to smile, "if you think your case stands thus."

The priest turned his head upon the pillow and looked the young man in the eyes. Olav felt that he went pale under the other's glance; a strangely impotent feeling came over him. He tried to say something, but could not find words.

"How you look at me—" he whispered at last. "How you look at me!" he said again a few moments later, and he seemed to be pleading for himself.

The priest turned his head again, and now he looked straight before him.

"Do you remember I always scoffed at Olav Half-priest for his talk of having seen so much of those things of which I had little knowledge? I think now that it may enter into God's counsels to open the eyes of one man to that which He conceals from another. I was never permitted to *see* aught of those things with which we are surrounded in this life. But now and again I have had an inkling of them, I too."

Olav looked at the priest attentively.

"Of *one* thing I have always had foreknowledge," said Sira Benedikt. "I have always known—almost always, perhaps it were well to say—when folk were on the way to fetch me to the dying. Above all, to such as had greatest need of help—such as were burdened by an unshriven sin—"

Olav Audunsson gave a start. Unconsciously he raised one hand slightly.

"Such things set their mark upon a man. Few are they who become so hardened as to show no trace that an old priest can note. This befell me one evening in this room, as I was putting off my clothes. I was about to climb into bed when it was borne in upon me that one was on the way hither and encountered great difficulties, and that he had sore need of intercession. I knelt down and prayed that he who was faring hither might find safe guidance—and then I thought to lie down and take a little rest before I had to go out. But when I had laid me down, I felt ever more strongly that someone was in great danger. At last it was clear to me that there was one present in the room with me, who aroused terror in my heart, but I knew it to be holy awe—'Speak, Lord,

Thy servant heareth,' I prayed aloud. And immediately it was as though a voice had called within me: I arose, clothed myself and waked one of thy servants, an old and trustworthy man. I bade him go with me up to the church, enter the belfry, and ring the midmost bell. I myself went into the church and knelt on the steps of the altar—but first I took a taper from the altar of Mary, lighted it and carried it to the church door, which I set open wide. The taper burnt with a calm, clear flame, though the night was wet and raw, misty and somewhat tempestuous.

" 'Twas not long before a man came and begged me to bring extreme unction and the viaticum to a sick man. The messenger had been so long on the road that he never thought he would arrive in time, for he had followed his own tracks in a ring and gone astray in bogs and rough ground. But we were able to bring succour in due time to one who needed it more sorely than most.

"Now I have been fain to think that even he who brought the message was one whose life had been such that evil spirits were more likely to guide his footsteps than his guardian angel, to whose voice he had ceased to listen. And it may well be that 'twas this angel, or the guardian spirit of the dying man, who turned to me and sent me to the church to ring the bell.

"But when I came home toward morning and went past the church, I saw that I had forgotten to close the door; the candle still stood there burning in its candlestick, and it was not consumed, nor had the wind and rain that drove in at the open door quenched it. I was afraid when I saw this sign, but I took courage and went in to bring the Virgin Mary back her candlestick and to close the door. Then I was ware that one bent over the candle and guarded the flame, for about it I saw as it were a reflection of the light falling upon something white—whether it was an arm or the lappet of a garment or a wing, I know not. I crept up the steps on my knees, and as I reached out my hand to take the candlestick, the light went out, and I fell upon my face, for I felt that one swept past me, whether it was an angel or a blessed soul—but I knew that this one had seen his and my Lord face to face."

Olav sat motionless, with downcast eyes. But at last he looked up, he could do naught else. And again he met Sira Benedikt's glance.

He knew not for how long they stayed thus, staring into each other's eyes. But he felt time passing over them like a roaring

stream, and he and the other stood at the bottom beneath the
stream, where was eternity, unchanging and motionless. He knew
that the other could see the secret sore that preyed upon his soul
and was eating its way out—but he was too cowardly to allow the
healing hand to touch the festering cancer. In extreme terror lest
the diseased spot might be disturbed, he summoned all his will and
all his strength—he closed his eyes. He sank into darkness and
stillness—time ceased to roar and sing, but he felt the room turning
round with him. When again he opened his eyes, the room was as
usual, and Sira Benedikt lay with averted head on the green-
spotted pillow. He looked weary and sorrowful and old.

Olav stood up and took his leave—knelt down and kissed Sira
Benedikt's hand in farewell. The old man took his firmly and
pressed it as he murmured some Latin words that were unknown
to Olav.

Then he went out, and the priest did not attempt to hold him
back.

A week after came the news of Sira Benedikt's death. The folk
of the parish counted it a loss—they had esteemed him as an able
priest and a bold and upright man. But the franklins had never
reckoned him to be endowed with any conspicuous mental gifts—
he was like one of themselves in manners and disposition and had
had no learning beyond what was necessary.

Olav Audunsson alone was strangely stricken in spirit when he
heard the news. It had seemed as though a door stood open—and
vaguely he had reckoned that one day he would be given courage
to enter it. But as yet he had not had the courage. And now the
door was closed for all time.

He had not had much talk with Ingunn about her visit to the
Upplands, and the child had not been mentioned between them.

But toward Yule, Olav again had fears that the worst had happened—so he called it in his own mind when Ingunn was clearly
with child.

Ever since Torhild Björnsdatter had been with them, Ingunn
had shown a more active spirit than ever before in all the years
they had been married. There was now no need for the mistress to
do anything herself; Torhild was so capable that she accomplished
all the household duties alone, and she had learned how everything
was done at Hestviken. But it seemed that the other's presence had

aroused a kind of ambition in Ingunn—Olav guessed that his wife had felt injured at his taking a housekeeper, and that without first consulting herself. And though Torhild was very accommodating, inquiring her mistress's desires in everything, keeping out of the way as far as possible and living with her children in the little old house on the east of the courtyard, where Olav's mother had once dwelt, the husband noticed that Ingunn did not like Torhild.

Fine needlework was the only thing in which Ingunn had excelled in her youth, and now she took it up again. She made a long kirtle for Olav—it was of foreign cloth, woven in black and green flowers, and she adorned it with broad borders. Her husband had little use for such a garment now—but she left the making of his working-clothes to Torhild. For the daily work about the manor she remained as useless as ever, but she insisted on taking part in it all, and for Yule she toiled at preparing the meat, brewing, and cleaning houses and clothes, running between the storehouses and the quay in driving snow-squalls that came in from the fiord and turned the whole courtyard and the road down to the sea into a mass of slippery green slush.

But the evening before Christmas Eve, when Olav came in, he found her standing by herself up on the bench, struggling with the old tapestry, which was to be hung on wooden hooks along the uppermost of the wall-logs. It was all in one piece and very heavy; Olav came up to help her, holding up a length at a time.

"I doubt if it be prudent for you to work so hard," he said. "If you think it will be well this time, all the more reason to be careful of yourself—so that it may turn out as we both desire."

Ingunn said: " 'Twill fall out, sure enough, as 'tis fated—and rather will I face now the suffering I cannot escape than go through months of torment in the prospect of it. Think you not that I know I shall never see the day when any child calls me mother?"

Olav looked at her a moment—they were standing side by side on the bench. He jumped down, lifted her after him, and stood for a while with his hands on her hips.

"You must not talk in that way," he said feebly. "You cannot be sure of it, Ingunn mine!"

He turned from her and began to clear away the hooks and pegs that were lying on the bench.

"I thought," he asked in a low voice, "that you had a mind to go and see that boy—when you were at Berg in the summer?"

Ingunn made no reply.

"I have sometimes wondered whether perchance you longed for him," he said very softly. "Do you ever long for him?"

Ingunn was still silent.

"Is he dead mayhap, the child?" he asked gently.

"No. I saw him once. He was so afraid of me—clawed and kicked—he behaved like a young lynx when I tried to hold him."

Olav felt old far beyond his years, weary and worn at heart. This was the fifth winter he and Ingunn had lived together—it might have been a hundred years. But the time must have seemed yet longer to her, poor woman, he reminded himself.

Meanwhile he tried to rouse himself—to hope. If this time it went well, that would indeed be the only thing that could make her happy again. And now she had been in good health longer than any time before—so maybe she was equal to going through with it.

As for himself, all desire of having children had been tortured out of him long ago. He thought indeed of his manor and his race —but now these affected him so little. And then there loomed before him a shadowy vision of something immensely far off in the future: when he had grown old, and his pain and anxiety and this strange morbid and uneasy love of his was no more— For she could not live to be old. And then his life might be like that of other men. Then he would be able to seek atonement and peace for his tortured conscience. And then there might yet be time to think of his manor and his race—

But when he had reached this point in his vague conjectures, a sharp pang went through his heart, as when a wound opens wide. Dimly he divined that, in spite of his having no peace, no joy, in spite of his soul being hurt to the death—he yet possessed happiness, his own happiness, even if it were unlike the happiness of other men. Sick and almost bled to death, his happiness yet lived within him, and his aim must be to find courage and means to save it, before it was too late.

Ingunn seemed to keep in good health, even into the new year. But by degrees it made Olav uneasy to see her so utterly unlike herself—in a continual state of futile bustling. That Torhild could have patience with such a mistress was beyond his comprehension; but the girl followed her mistress with calm endurance and made work for herself out of all Ingunn's restless confusion.

Matters stood thus when at the beginning of Lent word came to Hestviken that Jon Steinfinnsson, Ingunn's younger brother, had died unmarried at Yuletide. There was indeed no necessity for Olav to journey northward at this winter season in order to take up his wife's share of the inheritance. But to Olav Audunsson this thing came as a token.

For four nights he lay with lighted candles, scarcely closing his eyes in sleep. He was bargaining with his God and judge. Some means he *must* find now of saving himself and this unhappy wreck of whom he was so fond that he knew of no beginning or end between them. The whole of Hestviken as his patrimony and the name of his own son—that must surely be amends in full for the brat of the vagabond Icelander.

Olav had been twelve days at Berg when he spoke of this one evening as he sat in the hall drinking with Hallvard Steinfinnsson, while Tora was present: now there only remained his most important business, to fetch home his son.

Hallvard Steinfinnsson stared at him agape—speechless. Then he flared up:

"Your—! Do you tell me that you *yourself* were father to the brat Ingunn had to creep into the corner and give birth to like a bitch?" He smote the table, crimson with rage.

"You well know, Hallvard, how my fortunes stood at that time," replied Olav with composure. "Had my enemies had this against me, that I was here in secret while still under sentence of banishment, they would scarce have been easy to deal with. And it might have cost their aunt and Lady Magnhild dearly if it had come out that they had housed me, an outlaw."

But Hallvard swore till the sparks flew. "Think you not, Olav Audunsson, my aunt and Magnhild would rather have paid all they had in fines for your thrusting yourself upon them, an outlawed man, than that it should have been said that one of our women had disgraced herself so foully that she dared not name the father of her child?" He mimicked all the guesses folk had brought forward, each one uglier than the last.

Olav shrugged his shoulders. "I know not how you care to

speak of these rumours now. For now the truth will come to light
—and had you let me know a little sooner that such things were
said, I should not have waited so long. We deemed we ought to
keep silence about it awhile for Magnhild's sake—but you may be
well assured I have never had any other thought than to acknowledge my son."

"You had—God knows what you had!" the other mocked. All
at once he sat straight up, with a stiff stare: "You had so! I wonder
whether Ingunn believed it so surely—or that you would hold to
your boast that 'twas a lawful marriage you made when you went
to bed with her before you had hair on your chin? Why then did
she throw herself into the lake?"

"Ask Tora," said Olav curtly. "She thinks it was the milk that
had gone to her head."

"Nor do I believe," said Hallvard slyly, "that Haftor would
have sued Magnhild for this—for you and he were reconciled—"

"Believe what you will," said Olav. "To be sure Haftor and I
were reconciled—'twas on account of the Earl I was then an outlaw. A numskull you have been all your days, Hallvard, but you
can scarce be so foolish as not to see that for you and your kinsfolk the more profitable way is to believe what I have now told
you. Even if you should miss the inheritance you would have
gotten had your sister died childless."

Hallvard started up and made for the door.

But when Olav was left alone with Tora, he felt all at once that
this thing he had taken upon himself was intolerably difficult. As
she remained silent, he began with a kind of sneer:

"And you, Tora; do you believe me?"

Tora looked him straight in the face with eyes that betrayed
nothing:

"I am bound to believe you, when you say it yourself."

And Olav felt it as a physical pressure upon his neck. Weary
as he was, he had now taken upon himself a new burden, in addi-
tion to the old. Nothing of it could be cast off, and nowhere could
he turn for help. He must go through with it—alone.

On the evening of the next day Olav came down to Berg with
the child. Tora did her best to receive her sister's son kindly. But,
for all that, the boy seemed to feel he was not very welcome in
this house; he kept close to his new-found father, trotted at his

heels everywhere and stood by Olav's knee when the man sat down. Then if it chanced that he was allowed to hold his father's hand, or that Olav took him up and set him on his knees, Eirik's pretty little face beamed with joy—all at once he had to turn and look up at his father in glad wonder.

After this Olav stayed no longer at Berg than he was obliged. Already on the morning of the third day he was ready for the journey.

Eirik sat well wrapped in the sledge, turning this way and that, looking about and laughing with joy. Now he was to drive in a sledge again—he had had one drive when his father fetched him from Siljuaas; the sledge had been waiting for them at the last farm in the parish. Anki laughed and chatted as he made fast the baggage—the kind man who had carried him down on his back when his father fetched him. His father looked shapelessly huge in his fur mantle—and the rime on the fur of his own cape showed as white as it did on the hairs around the men's hoods.

Tora stood looking at the boy's red and happy face—his brown eyes were bright and quick as those of a little bird. There sprang up in the woman's heart a few drops of the tenderness she had felt for Eirik when he was a baby. She kissed him farewell on both cheeks and bade him bring greetings to his mother.

Olav came home to Hestviken early one day, as the pale sun shone red through the frost fog; he had driven from Oslo in the pitch-dark early morning. When they came into the valley he gave the reins to Anki, lifted the sleeping boy out of the sledge, and carried him up the slope to the house.

Ingunn sat by the fire combing her hair when Olav came in. He set down the child on the floor and pushed him forward:

"Go on, Eirik, and bid your mother good-morrow as you ought"—whereupon he turned back into the anteroom. From the door he saw with the corner of his eye that Ingunn crept toward the boy on her knees, stretching out her thin, bare arms; her hair swept the floor behind her.

He was out in the yard by the sledges when she called to him from the doorway. In the dark anteroom she threw her arms about his neck, weeping so that it shook her as she clung closely to him. He laid his hand upon her back—underneath the hair and the shift he felt her shoulder-blades standing out like boards. With that wealth of unbound hair streaming over the weak, drooping shoulders she reminded her husband in a strange way of what she had been like when she was young. Heavy and awkward she was now in her movements—it was not easy to see traces of her freshness and beauty in the tear-swollen, wasted face. And yet it was not so many years since she had been the fairest of all.—For the first time he felt the full wretchedness of her useless fecundity. He put his arm around her again.

"I thought 'twould make you happy," he said, for she wept and wept.

"Happy—" she trembled, and now he found that she was laughing through her sobs. "I am surely happier than the angels—though you know full well, Olav, I love you more than ten children—"

"Go in and dress yourself," he begged her; "you will take cold here."

When he came in she put on her clothes and her wimple and was carrying in food from the closet where they kept it in winter. Eirik still stood where Olav had put him down, but his mother had taken off his leathern jacket. When he saw his father coming, he turned to him quickly and tried to take his hand, smiling a little anxiously.

"Nay, go to your mother now, Eirik," said Olav. "Do as I tell you," he repeated, rather sharply, as the boy shyly drew nearer to him.

8

EIRIK was nearly five years old, and he was beginning to find out that it was counted a great blemish in him that he had no father. A year before, when they had been down to the village for Lady Day in the spring, he had heard certain folk saying that he was base-born; the same word had been used by the men who called at Siljuaas on their fowling—and it was surely said of him. But when he asked his foster-mother what it meant, she boxed his ears. Afterwards she had muttered angrily that they had better deserved the blows who said such things to the poor little creature—ay, and his mother too—'twas not the boy's fault that he was a bastard and a straw-brat. But Eirik guessed it was better not to ask more questions about these queer words. They meant something it was wrong to be, and that was why Torgal did not like him—he could not tell how he knew it, but it had come to him in some way that Torgal, the father of the house, was not *his* father.

Torgal, the crofter of Siljuaas, was a kindly, home-loving man. He trained up his sons: the eldest of them already went hunting with him in the forest, the younger ones had to work on the clearing at home, and their father showed them what to do and chastised them when they needed it. But Eirik he heeded not at all, whether for good or for evil. He showed his wife the honour of never meddling with her affairs, and he reckoned this adoption of the bastard of a great man's daughter to be a venture of hers with which he had nothing to do—he left her a free hand both with the child and with the payment for his fostering.

Eirik knew well enough that Hallveig was not his mother, but he thought nothing of it, for Hallveig never made any difference between him and her own children. She was just as ready with blows and angry words whichever of them might get in her way while at work. And on the eve of holy-days she bathed them all in order of age in the big tub, and he was clad in a sheepskin coat the day before winter night,[8] and as soon as the cuckoo was heard he had to be content with a homespun shirt and nothing else, like the other children, whatever the weather. On those days in the year when the people of Siljuaas went down to the village to mass, and Hallveig had the use of the horse, Eirik was allowed to ride behind her just as far as each of the other children, and she kissed them all with equal affection when she had received *corpus Domini.*

They never went short of food—cured fish or game; with it a piece of bread or a ladleful of porridge, small beer now and again, and water when milk ran short in winter. Eirik had been very well off and quite content with his lot in the lonely clearing far away in the forest.

Every hour of the day something happened, so many people and animals were there in the little homestead. And round about its fences the forest was thick on every side: within it, behind the wall of murmuring fir trees and glistening bushes, was a teeming, hidden life. Creatures lived and moved in there, keeping an eye on them from the edge of the wood, luring the boy and drawing him right down to the fence: at the slightest movement or sound

[8] October 14

within the forest the whole flock of youngsters would spin round and take to their heels across the turf, back to the shelter of the houses. Not much had the children seen of the folk from beyond, but they heard the grown-ups tell tales of strange happenings, so they knew of the troll of Uvaas and the pixy who mostly haunted the mossy rocks by the Logging Stone, and of the bear—one year he had appeared at the byre and tried to break through the roof on a frosty night—but that was before Eirik could remember. Under a fixed rock in the meadow there dwelt little men and women in blue, but with them they were good friends—Hallveig carried out food to them now and then, and they did her many a good turn in gratitude. Eirik had often seen their footprints in the snow. Those who dwelt outside the fences were of course more evilly disposed. There was no great difference, to the boy, between the beasts of the forest and these others who haunted it.

The sound of something moving within the thicket on a summer's day, the calls of beasts and other noises from the forest at nighttime, tracks in the snow on winter mornings. Beisk, the dog, who would start up and bark furiously on dark evenings, without Eirik ever finding out what made him do it—all such things made up the wonderful world outside the homestead which greeted the child. It was misty and dreamlike, but it was real enough, only he was so small that he had to stay inside the fence. But Master Torgal and the big boys went in and out of it and told of the strange things that happened there.

Eirik never came into the forest except on those days in the year when Hallveig took him with her to church. Then they passed through it, a long, long way down. At last they came to a new world that was even farther away and more dreamlike. The bells that pealed and rang again across the great open fields with big houses on them; the church hill where stood horses and horses and yet more horses—little shaggy ones like their own on the lower side, but up by the churchyard fence there was a neighing of big, shiny colts with hog manes and red, green, and violet harness glittering with gold and silver. Within the church stood the priests with gilt cloaks on their backs, singing before the lighted candles on the altar, and some young ones in long white shirts swung the golden censers so that the church was filled with the sweetest fragrance. His foster-mother pushed her flock down on their knees and hoisted them up, according to the movements of those in the brilliant light of the choir. At last came God, as Eirik knew, when the priest lifted up the little round loaf and the bell in the tower above began to ring, chiming with a sharp note of joy.

At the upper end of the church stood a whole crowd of men and women in bright-coloured clothes, shining belts, and big brooches, and Eirik knew that it was they who owned all the horses with the fine saddles and the gleaming arms that were left in the room under the tower. Eirik believed they were a kind of fairies—only that they lived and moved even farther away from his life than those others in the woods at home. One day Hallveig pointed to one of them, the bulkiest of all the women, clad in flaming red, with a triple silver belt about her big stomach and a brooch like an ale-bowl in the middle of her mighty bosom: that was his aunt, said Hallveig. Eirik was none the wiser, for he did not know what an aunt was. Fetches he had heard of and angels; nay, sometimes a woman came to Siljuaas whom the children called Aunt—her name was Ingrid and she had a great hump on her back—but this one did not look like anything of that sort.—

He had been properly scared when that lady in blue came. And it was for him she had come—she was his mother, they said. It made him extremely uncomfortable, for it seemed to be not only a great danger but a disgrace. She was certainly one of the women who stood in front at church—fairies of the farthest-off kind. And now he had got his eldest sister to tell him what a straw-brat was: when women lie with men out in the woods, they get a straw-brat. The blue woman had had him, just as Mother had had little Inga in the spring; all the other children in the house Mother had had, but not him. The child had a horrified suspicion that he had been born out of doors and carried in from the woods. But now he was mortally afraid he would be taken out there again, and he did not want that at all. For a long time he was haunted by a terrible dread lest the blue woman should come back and fetch him out to where she lay—with a man whom he imagined to be like a tree blown down by the storm, with tangled roots in the air. They passed a tree like this on the way to church; it lay on a flat piece of dry ground under a knoll, and Eirik had always been afraid of this dead, fallen fir tree, for it had something like an ugly man's face amid the tangle of its roots. The boy imagined that the blue woman lived in a little glade like this among the woods, and there he would be alone with her and her tree-man and the big sorrel horse with bright things on its bridle; never would anybody else come there, neither people nor animals. But he would not have that—he wanted to stay at home in the safe, open clearing and sleep indoors, and he would never be parted from Mother and Gudda, his foster-sister, and Kaare and the other children and Beisk and the horse and the cows and the goats and Torgal—and he would not be squeezed and kissed as he had been by the strange woman. For a long time he scarcely dared to go three steps from the house door, so frightened was he that she would come again, this mother of his. But if he had had a father, she could not have done anything to him—for sister had said that only those children who had no father could be straw-brats.

All the same, as time went on, Eirik thought less of that visit. But one day in the winter some men who were following a ski-track through the forest to Österdalen called at Siljuaas. Again he heard that they were talking about him, but this time they mentioned his mother by name: "Leman" they said she was called. Eirik had never heard that word before, but it sounded strange and unsafe—as if she were not human, but rather some kind of great bird. He imagined vaguely that Leman might come flapping her great blue cloak like a pair of broad wings and pounce down on him. It grew more and more clear to him how evil was his plight, since he had no father to own him, so that nobody would dare take him away.

Then one day there came a father to him. Eirik was not very surprised at this. When he was led up to the man, he took a good look at him. It must have been the fact that Olav's complexion was so fair that made the boy feel confidence in him from the first. This father with the broad, straight shoulders and the up-right bearing—Eirik felt at once that he knew this was another of those who stood in front at church—but he was not afraid of him. Gay clothes he wore—a leaf-green kirtle, a silver clasp in the breast of his jerkin, bright metal on his belt and on the long sheath of his dirk. And then Eirik took such a fancy to the queer big axe his father held between his knees as he sat; the hand that rested on the head of the axe was covered with rings. The more he looked at him, the more pleased he was with his father. He stood calmly meeting the other's searching glance—at the first sign of something like a smile on the man's face Eirik beamed and went up close to Olav's knee.

"He is small, this son of mine?" said the father to Hallveig, holding the boy's chin a moment. Beyond that he said nothing to Eirik while he was at Siljuaas, but that was enough for the boy. Hallveig wept a little, Torgal lifted him up when he said farewell, the brothers and sisters stood staring at him who was to go away with the two strange men. Eirik felt a little clutch at the heart when he saw his mother cry; he put his arms about her neck, and his lips began to quiver—then his father called, and at once he turned and trudged to the door, clumsy in his new fur coat that came down to his feet.

Eirik and Olav became good friends on the journey. It was not much that his father said to him; he let Arnketil, his man, look after the boy. But all the strange new things he met with, the sledge and horses, a fresh house to sleep in every night, all the good food, and then the many people everywhere, who talked to him, many of them—Eirik knew that all this was his father's doing. And his father wore a shirt and breeches of linen next his skin, and he did not take them off at night.

The new mother that he found when he came to the end of the journey made much less impression on Eirik. He did not know her again; when she asked if he remembered that she had been at Siljuaas, he answered yes, for he guessed that was what he ought to say. But he had no feeling that she was the same. This mother here had brown clothes, she was thick about the waist and trod heavily and slowly as she went ceaselessly in and out, busying herself between the houses. The tall, blue mother, Leman, with the quick, birdlike movements, he imagined standing in the little clearing in the forest, where she dwelt with her tree-man and the big sorrel horse. Only when the new brown mother crushed him to her and smothered him with kisses and wild words of endearment did he know in a way that she and Leman were one and the same—although they called this one Ingunn.—Eirik did not like being kissed and squeezed in this way—he had never in his life been given other kisses than those which went with a mass Sunday and fresh meat and a drink from the ale-bowl when they came home—rare and festive occasions.

But here the way of it was that he got ale every day, and these folk ate cooked fresh food, fish and meat, day after day for many days, so maybe the women had the habit of kissing every day too.

When Eirik came up to Olav, laid his hands in his lap, and asked him all kinds of questions—whether the seal lived in the forest that he could see straight across the fiord, and why his two horses were white, and why he was not the father of Torhild's children, and what they were to do with the train-oil they were boiling, and where the moon was going when it flew so swiftly across the sky —Ingunn watched the two with a strange tension. For one thing, she was afraid Olav might be impatient with the boy. She was so unspeakably humble in her gratitude for this thing her husband had done for her in bringing home the child for whom she had longed to the very death; and now she was only afraid the boy might worry Olav, or that he might be angry at the sight of her child if he saw too much of him. She could not discover that Olav entertained any dislike for Eirik. He took little notice of him, unless the boy sought him out, but then he was always friendly and replied as well as he could to Eirik's endless questions. But it was not easy to make Eirik understand the nature of anything. The boy seemed to have no grasp at all—he made no difference between living and dead things, asked whether the big rock on the beach was fond of the gulls and why the snow wanted to lie on the ground. He could not make out that the sun that glimmered through the fog was the same as shone in the sky on a clear day, and once he had seen a moon that was quite unlike all other moons. —The priest came to see them one day, but Eirik never guessed that he was the same person he had seen up at the church—that his vestments could be taken off and that he could ride about like other men. Sometimes Eirik would take it upon himself to hold forth to them, but all his stories were strange and absurd—impossible to find any sense in them. Ingunn feared the boy was very stupid and backward for his age—and she was afraid Olav would dislike him still more for having so little sense. He was so pretty and so sweet that she thought she could never feast her eyes enough on him—but clever he was not.

The secret pang of disappointment and pain that she felt because the boy showed so openly that he liked his father better than her was another reason for her seeking to keep her husband and her son away from each other as much as she could.

At the outset Olav entertained no ill will toward Eirik. The violent mental tumult that had shaken him when he heard of Ingunn's infidelity, and afterwards time after time when he recalled that another man had possessed her—this had become a thing of the distant past during these years of their joyless life together. His love of her was a fixed thing and a habit; it was intertwined with his whole being as the mould of a meadow is intertwined with a mass of roots. But now he did not feel this love otherwise than as an infinite compassion with this poor sick creature, whose life was his own life. What was now the living warmth in his feelings for Ingunn—what throbbed, flared up, and sank again— was tenderness and anxiety for her; desire only stirred sluggishly and lukewarm, as in a doze. But thus it was that his jealousy had also grown weak and numb—it was but rarely that he thought of what she had gone through in the past, and then it seemed very far away. And Olav could not realize any connection between the shame and agony of that time and this little boy whom they had brought into their home. Eirik was there, that was to be—God had made known to him that he was to take Eirik to himself, and that was an end of the matter. And Olav was more inclined than not to like the boy in himself—he was a pretty boy, and he wooed his father's affection so openly. Olav, himself slow in taking to others, was always surprised and glad when any sought his friendship.

Olav often guessed the train of thought behind the boy's strange jumble of talk much better than his mother did. And when she interrupted Eirik's faltering explanations with inappreciative words and would not leave the boy alone so that he and Olav might reach an understanding, her husband more than once felt a kind of fretful impatience. *He* remembered—not in such a way that he could form clear images of it, much less put it into words, but in brief and fleeting visions he remembered a great deal of how the world had appeared to himself when he was a child.

9

THE ICE broke up and the spring came. The dull-red rocks down by the fiord were baked in the sunshine, and the spray gleamed white under the Bull Crag, as though new-born. The soil turned green and breathed its sweet smell of grass and mould, and then came the time of bursting buds, filling the evening air with a cool and bitter scent of young leaves along the valley.

One morning in May, Olav came across a nest of vipers on a slope; he killed three of them. He brought them home in a closed wooden cup and during the midday rest he stole to the cook-house with them. Snakes' fat and snakes' ashes are good for many things, but they have much more power if one goes secretly about the preparation of them.

He was about to slip into the cook-house when he heard voices. Ingunn was there, and the boy. The child's voice said:

"—because father gave me the breast, you see."

"He gave you the breast?" his mother wondered. "What nonsense are you talking now?"

"Oh yes, he did. And then Father said I might eat up the wings too, if I had not had enough, but there was nothing left of the cock but the wings—"

Olav laughed quietly to himself. Now he remembered: in the inn at Oslo the woman had set before him a roast cock, and the boy had liked the meat hugely.

Then he heard Ingunn say: "A whole cock I will roast for you, Eirik—will that make you think I am as kind as your father? You shall have it next time he goes away from home—"

Olav stole back across the yard and went east to the smithy. He felt a strange sense of shame on her behalf. What was the use of such talk? Surely she could roast one of her own cocks for the child, whether he were at home or not.

Whether it was that the unaccustomed food was too rich for Eirik's stomach or from some other cause, as spring went on the child took to waking up and screaming nearly every night. Olav heard Eirik start up with a shriek, crawl around and grope this way and that in the big north bed, where he slept alone—then he shrieked again, even louder, as though in utmost terror.

Ingunn tumbled out of bed and went to him. "Eirik, Eirik, Eirik mine, hush, hush, hush, you will wake your father—oh be quiet now—there is nothing here that you need be afraid of, my little son!"

"You had better bring him over to us," came Olav's voice, wide awake, from the darkness.

"Oh, has he waked you again!" complained Ingunn as she came back with the boy and lay down—the two tossed and wriggled till they were comfortable.

"I was not yet asleep. What have you dreamed of this time, Eirik?"

But at night it was only his mother who would serve Eirik's turn. He simply nestled closer to her and did not answer his father. They never got to hear anything of his dreams. He made a gesture of wiping something from his hands and throwing it from him two or three times. Then he gave a sigh of relief and lay down to rest. Very soon they were both asleep.

Olav was always more sleepless in spring than at other seasons; he seldom fell asleep before midnight and woke very early. On these early summer mornings the fiord often lay smooth as a mirror, pale blue and glistening in the sunlight, and the desolate shore opposite seemed bright and tranquil as a mirage. Olav was absurdly happy and light-hearted when he went out on such a morning. Torhild Björnsdatter was singing somewhere in the outhouses; she had already been long at work. Olav and the girl met in the yard; they stood and talked together in the morning sunshine.

When he came in again some hours later he sometimes stood for a moment looking at the two, mother and child, who were still asleep. Eirik lay with his face against his mother's neck, breathing with half-open mouth. Ingunn held her narrow hand, heavy with rings, about his shoulder.

A fortnight before St. John's Day, Ingunn gave birth to a man-child. Olav had him christened at once, Audun.

It was a tiny boy, purple and skinny. Olav put two fingers around his son's hand one day, when he lay in Signe Arnesdatter's lap and was being washed—it was so thin, that little hand, almost like a chicken's leg, and just as cold.

Olav felt no very deep affection for his son or joy that at last he had one. The waiting had been so long that the bare suspicion that Ingunn might be with child again had struck him with black despondency. He had grown so unused to the hope that all this misery might end at last in rejoicing that he had to have time to take it in.

But he saw that it was not so with the mother. In spite of her having expected nothing but bitter pain, against her own will her heart had trembled each time with hopeless and despairing love for the little unborn creatures. Now Audun inherited this love from all his brothers, who had left behind them not even a name or a memory.

Eirik was boisterously happy at having a brother. He knew from Siljuaas that the birth of a child was the greatest of great events. Then there were two or three strange women in the house, and they brought with them good food, and candles were burning in the room all night long. The child in the cradle was tended as a most precious thing—those outside the fence were lying in wait to steal it—and its health and well-being were constantly inquired after. That it was the worst off of all in the home when the next child came and took its place in the cradle—the child of yesteryear was abandoned to the care of its little sisters, always in the way and always in danger—of this Eirik took no account. Here in this house the time was one of immense festivity, so many wives, each with her maid, and masses of food—but the candles at night he and his father were cheated of; his mother and the new brother lay in another house.

"It's my silken brother, but it's only your woollen brother," he said to Torhild's two youngest children as they stood together watching Audun being dressed.

Olav was sitting with his wife at the moment; he heard it. He glanced at Ingunn. She lay looking at her two sons, radiant with joy.

His son—that little creature there, that the maid was pulling about. The other bent his healthy, beaming face over him and prattled to the little brother, whom all unwittingly he had deprived of his birthright.

• • •

ThE SNAKE PIT

It had caused a certain mild stir in the neighbourhood when the people of Hestviken so unexpectedly produced a big son of five who had been hidden away all this time.

Olav was not very well liked in the neighbourhood. He had been received with evident and cordial goodwill when he came home to his own—but little by little a feeling grew up among the people of the countryside that he had repelled their offers of friendship and good-neighbourship. Olav kept to himself more than they liked, and in company he was little inclined to be sociable; never discourteous—and this did not make him more popular, for it was taken as a sign that he thought himself something above the other franklins—but taciturn, quiet, and unapproachable. It was hinted in private, with a slight sneer, that Olav must think himself something like a courtier, since he had been Earl Alf's man and was kinsman on his mother's side to these great Danish lords who lay here in Norway half a year at a time and fed at the Duke's table. Ay, ay. He owned his fathers' manor yet, whole and undivided—but let him wait and see how long that would last, in days such as these. Although he never shirked doing anything that was his due, and was not ill-natured when it was a question of helping anyone, nobody *cared* to ask Olav Audunsson to do him a favour. For if folk who were in difficulties went to the rich Master of Hestviken, it was as though he scarce troubled himself to listen to them. When they had explained to him their situation at length, he would ask at the end of it all, as though he had been thinking of other things: ay, what was it they wanted—? No one could deny that Olav was generous in both giving and lending, but if anyone would ease his heart and discuss his affairs with him, there was no comfort to be had of it in that house—he gave such answers that one knew not whether the man was foolish or indifferent. So that unless folk had the most crying need of a helping hand, they preferred to go to another, who would listen to what they said, express an opinion, and give them counsel and consolation, even if this man might not grant them help without some hanging back, saying he was badly off himself—but in God's name—

Another matter which had been remarked by the neighbours was that no man had seen Olav get honestly drunk or free-spoken in a carouse. He drank no less than other good men at a banquet. But it seemed that God's gifts did not bite on him.

111

And by degrees there grew up a feeling in the countryside—vague and formless, for no one really knew on what they based it, but with all its obscurity it was strong as a certainty—that this man had something on his mind, a secret misfortune or a sin. The handsome, erect young master, with the broad, fair face beneath his curly flaxen hair, was a marked man.

It was a strange thing too about his wife, that she could not give birth to living children. Little it was that one saw of Ingunn Steinfinnsdatter, and the poor thing was not much to look at either. But folk still remembered how fair she had been—and that not so many years ago.

And now it came out that they *had* a child. For all these years they had had a son hidden away, the Fiend knew where, far in the north in her home country.

Begotten while the father was an outlaw, ay, that was it. Olav had made that known, briefly and clearly. Folk knew that his quarrel with his wife's kinsmen had arisen from this, that Steinfinn on his deathbed had given into Olav's charge the daughter to whom the lad had been betrothed since their childhood. Olav had accepted her as his wife, and it was impossible to interpret Steinfinn's words otherwise than that this accorded with his wishes. But the new sponsors had thought they might dispose of the fair and wealthy maid in another manner. Now Olav declared that the summer before he made final reconciliation with his wife's kinsmen, he had secretly visited the house where she dwelt. But in the meantime this had had to be kept secret.

So said Olav Audunsson. But folk began to wonder. Perhaps it was not so sure that Olav had accepted purely of his own free will the wife he was made to marry by Steinfinn's order, while he was a mere boy and subject to Steinfinn's authority. Had he not rather tried to shuffle out of a marriage into which he had been forced in childhood? Folk who had seen a little of their life together—their serving-folk and the neighbours' wives who had been with Ingunn when she lay sick—spoke of what they knew. True enough, Olav was good to his wife in a way, but he was sulky and silent at home as he was abroad; days might pass when he spoke not a word to his wife even. Ingunn never looked happy, and that was not so strange either—a woman who was tied to this cross-stick of a husband, always in bad health and giving birth to one dead child after another.

One day the new priest, Sira Hallbjörn, came to Hestviken.

He was a fairly young man, tall and slight, with a handsome face, but his hair was fiery red and folk thought he had a haughty look. He had made himself somewhat disliked in a short time. Scarcely had he come to the parish when he raised dissension on every side, over the property of the Church and the incomings of the glebe, over old agreements which Sira Benedikt had made with the owners of the land, but which this new man found to be unlawful. Both the monastery on Hovedö and the nuns' convent of Nonneseter owned farms and shares of farms in the parish, as did several of the churches and pious foundations in Oslo. The deputies of these institutions were for the most part wise and kindly men who were on good terms with the country folk, many of whom had bought themselves a resting-place within the walls of the convents; and when it happened that any of the Hovedö monks themselves came to visit their farms, the franklins flocked from far around to hear mass in their chapels. And then it was not long before Sira Hallbjörn fell out with the convent folk. On the other hand the priest had set his whole heart upon some monks of a new order that had just come into the country: they went barefoot, in habits that were like sackcloth and ashes, and the virtues they chiefly practised were said to be humility, meekness, and frugality—ay, 'twas said these friars begged their daily bread as they went about teaching rich and poor the true fear of God, and had they aught left in their bag after vespers, they were to share it among the poor and themselves go out each morning with empty hands. Now it was sure that Sira Hallbjörn was neither humble nor meek, but proud of his birth—he came of noble stock far away in Valdres—and he was little fitted to teach the fear of God, for he was so learned and his speech was so hard to understand that folk had no great benefit from listening to him. But he could never praise these beggar friars enough—Minorites they called themselves—and made himself as it were their protector, gave great gifts to the house they had set about building in the town, and tried to persuade his parishioners to do the same. But folk found out that this must be because the Duke favoured these new monks greatly, while the Bishop and most of the priests and learned men in the town liked them ill and thought that the rule of this order was dangerous and unsound. And folk knew that Sira Hallbjörn had been sent out to this parish because he, a man who by his birth and rare learning seemed destined for the highest offices of the Church, had fallen out with the Bishop and the whole chapter of Oslo, through being so proud and quarrelsome and thinking he knew and understood and could teach everything better than all the others. But they were not able to do any worse thing to him than banish him to this good call—his conduct was blameless in all else, he had studied in foreign lands for many years, and he knew all that was to be known of the law and justice of the land, from the oldest times down to his own day.

It was in order to hear what Olav knew about a right to salmon-fishing in a little river over on the Hudrheim side that he had come today. Olav could not tell him much—the farm with which the right went had been sold by his grandfather to his son-in-law and since then it had been divided and had passed into many hands. He could see that Sira Hallbjörn was vexed because he could tell him so little of the matter; nevertheless Olav asked, while the priest sat at meat, if he could throw light on a question that weighed on his mind. "It concerns my sons—"

It was thus: he had heard that a child begotten while the father is under ban of outlawry is outside the law and has no rights, even if the mother be the outlaw's duly married wife.

"Nay, nay," said Sira Hallbjörn, with a sweep of the hand. "You have heard of the wolf's cub—such was the name they gave to an outlawed man's child in old days. Then it was so that the outlaw was treated as a dead man: his estate was divided and his wife held to be a widow; and if he were granted grace, he had to ask her again of her kinsfolk and wed her anew. But you know full well that such a law cannot hold among Christian men—among us no sin and no sentence can sever the bond of wedlock between man and wife."

"Her kinsmen would not have it that 'twas lawful wedlock, that which had been made between us when we were young," said Olav. " 'Twas only after Eirik was born that I got her with her kinsfolk's consent."

"You need have no fear on that score now. Whether the boy were true-born or not, he enjoys the same rights now that you are married with her kinsfolks' consent, so none can dispute with you whether 'tis lawful marriage."

"Then is it certain," asked Olav, "that Audun can never come forward and oust Eirik from his right as our first-born?"

"Certainly he cannot," said the priest decisively.

"Nay, nay. I wished but to be sure how this matter stood."

"Ay, 'twas natural enough," replied Sira Hallbjörn.

Olav thanked him for his information.

While his mother was lying in, Eirik took to talking of one he called Tötrabassa. At first the grown people thought this was a beggar woman—one of those who came in greater numbers now that the house was overflowing with food and drink.

Ay, Tötrabassa was a woman with a bag, said Eirik. But another day he said that Tötrabassa had been there and had played with him in the field behind the barn. There was a little hollow in the meadow where he was fond of going with his things. Tötrabassa was a little maid. No one paid much attention to this—they were all used to the queer nonsense Eirik so often talked.

But after a while he began to tell of more playfellows, and they all had strange names like Tauragaura, Silvarp, Skolorm, Dölvandogg, and Kolmurna the Blue—whether they were men or women, grown-up or children, it was not easy to make out.

The house-folk grew alarmed. It still happened sometimes that a whole household left croft or cabin, great and small, and took to the wood, either because they were pursued by the law or from sheer poverty, and chose a vagabond life, in summer at any rate, rather than be brought to justice. Just at this time a fat sheep was lost that had been kept in the home pasture, and now the house-carls thought that these friends of Eirik's must be vagabonds of this sort, who lived chiefly by pilfering and stealing. Folk kept an eye on Eirik, when he was playing in the hollow, whether any unknown children or grown people might come to him. But nothing was seen. And one day the sheep's carcass was washed up in the bay—it had fallen from the cliff.

And now the people of Hestviken were afraid in earnest. This must be some of the underground folk. They asked Eirik if he knew where they came from. Oh, from away under the crag. But when he saw how frightened the others were at this, he was a little scared himself. Nay, they came from the town, he said—in a sledge they came. Or maybe they sailed, he corrected himself, when Olav said no one could drive a sledge from Oslo in summertime, he must not talk such nonsense. Anyhow, they came from the woods—ay, they dwelt in the woods, Tauragaura had said. Tauragaura was the one he talked most about.

Ingunn was quite beside herself with despair. These must be the evil spirits who had turned all luck from this house, generation after generation; now they were surely after her children. Eirik was shut up in the women's house and watched—and then he talked and talked of these friends of his, till it looked as if his mother would lose her wits with despair. She would have Olav fetch the priest.

"Now, you are not lying, Eirik, by chance?" asked Olav severely one day when he had been listening while Eirik replied to his mother's anxious questions.

Eirik stared in terror at his father with his great brown eyes and shook his head vehemently.

"For if I find out one day, boy, that you bear untruthful tales, it will go ill with you."

Eirik looked at his father in wonder, seeming not to understand.

But Olav had conceived a suspicion that the whole story was a thing the boy had invented—unreasonable as such an idea appeared to himself, for he could not make out what object the child could have in spreading such vain and purposeless lies. And the next day, when Olav and a man were to mow the meadow that lay below the hollow, he let Eirik come with them, promising Ingunn that they would keep a sharp watch on the child all the time.

Olav did so, looking out for the boy now and then. Eirik pottered about, good and quiet, up in the hollow, playing with some snail-shells and pebbles that the boatmen had given him. He was quite alone the whole time.

When the other man and the girls went up to the morning meal, Olav came up to Eirik. "So they did not come to see you today, Tötrabassa and Skolorm and the rest?"

"Oh yes," said Eirik radiantly, and he began telling of all the games he had played with them today.

"Now you are lying, boy," said Olav harshly. "I have watched you the whole time—none has been here."

"They took to their heels when you came—they were afraid of your scythe."

"Then what became of them—where did they run to?"

"Home, to be sure."

"Home—and where may that be?"

Eirik looked up at his father, puzzled and a little diffident. Then his face brightened eagerly: "Shall we go thither, Father?" and he held out his hand.

Olav hung his scythe on a tree. "Let us do so."

Eirik led him up to the manor, out of the yard and on to the rocks to the west of the houses, where they could see over the fiord.

"They must be down there," he said, pointing to the little strip of beach that lay far below them.

"I see nobody," said Olav shortly.

"Nay, they are not *there*—now I know where they are—" Eirik first turned back toward the manor, but then he took a path that led down to the waterside. "Now I know, now I know," he called eagerly, hopping and skipping as he waited for his father; then he ran on ahead again, stopped and waited and took his father by the hand, dragging him down along the path.

He showed the way to the farthest of the sheds by the quay. Olav hardly ever used this one—there was not so much trade at Hestviken now. Only in spring, when Olav was preparing to visit the Holy Cross fair at Oslo, did he store some of his winter goods here. Now the shed was empty and unlocked. Eirik drew his father into it.

The sea splashed and gurgled about the piles under the floor of the shed. This was leaky and the walls were gaping, so that reflections of the sunlight from the water rose and fell in bright streaks on walls and roof. Eirik sniffed in the salt smell of the shed, and his face sparkled with excitement. He looked up into his father's eyes with a smile of expectation and, stealing on tiptoe, led him to an old barrel standing bottom-upwards, which Olav used to pack skins in.

"Here," he whispered, squatting down. "In *here* they dwell. Can you see them—now the cracks have grown so big again, else we could see better, but they are sitting there eating—can you see them?"

Olav turned the barrel on its side and gave it a kick so that it rolled away. There was nothing underneath but some litter.

Eirik looked up smiling and was about to say something—when he noticed the expression of his father's face and stopped in terror, open-mouthed. With a scream he put up his arms to ward off the blow, bursting into a heart-rending fit of weeping.

Olav let his hand drop—felt it was unworthy of him to strike the boy. So puny and miserable Eirik looked as he stood there in tears that his father was almost ashamed of himself. He just took the child's arms, drew him away, and sat down on a pile of wreckage, holding Eirik before him.

"So you have lied, I see—'twas a lie every word you said of these friends of yours—answer me now."

But Eirik answered nothing; he stood staring up at the man's face, clean dazed—it seemed he could not make it out at all.

The end of it was that Olav had to take Eirik on his knee to stop his bitter weeping. He said again and again that Eirik must never say what was untrue or he would get a beating—but he spoke much more gently now, and between whiles he stroked the boy's head. Eirik nestled close to his father's chest and put his arms tightly about his neck.

But he did not understand—Olav was sure of that, and it affected him almost uncannily. This boy that he held in his arms seemed to him so strange and odd—what in God's name had come over him that he could invent all these lies? To Olav it was so utterly aimless that he began to wonder: was Eirik altogether in his right senses?

Ingunn stayed indoors for nearly nine weeks after her lying-in. She was not notably sick or weak; it was rather that she had grown too fond of her life in the narrow chamber, where all was done for the comfort of herself and the infant, and all was shut out that might disturb her. She let herself sink deep into this new happiness—the infant she had at the breast, and Eirik, who ran in and out of her room all day long. Toward the end Olav began to grow impatient—they had passed so many bad years together, and in all that time she had clung to him. Now she was happy and well, ay, she had recovered some of her youthful beauty, and she barred herself in from him with the children. But Olav allowed nothing of this to appear.

At last, on the Sunday after St. Laurence's Mass, she kept her churching. Eirik was asleep when the company left home in the early morning, but he was out in the yard when the church folk came back.

A new custom had grown up—although many liked it not, nay, said it was tempting God with overweening pride: young wives at their first churching, especially if the child was a son, wore again on that day their golden circlet, the bridal crown of noble maids, outside their wedded women's coif.

Ingunn had fastened her white silken kerchief with the golden garland; she wore a red kirtle and her blue mantle with the great gold brooch in it.

Olav lifted his wife from her horse; Eirik stood rapt, gazing at his mother's loveliness. She seemed much taller in this splendid dress, with the silver belt around her slender waist; her movements were lithe and supple, light as a bird's.

"Mother!" Eirik exclaimed, beaming; "you *are* Leman after all!"

In an instant his father seized him by the shoulder; the blow of a clenched fist fell on his cheek-bone, making his head swim. Blow followed blow, leaving the child no breath to cry out—only a hoarse whistling came from his throat—till Una Arnesdatter came running up and caught the man by the arm.

"Olav, Olav, curb yourself—'tis a little boy—are you out of your senses, to strike so hard?"

Olav let go. Eirik let himself fall backward flat on the ground; there he lay, panting and whining, black and blue in the face. It was no swoon—half on purpose, the boy behaved as if he were dying. Una stooped down to him and lifted him to her lap; then his tears began to flow.

Olav turned toward his wife—he was still trembling. Ingunn stood bending forward; eyes, nostrils, the open mouth were like the holes in a death's-head. Olav laughed, a harsh and angry laugh —then he took her by the upper arm and drew her into the hall, where the maids were now bringing in the banquet.

None of the company had heard what the child said. But all thought the same—no matter what he had done, it had been an ugly sight to see the father correct the little boy so roughly. They sat about on the benches, waiting to be bidden to table, and all were ill at ease.

At last Una Arnesdatter came in, carrying Eirik in her arms.

She set him down beside his father's knee. "Eirik will not disobey you again, Olav—you must tell your son you are angry no longer."

"Has he told you why I chastised him?" asked Olav without looking up.

Una shook her head. "Poor little fellow—he has cried so he had no power to speak."

"Never more shall you dare to say that word, Eirik," said Olav hotly in an undertone. "*Never* more—you understand?"

Eirik was still hiccuping spasmodically. He said nothing, but stared at his father, frightened and bewildered.

"Never again are you to speak that word," his father repeated, laying a heavy hand on the boy's shoulder. Till the child nodded. But then Eirik's eyes wandered longingly to the dinner-table, which was groaning with good things.

And so the company seated themselves.

Eirik was to sleep in Torhild's house that night, for there were so many guests at the manor. In the evening, when he was going across, his father came after him into the yard. Eirik stopped short, trembling violently—he looked up at the other in such mortal fear.

"Who taught you to say that ugly word—of your mother?"

Eirik looked up, frightened; the tears began to rise. Olav could get no answer to his question.

"*Never* say it again—do you hear, *never* again!" Olav stroked the boy's head—saw with something like a sense of shame that one side of Eirik's face was all red and swollen.

The boy was on the point of falling asleep when he felt that someone was bending over him—his mother; her face was burning hot and wet.

"Eirik mine—who has told you this—that your mother was a leman?"

The boy was wide awake in a moment:

"But *are* you not Leman?"

"Yes," whispered his mother.

Eirik threw his arms about her neck, nestled up to her, and kissed her.

THE SNAKE PIT

10

AUTUMN came early that year. Bad weather set in about Michael-mas, and then it rained and blew, day in, day out, except when the gale was so high that the clouds could not let go their rain. This weather lasted for seven weeks.

At Hestviken the water rose above the quays. One night the sea carried away the piles under the farthest shed: when the men came down in the grey dawn, they saw the old house lying with its back wall, which faced the rock, leaning forward, and the front wall, toward the fiord, sunk half under water. It rocked in the heavy seas like a moored boat, and every time the wreck was lifted by a wave and sank again, the water poured out between the timbers, but most of all through a hatch under the gable. It looked like a drunken man hanging round-shouldered over the side of a boat and spewing, thought Anki.

With axes, boathooks, and ropes the men now had to try to cut the wrecked shed adrift and warp it out of the way; otherwise it was likely to be flung in against the quay and the shed in which Olav stored all the salt he had dried during the summer, and his fish—of this there was not much, for the autumn fishing had failed. In the course of this work Olav bruised his right arm badly.

He paid little heed to it while he was toiling in the spray and the storm, which was so violent that at times the men had to lie flat and crawl along the rocks. But at dusk, as they walked up to the manor, he felt his arm aching and it hurt when he touched it. As he was shutting the house door a gust of wind blew it in, carrying Olav off his feet; his bad arm was given a violent wrench as the man stumbled over the threshold and fell at full length on the floor of the anteroom. He had to call for help to be rid of his soaking sea-clothes, and Torhild bound up his arm in a sling.

It was unbearable in the hall that evening; the room was chock-full of smoke, for it was impossible to open door or louver in this wind. Eyes smarted and chests were racked; and when the men's wet clothes began to steam on the crossbeams, the air was soon so thick that it could be cut with a knife.

Ingunn lay in the little closet with both the children—there was less smoke, but it was so cold that they had to creep under the bedclothes. The men went out as soon as they had supped. Olav threw some skins and cushions on the floor by the hearth and lay down there, to be below the smoke.

His arm was now swollen. His face was burning from the weather and his head and body were hot and cold by turns. Feverish and light-headed, he heard the storm as a multiplicity of voices—it howled about the corners of the house, slamming a loose shutter somewhere—now and then he could distinguish its roaring in the trees on the crag above the manor. The deepest note was that of the raging fiord; where he lay he thought he could hear the thunder of the waves breaking on the rock on which the houses stood as though the booming came from beneath him, up through the rock.

In a doze he saw the huge white-crested seas coming, their water brown with mud; and he crawled again up the wet rock on hands and knees, with the boathook gripped under him, and the rope he had to fasten in a cleft of the rock. The spray, thick as rain, lashed him even up here. The black welter of clouds was split at that moment with a brassy yellow rift, and far beneath him, where the black and foaming fiord seemed hollow as a cup, a single shaft of sunlight fell glittering upon the racing waves.

Then another vision appeared under his closed eyelids—a great bog, pale with rime, grass and heather frosted and white. But a kind of light glimmered within the morning mist, and he could tell that as the day wore on, the sun would break through. Never is there such a day for riding out with hawk and hound: bog-holes and tarns scattered over the moor are held fast in dark, smooth ice with little white air-bubbles that crack. The wooded hillsides are clear and carry sound, for trees and bushes are bare, and the fallen leaves are bright over the ground, but the fir forest stands dark and fresh after the rime has thawed—and then there is the suspense, whether the bird will make for impassable ground or will take to the bogs and the frozen water.

The only hawk he owned now was in the loft of the men-servants' house, sick and reddish about the feet, nor did it breathe as it should either. It would be as well to make an end of it now—it would never be fit for hunting again. And he had lost his falcon last autumn.

Now Audun was fretting again. Ingunn hushed him and lulled him to sleep in there.

Torhild Björnsdatter came up and spread some blankets over her master. Olav opened his eyes—from where he lay he could see the girl's strong figure moving in the red glare from the embers on the hearth. Torhild was putting things straight—moving the clothes on the crossbeams.

"Are you not asleep, Olav—are you thirsty?"

"Oh, ay. Nay, I will rather have water—"

Olav raised himself on his elbow. His bandaged arm hurt him when he tried to stretch it out and take the cup of water. Torhild sat on her haunches and held it to his mouth. When he lay down again, she drew the coverlet over his shoulder. Then he heard her asking in the closet whether the mistress wanted anything.

"Hush, hush," Ingunn whispered impatiently in reply; "you will wake Audun for me—he was almost asleep."

Torhild covered the embers and went out. Olav lay on the floor all night.

The severe autumn weather was not good for Audun. He got sore eyes from being always in the pungent smoke, and he coughed a great deal.

On the approach of Yule the weather fell calm; the sun glowed red behind the frost fog every morning. Early in the new year the fiord froze over, but the cold increased. In the farms round about, folk had to move all into one house and keep the fire burning on the hearth night and day.

It had been a good spring the year before, so the farmers had as much live stock as they could in any way find room for. But in spite of their byres and stables being overfilled, the beasts suffered so much from the cold that folk had to wrap in sacks and cloths those it was most important to save, and they had to spread the floor with spruce boughs, lest the animals should freeze fast in the clay. The dung was frozen stiff every morning, so it was almost impossible to clear it away.

About the time of St. Agatha's Mass [9] it was said in the countryside that now men could drive on the ice right down to Denmark. But now no man had business in that land; peace had been concluded between the Kings the year before.

About this time Olav was called upon to show cause why he had stayed at home in the summer, when the Duke proceeded to

[9] February 5.

Denmark to negotiate the peace of Hegnsgavl. The matter was thus: that Olav, who had been out for three summers in succession with the war fleet as one of the lesser captains, had been given a half-promise of furlough by Baron Tore Haakonsson for the fourth summer; but Tore ordered him to provide two fully armed men and their victuals for the Baron's service instead. Olav had not been able to do this, but in spite of that he had not presented himself at the muster of the army in the spring—the levy this year was much smaller, since the Duke only went south to negotiate. Now Olav found himself in trouble over this, and in the bitter cold about mid-Lent he had to ride once to Tunsberg and then several times to Oslo, first to account for his absence and then to raise ready money. He lost much cattle that winter, and the white horse died that he had bought of Stein.

The two little children filled the crowded house with commotion.

Eirik had a bad fault: Olav found out by degrees that this boy was greatly given to lying. If his father asked whether he had seen this or that member of the household, Eirik was always quick to answer yes, he had just spoken with the other in the house or out in the yard, and gave an account of what had been said or done. Usually there was not a word of truth in it. Some of the serving-folk, and his mother too, hinted that perhaps the child had second sight—Eirik was not like other boys. Olav had not much to say to this, but he kept an eye on him—he could see no sign that it was anything but mendacity.

Another bad habit of Eirik's was that he would sit humming or singing some rigmarole that he made up himself, interminably, till Olav's head ached and he felt inclined to beat the boy. But he had grown wary of laying a hand on the child since he had thrashed him so pitilessly the day Ingunn came home from her churching.

Eirik knelt before the bench in the evening, arranging these snail-shells and animals' teeth of his in rows and chanting:

> *"Four and five of the fifth dozen,*
> *Four and five of the fifth dozen,*
> *Fifteen mares and four foals*
> *I got in the daytime and got in the nighttime.*

Four and five of the fifth dozen
Were the horses I owned upon the morrow."

He repeated this about cows and calves, sheep and lambs, sows and pigs.

"Be still," his father checked him sharply; "have I not told you I will have no more of these gowling cantraps of yours?"

"I had forgotten, Father mine," said Eirik in alarm.

Olav asked him: "How many horses would you choose to have, Eirik—four and five of the fifth dozen or a hundred horses?"

"Oh, I would have many more," replied Eirik. "I would have—seven and twenty!"

So little did he understand of his own crooning.

Audun was fretful and ailing. Ingunn boasted of her son and said there was no fairer child, and indeed he had been better of late; but Olav saw the smouldering anxiety in her eyes when she spoke thus. Eirik repeated what he heard his mother say, hung over the cradle, rocking and wheedling his silken brother, as he always called Audun.

Olav felt a strange distress when he saw it. Audun seemed to him a most miserable little creature—always scurfy about the scalp, sore about the mouth, lean and raw about the body, which was backward in its growth. Never had this son made him feel anything like paternal joy; but that he was father to this poor sick, fretting child gave him a feeling of bitter pain when Eirik was bending over the cradle: the other was so fair and full of life, with his glistening nut-brown locks falling about Audun's wrinkled face.

One day Olav asked Torhild what she thought of Audun.

"He will surely mend, when the spring comes," said Torhild; but Olav felt in himself that the girl did not believe her own words.

They had turned loose the cattle at Hestviken and drove them up to the old moss-grown pastures in Kverndal in the daytime, when Audun fell very sick. He had coughed the whole winter and had had many fits of colic, but this time it was worse than ever before.

Olav saw that Ingunn was ready to drop with fatigue and anxiety, but she kept wonderfully calm and collected. Untiringly she watched over the child night and day, while every remedy was tried to help Audun—first those familiar to the people of the house, and then all those known to the neighbours' wives for whom Ingunn sent.

At last, on the sixth day, the boy seemed to be much better. By supper-time he was sleeping soundly, and he did not feel so cold to the touch. Torhild put warm stones underneath his cradle clothes; then she went out, taking Eirik with her. She had watched nearly as much as the mother and had had all the housework in the daytime; now she could do no more.

Ingunn was so tired that she neither heard nor saw—at last Olav led her away by force, took off her outer garments, and made her lie down in the bed. He promised that he himself would sit up with the maid and would wake her if the boy was restless.

Olav fetched three tallow candles, set one on the candlestick, and lighted it. But, though he was usually such a bad sleeper, he felt heavy and drowsy tonight. If he stared at the flame of the candle, his eyes began to smart and run, and if he looked at the maid, who had taken her distaff and was spinning, he grew sleepy from seeing and hearing the spinning-wheel. From time to time he made up the fire, snuffed the candle, gave a look to the sleeping child and to his wife, drank cold water, or went outside for a moment, to look at the weather and refresh himself with a breath of the calm, cold spring night—bringing in a piece of wood, which he whittled as he sat. Thus he kept himself awake till he had set the third candle on the stick.

He started up on hearing the cradle rockers bumping queerly against the clay floor; such a strange sound was coming from the child. It was almost dark in the room; the candle-end had fallen off the spike, almost burned out—the wick flickered and smoked in the molten tallow on the iron plate. On the hearth there was still a faint crackling amid the smoke of the wood ashes. Olav was beside the cradle in two noiseless steps; he lifted up the child, wrapping him in the clothes he lay in.

The little body struggled, as though Audun would free himself from his swaddling-clothes—in the dim light Olav thought the boy gave him a strangely accusing look. Then he stretched himself, collapsed limply, and died there in his father's arms.

Olav was benumbed, body and soul, as he laid the corpse down again and covered it over. It was vain to think when Ingunn would wake.

The maid had fallen asleep with her head in her arms over the table. Olav waked her, hastily hushing her as she was about to utter a cry. He bade her go out and tell the house-folk, begging them not to come near the house—Ingunn must be allowed to enjoy her sleep while she could.

He opened the smoke-vent—it was daylight outside. But Ingunn slept and slept, and Olav stayed sitting with her and their dead son. But once when he got up to look at her, he chanced to jerk her belt onto the floor. It made a clanging noise, and the woman started up and looked into her husband's face.

She sprang up and pushed him aside when he tried to hold her back, threw herself upon the cradle so violently that it looked as if the dead child was upset into her arms.

As she sat on her haunches, rocking the corpse in a close embrace and weeping with a strange, spluttering sound, she checked herself all of a sudden and looked up at her husband:

"Were you two asleep when he died—were you both asleep when Audun drew his last breath?"

"No, no, he died in my arms—"

"You—and you did not wake me—Lord Christ, how had you the heart not to wake me—in *my* arms he should have died, 'twas me he knew, not you—you never cared for your child. Is it thus you keep your word!"

"Ingunn—"

But she leaped up, holding the child's corpse high above her head with both hands and screaming. Then she tore open the dress over her bosom, pressed the little dead son to her bare body, and threw herself on the bed, lying over him.

When Olav came up after a while and tried to talk to her, she put her hand against his face and thrust him away.

"Nevermore will I be parted from my Audun—"

Olav knew not what to do. He sat over on the bench with his head between his hands, waiting if perchance she should recover her senses—when Eirik burst open the door and ran to his mother, in a flood of tears. He had been told it when he awoke.

Ingunn sat upright—the child's corpse was left lying on the pillow. She drew her son to her in a close embrace, let him go and took his little tear-stained face in both hands, laid her own against it and wept, but much more quietly.

The day Audun was borne to the grave was gloriously fine.

During the afternoon Olav stole away from the funeral guests, down to the fence around the farthest cornfield. The sea gleamed and glistened so that the air seemed all a-quiver with it; the quiet surf at the foot of the Bull shone fresh and white. The smell that came up from the quay was so good and full-laden today, and it was met by the scent of warm rocks and mould and young growth. The little waves breaking on the beach trickled quietly back among the pebbles, rills were gushing everywhere, and from Kverndal came the murmur of the little stream. The alder wood up there was brown with bloom, and the hazel thickets dripped with yellow catkins. Summer was not far off.

He heard it was Ingunn who came up behind him. Side by side they stood leaning over the fence, gazing at the reddish rocks on which the sun was blazing and at the gleam of blue water.

All at once Olav felt strangely ill at ease, oppressed with longing. To be on board ship, at sea, with a clear horizon on every side. Or at home upcountry, where the scent of mould and grass and trees welled out of broad hills and ridges as far as one could see. Here all was cramped and small, this narrow fiord with its strips of land bordering the lonely creek.

He said gently: "Do not grieve so much over Audun, Ingunn. It was best that God took home His poor innocent lamb, whose only heritage was to bear the burden of all our misdeeds."

Ingunn made no answer. She turned from him and went back toward the houses, quietly, with bowed head. Up by the houses Eirik came rushing to meet her—Olav saw that his mother hushed him as she took his hand and led him with her.

I I

In the summer the year after they had lost Audun, Olav and Ingunn were at a working meeting on a farm in the neighbourhood; they had Eirik with them. The boy was now seven winters old, and he was apt to be unmanageable when amusing himself.

When work was over in the evening the people sat in a meadow near the house they had been roofing. Some of the younger ones then began to dance. Eirik and some other little boys ran about and made a noise; the ale had gone to their heads—they ran straight at the chain of dancers and tried to break it, shouting and laughing as they did so. They mixed among the older folk, jostling one after another, and interrupted the men's talk. Olav had spoken to Eirik time after time, rather sharply at last—but it only kept the boy quiet for a little while.

Ingunn had not noticed it—she was sitting a little way off by the wall in company with other women. All at once Olav appeared before her, dragging Eirik with him; he lifted him by the back of his shirt, so that the boy hung from Olav's hand as one takes a puppy by the nape of the neck. Olav was red in the face, somewhat drunken—his ale was apt to tell on him more than usual when these fits of sleeplessness had been very frequent.

"You must look after your boy and keep him in order, Ingunn," he said angrily, giving Eirik a shake. "He will not obey me, unless I thrash him—take him, he belongs to you—" and he flung the boy so that Eirik pitched into his mother's arms. With that he went away.

In the course of the evening, when folk sat drinking in the shed after supper, some of them began to tell stories. And Sira Hallbjörn told the tale of Jökul:

"A rich merchant fared forth and was away from home three winters. So every man may judge whether he was more surprised or joyful when he came home and found his wife abed and with her a little boy of one month old. But the traveller's wife was a crafty and quick-witted woman; she said:

" 'A great miracle has befallen me. Sorely have I longed for you, my husband, while you wandered so far abroad. But one day last winter I stood here at the door of the house and the icicles hung from the eaves; I broke one off and sucked, yearning for you the while with keen and ardent desire—and then I conceived this child; judge for yourself whether you and none other are not his father, Jökul [1] I have had him called!'

"The traveller had to rest content with that; he spoke her fair, this loving wife of his, and seemed to have great joy of the son,

[1] *Jökul:* icicle.

Jökul. He would have the boy ever near him when he was at home. And when Jökul was twelve years old, his father took him out on one of his voyages. But one day, when they were in the midst of the sea and Jökul stood at the ship's side, the merchant came behind him, while no man saw; he dropped the boy overboard.

"On returning to his wife he told his tale with sorrowful mien and mourning voice:

" 'A great misfortune has befallen us and a heavy loss have we suffered, my sweet one—Jökul is no more. Know that I lay becalmed in the midst of the sea, the day was hot and the sun poured straight down. Our Jökul stood upon the deck and he was bareheaded. We begged him hard that he would cover his head, but he would not—so he thawed in the heat of the sun, and there was nothing left of Jökul, our son, but a wet spot on the deck-planks!'

"With that the wife had to rest content."

Folk laughed greatly at this tale. None took note that Olav Audunsson kept his eyes on the floor, while blushes overspread his face. If his life had depended on it, he did not believe he would have dared to turn his eyes to the dais, where his wife sat among the other ladies. Then there was a disturbance up there—Olav leaped over the table and forced his way through the crowding woman. He lifted up his wife, who had slipped from the bench in a swoon, and carried her out into the fresh air.

The best thing Eirik knew was to be allowed to go out with his father—in a boat when Olav rowed out alone to fish with a handline, as he did now and then, mainly for pastime, or across the fields. Afterwards he always came to his mother and told her about it—with beaming eyes, so eagerly that he stumbled over the words—all that had happened to them and all that he had learned of his father: now he could both row and fish, make knots and splice ropes after the fashion of seafaring men; soon he would be able to go out and fish in earnest with his father and the men. He had become such a good hand at shooting and casting—his father said he had never seen his match.

Ingunn listened to the boy's chatter, perplexed and distressed. Her poor, simple-minded little boy loved Olav more than anyone else on earth. It was as though the man's unfriendliness did not bite upon Eirik: he was given curt answers to all his questions, and at last he was told to hold his tongue. Olav coldly chid him when the boy was wild and wanton, and harshly bade Eirik speak the truth, when his mother guessed that only the child's memory was at fault. But she dared not say that to her husband, dared not take Eirik's part and remind Olav that he was so young—or tell the man Eirik called father how dearly the child loved him. She had to bow the neck and keep silence; only when she was alone with her son did she dare to show her love for him.

Ingunn did not know that what Eirik said was true, and that it was for this that Olav's bad humour neither frightened the boy for long at a time nor lessened his love for his father. They agreed much better when they were alone together. Eirik was then more obedient and not so restless, and even if he was too fond of asking odd questions, there was often some sense in them. He swallowed every word from his father's lips with eyes and ears, and this made him forget to come out with his fables and rigmaroles. Without being himself aware of it, Olav was warmed by the affection the child showed him; he forgot his dislike of other days and let himself be warmed, just as he had felt warmed whenever anyone showed him the friendship he found it so hard to seek for himself. So he met Eirik halfway with calm goodwill; he instructed the boy in the use of weapons and implements, which were still more like playthings, smiled a little at Eirik's eager questions, and chatted with him as a good father talks to his little son.

They fished for wrasse under the cliff north of the Bull, and Olav showed the boy the cleft in the rock where an old she-otter had her lair. Every year Olav took the cubs—one year two litters —and the dog-otter. As soon as the dog was gone she got a new mate, said Olav, and he mimicked for the boy the otter's cry. Yes. Eirik should come with him after the otter one night, when he was a little older—ah, when it would be, his father could not say.

One day when they were up in his father's game-covert to see to some traps, Olav chanced to speak of his own childhood at Frettastein, while he and Eirik's mother were young. "Your grandfather," said Olav, telling some story of Steinfinn at which he himself smiled and Eirik roared with laughter. "One day I had coaxed Hallvard, your uncle, with me—he was very small at that time, you must know, but all the same I had taken the boy with me up to the tarn, where we had a dugout we used to row in—"

Till Eirik mentioned Tora of Berg; he remembered her. Olav broke off his story, answered absently when the boy went on asking questions—at last he bade him hold his tongue. It was as though the sky had suddenly clouded over.

But whenever Olav was with his own house-carls, either on the quay or up at the manor, and Eirik ran about among them, he was at once more impatient with the boy. It was the way with Eirik that the more people he saw about him, the more noisy and foolish and disobedient he became. The men were amused at the boy, but they noticed that the master disliked their laughing at the things he said, and they thought Olav was very short-tempered and strict with his only son.

But it was when the mother was there that Olav felt most provoked to an intolerable ill will toward the boy. Many a time he itched to give Eirik a thrashing, to break him roughly of all his bad habits.

One thing was that Ingunn provoked him to a dull exasperation when she fussed with the child—he was to be quiet and behave in a seemly way, she said severely. Olav knew only too well that the moment his back was turned on the two, she would be on her knees trying to please Eirik. He saw how deeply she distrusted his feeling for the boy; she spied on him secretly when he was occupied with Eirik. He knew in himself that he had never done the child any harm—he might surely be trusted to punish the boy when he needed it. It was Ingunn who egged him on to anger, but it was his lifelong habit, when she was concerned, to hold himself in—and of late years it had come to this, that she was a poor, sick creature, and he had to be doubly careful not to make things worse for her. So when Ingunn tried Olav's patience too far, it was usually Eirik who suffered.

The boy had come between man and wife, and he was the first who had sundered their hearts in earnest. In their youth Olav had had to leave his playmate and fly the country—and in a way he had felt that Ingunn had gone astray simply because he had been forced to abandon her. Far too great a burden of evil fortune had been thrown upon her when she had to have recourse to her angry kinsfolk, who refused to count her as anything but a disobedient and dishonoured woman. Young she was, weak-shouldered and pampered—but her nature was not such that she could have been unfaithful to a husband with whom she shared bed and board, he knew that. He had had a feeling that Teit was but an unhappy accident—and in making an end of this confiding fool he had acted more from a belief that it would be so hopelessly difficult to remedy the disaster so long as he was alive and could blurt out the truth than because he had felt himself wronged by Teit. But even when the slaying had been accomplished, this had not done much to allay his pain of mind. His thirst to avenge the destruction of his happiness—this the poor corpse in the sæter had not been able greatly to assuage.

Now Olav saw that Ingunn loved another, and he guessed how often she had wished him out of the way, so that she might freely shed her affection upon Eirik—as one smuggles food to an outlawed friend behind the back of the master of the house.

And together with this bitterness and unrest something like a ghost of his youthful desire awoke in Olav's heart and senses; he longed to possess Ingunn as he had possessed her in former days, when they were young and healthy and could find happiness in each other's arms in spite of all their cares. Olav had never quite forgotten that time; the memory of her sweet beauty had warmed his pity to a painful tenderness—this poor faded wreck to whom he was bound was the wreck of the lovely, useless Ingunn he had once loved, and his will to protect her became stubborn and intense, as had once been his will to defend his right to his wife.

Now there blazed up in him a desire to feel that she too remembered the madness of their youth. Year in, year out a latent repugnance had smouldered within him when she clung to him with her morbid and insensate demand for caresses which, he knew, ought to be withheld from his sick wife. Now, when she avoided him, hiding herself away with what was her own, what she thought he could have no share in, it was Olav who felt he would fain have crushed her to pieces in his arms in the effort to make her answer such questions as these: Have you forgotten that I was once your dearest friend in all the world?—Why are you afraid of me?—Have I ever willingly brought sorrow upon you in all these years? For it cannot be *my* fault that we have had so little happiness in our married life?

And then his fear awoke, when he touched upon the sick spot in his mind; the dull ache became a pain that shot through his whole being: whether it was so that he *might* all the time—have

averted her misfortunes. If he had had the courage to hand himself over—to men's justice and God's compassion.

Olav noticed that his unwonted impetuosity now frightened
Ingunn and made her shrink; so he withdrew into himself, while
his secret wound throbbed and stung. "Why is she afraid of me?
Does she know—?"

There were times when he almost believed it—believed that all
knew it. For he had not a friend here in his native country. It
could not be helped; but that was not all: Olav guessed that no
one *liked* him. Coldness and distrust met him everywhere, and
often he thought he could detect a hidden malicious satisfaction
when things went ill with him. Yet in this part of the country he
had always acted rightly and had never done any man an injustice. He could not even bring himself to be angry at this—he
received his sentence without wincing. It must be that folk saw
the secret mark upon his brow.

But when he thought of Ingunn, the fear quivered through him:
did *she* see it too? Was it for that she turned cold in his arms, and
was it for that she seemed to be afraid when he came near her son?

On the day of St. Olav's Mass,[2] Olav always held an ale-feast.
He never prayed to his patron saint—the lawmaker King would
certainly not aid him with his intercession except on one condition. But nevertheless he thought himself bound to show Holy
Olav due honour.

The floor was strewed with green and the hall was decorated
with hangings—the old tapestry that otherwise only appeared at
Yule.

On St. Olav's Eve, Olav himself was busy hanging up the
tapestry. He moved along the bench and fastened the long piece
with wooden hooks, which he drove in between the topmost log
of the wall and the roof. Eirik followed him on the floor, gazing
at the worked pictures: there were knights and longships with
men on board. He knew that soon the best picture of all was coming—a house with pillars and shingled roof like a church and a
banquet going on inside with drinking-horns and tankards on the
table. Eirik had to peep into the roll of stuff that still lay on the
bench—and in so doing he chanced to pull down a long piece of
that which his father had just made to hang right.

[2] July 29.

Olav jumped down, pulled the boy from under the folds of tapestry, and flung him on the floor:

"Out with you—you are ever in my way, bastard, doing mischief—"

At that moment Ingunn appeared in the door of the anteroom with the lap of her gown full of flowers. She let her burden fall straight on the floor.—He saw that she had heard.

Olav did not get a word out. Shame, anger, and a confused feeling that soon he would not know which way to turn made a tumult within him. He stepped up on the bench and began to hang up the tapestry that had been torn down. Eirik had fled out of the door. Ingunn picked up her flowers and strewed them over the floor. Olav dared not turn round and look at her. He did not feel equal to talking to her now.

One morning a few days later Ingunn was sitting with Eirik on the top of the crag behind the houses of Hestviken. She had been down to Saltviken—a path led over the height; it would serve at a pinch for riding, but was little used: the common way between Hestviken and Saltviken was by boat.

There was sparkling sunshine and a fresh breeze; from where Ingunn sat she saw the fiord dark blue, dotted with white foam. The breakers dashed up in spray, glittering white along the reddish rocks that planted their feet out into the water all along the coast. The morning sun still lay over Hudrheimsland. From the height where she sat she could see a little of the cultivation on the hillside—it was for that she liked this spot. And up here it sounded fainter and farther off, that intolerable roar of the sea which tormented her at home at the manor till she thought it must come from within her own weary, bewildered head. But there was a kind of taste of salt, and that flickering of light from the sea in the uneasy air—she could never accustom herself to that. She grew tired of it.

Eirik lay half in his mother's lap playing with a bunch of big bluebells. One after another he tore off the flowers, turned them inside out, and blew into them. Ingunn laid her thin hand on his cheek and looked down into his sunburned face. How handsome, how handsome he was, this son of hers—his eyes the shade of bog water in sunshine, his hair as fine as silk! It had grown much darker in the last year; it was brown now. Eirik scratched his head.

"Louse me now, Mother mine. Ugh, they bite so hard in this heat!"

Ingunn gave a little laugh. She took out her comb from the pouch at her belt and began to clean the boy's head with slow, caressing strokes. It made Eirik sleepy—and the scent of the fir woods in the sun's heat and the sourish fragrance of the hair-moss on which she was lying, the clanging of bells from the cattle moving on the slope farther up the valley, lulled Ingunn to sleep.

She started at the little sound of a dog that came swimming through the high bilberry bushes. It sniffed at the two, jumped without a sound over their knees, and set off again down the path.

Her heart still trembled from being waked so suddenly. Now she heard horse's hoofs on the rock far below. Her head fell back against the trunk of the fir tree by which she sat—oh, that he should be back already! She had felt so sure he would not come home before evening at the earliest, perhaps not before the morrow.

They came over her again, the same thronging fears and despair. This thing that she had gone in dread of the last month—she could not face it, she felt that; it would be her death this time. And she could almost have wished it—had it not been for Eirik's sake; then he would be left alone with Olav. And in the midst of her great dread this little anxiety started up—why had Olav come home so soon? Had he not been able to accomplish his errand in the neighbouring parish, or had he fallen out with those folk?—and maybe he came home in yet worse humour than when he set out.

Instinctively she had thrown her arm about her child, as though to protect and hide him. Eirik struggled and freed himself:

"Let me go now—father is coming." He got on his feet, and his mother saw that he turned red as he went along the path, seeming a little uncertain and hesitating. Ingunn followed.

She saw the white horse among the trees; Olav was walking by its side. When Ingunn came up he was showing Eirik something that lay at his foot—a great lynx.

"I found her over on the mountain here to the south—she was out in broad daylight. She has young in her lair—her teats are full of milk." He turned over the dead lynx with his spear, shooing off the dog, which lay on its front paws barking, and holding the uneasy horse. Eirik cried aloud with joy, squatting down over his father's quarry. Olav smiled at the boy. "We could not find the lair—though it cannot have been very far away. But there was a scree with fallen trees on it—she must have had her track among the trees."

"Will they starve to death now, the young ones?" asked Ingunn. Eirik fumbled in the light fur under the belly of the lynx, found the swollen teats, and squeezed them—the boy's hands were all bloody. Olav was telling him how it was easy enough to get the lynx when it strayed out in broad daylight.

"Starve to death?—ay, or else they will eat each other in the lair, the strongest will come through. Unless they were born very early in the summer—that is like enough, since the dam was not with them."

Ingunn looked at the dead beast of prey. A soft and warm place the young had had as they huddled together, nosing for the sources of milk in the light fur under her soft belly. The heavy thigh that she had protected them with was tense with muscle and sinew, the claws were like steel. When she licked her young, the cruel white fangs showed up. The tufts of hair in the ears had been given her to make her the more wary and sharp of hearing; the black streaks in her yellow eyes had been like keen slits. She had been well fitted to protect and defend and discipline her offspring.

Her own child, he had such a poor wretch of a mother, unable to defend her own. And she herself had brought it to such a pass that he had none to protect him, and most he needed protection against the man he called father.

"I cannot believe even Mary, God's Mother, will pray for a mother who betrays her own son," Tora had said. And she had already betrayed her child when she suffered him to be begotten; she saw that now.

Olav and Eirik were pulling up bunches of moss and wiping away the blood that had got on the saddle and had run down the side of the white horse. Olav helped the boy into the saddle and placed the reins in his hand.

"He is so quiet, Apalhvit; Eirik will be able to ride him home, though it is a little steep below here." He walked a few steps down, cheering the boy and the horse with kind words. Then he returned to the lynx, bound its limbs together with thongs; now and again he looked up, watching the boy on the big white horse, till they were lost among the trees.

"Nay, we came to no agreement—'twas vain to stay there disputing with those Kaaressons," he said. "I think that Eirik ought to have Apalhvit—is he not seven winters now, the boy? 'Twill soon be time he had his own horse—and 'tis unsafe to let the boy ride Sindre, he is too skittish.—What are you crying for?" he asked rather sharply, as he rose to his feet.

"If you gave Eirik the fairest colt ever bred—with saddle of silver and bridle of gold—what would that serve, Olav, if you cannot alter your feelings—can never look at the boy without a grudge?"

"That is not true," said Olav hotly. "You are heavy too, you sow of Satan"—he had got the lynx on his spear and hoisted it over his shoulder. "Do use your wits, Ingunn," he went on, rather more gently. "Can I have any joy of the son who is to take this manor after me, if he is always to hide behind your skirt, now that he is of an age to need a father's teaching and discipline? You must venture it now, to let *me* take Eirik in hand; else there will never be a man of him."

The breeze up here on the height fluttered his long grey cloak; the wide brim of his black cloth hat flapped. Olav had come to look much older in the last few years; he was no stouter than before, yet his figure seemed much more burly, broader and rounder behind the shoulders. And the pale eyes looked smaller and even sharper than of old, as his face was now browned by the weather. The whites were somewhat bloodshot, no doubt because the man had too little sleep.

He felt her staring at him, till he was forced to turn his head. He met her complaining glance with a hard eye.

"I know what you are thinking of, Ingunn, I spoke a word in wrath—God knows I wish it unsaid."

Ingunn crouched as though expecting a blow.

Olav began again, forcing himself to be calm: "But you must not act so, Ingunn, as to entice him away from me, as though you were afraid I should— Never have I chastised Eirik excessively—"

"I do not remember that my father ever laid a hand upon you, Olav."

"No, Steinfinn cared not to trouble himself so far on my account as to correct me. But I have never departed from my own word—not from my word to you, Ingunn, in any case. And now I have let all men know that Eirik is *our* son—yours and mine."

He saw that she was ready to faint. But it seemed to him that this time he *could* not turn aside—saying some new thing to blot out the traces of what he had already said. He went on:

" 'Tis worst for us all if you steal away with your motherly love and dare not take Eirik on your lap when I am there to see. Deal with the boy in hole-and-corner fashion, as though you crept away by stealth to meet a leman."

He took her hand, pressed it hard and kept it. "Remember, my dear—by so doing you serve Eirik worst."

On the Eve of St. Matthew,[3] early in the day, Eirik came rushing in to his parents, who were in the hall. He was screaming at the top of his voice. Kaare and Rannveig, the two children Björn had left, who were still with Torhild, came after him, and Olav and Ingunn heard from them what had happened.

The stoat that lived in the turf roof of the sheepcot had had another litter of young, and Eirik had tried to dig out the nest— though Olav had said they were to be left in peace this summer. Eirik had been bitten in the hand.

Olav seized the boy, lifted him up, and carried him to his mother's arms. Hurriedly he took the child's hand and looked at it—the bite was in the little finger.

"Are you able to hold him—or shall I fetch in Torhild? Be quiet—say nothing to Eirik. He can be saved if we are quick enough about it."

The stoat's bite is the most poisonous of all animals'; the flesh of him who is bitten by an enraged stoat rots and falls from the bones till the man dies, or else he gets the falling sickness, for all stoats have falling sickness. Only if one be bitten in the tip of one finger there may be a chance of saving life and health, if the finger be cut off and the wound burned out.

Quick as lightning Olav made all ready. Among the smaller implements kept in a crack of the wall he found a suitable iron and put it in the fire, bidding Kaare Björnsson blow. Then he drew his dagger and set to sharpening it.

But the serving-maid who had been called in to hold the boy began to scream loudly. Eirik was scared already—now he guessed

[3] St. Matthew's Day is September 21.

what his father would do to him. With a howl of the utmost terror he tore himself away from his mother and ran like a rat from wall to wall howling worse and worse, and Olav after him.

A ladder stood leading to the loft above the closet. Eirik ran up it, and Olav followed him. In the darkness among all the piled-up chattels he got hold of the boy at last and came down the ladder carrying him. Eirik kicked and sprawled and yelled inside the flap of his father's kirtle, which Olav had had to wrap about his head so as not to be bitten by the maddened child.

Ingunn did not look as though he could expect help of her. Torhild had come in—Olav gave Eirik to her, and the two other serving-women also took a hand. Eirik fought and screamed in mortal fear as they struggled to wind a cloth about his head.

Then the father pulled the cloth from the boy's eyes.

"Your life is at stake, Eirik—look at me, boy—you will die, if you will not let me save you—"

Olav was in a raging tumult. This was the last of her children and she loved the child as she had never loved him—if she were to lose Eirik, it would be the end of all. He must and would save the boy; if it might cost his own life, he must! At the same time he felt a cruel desire and longing to get home at last on this flesh that had come between him and her, to maim and burn it—and in spite of that, something arose from the innermost depths of his being and forbade him to harm the defenceless child.

"Do not scream like that," he yelled in fury. "You wretched whelp—do not be so afraid—it is no worse than—look here!"

He set the point of his dagger to the lining of the sleeve at his left wrist and slit and cut till his shirt and the sleeve of his kirtle hung in tatters right up to the shoulder. He quickly wound the rags about his arm, so that they should not be in the way, took the red-hot iron by the tongs, and pressed it against his upper arm.

Eirik had stopped howling from fear and surprise at what his father was doing; he lay limply in the women's arms and stared. But now he set up a fresh shriek of terror. Olav had had a vague idea of putting heart into the boy, but all he had done was to scare away the rest of his wits: the smell of the scorched flesh, the sight of the spasm that passed over Olav's face as he withdrew the iron from the burn, made the boy clean mad. A straight stream of blood ran down the man's white arm as he let it drop; his dagger had entered the flesh as he started.

Then all at once Ingunn was there. She was white in the face, but perfectly calm now as she took the child on her lap, held his legs tight between her knees, threw the end of her coif across his face, and caught it under one arm. With her other hand she took him by the wrist and held the little fist against the table. The serving-maids helped to hold the boy, smothering his hideous screams of pain with more cloths, while Olav took off the damaged finger at the inner joint, burnt out the wound, and bound it up—he did it so rapidly and so neatly as he had never guessed himself able to accomplish leechcraft.

While the women attended to the wailing child, got him to bed, and poured strengthening drinks into him, Olav sat on the bench. Only now did he feel the pain of his burn, and he was ashamed and furious with himself for being capable of such senseless conduct—maltreating himself to no purpose like a madman.

Torhild came up to him with white of egg in a cup and a box of fuzz-ball fungus. She was going to tend his arm; but Ingunn took the things from the serving-woman and pushed her aside:

"I shall tend my husband myself, Torhild—go you out, find a tuft of grass, and wipe the blood from the table."

Olav stood up and shook himself, as though he would be rid of both women. "Let be—I can bind this little thing myself," he said morosely. "And find me some other clothes than these rags."

Eirik recovered rapidly; that day week he was already sitting up, eating with a good appetite of the dainties his mother brought him. It looked as though he would escape from the stoat's bite with no worse harm than the loss of his right little finger.

At first Olav would not allow that the burn on his arm troubled him; he tried to work and use the arm as if nothing had happened. Then the wound began to gather and he had to bind up his arm. After that he had fever, headache, and violent vomiting, and at last he had to take to his bed and let a man practised in leechcraft tend his arm. This lasted till near Advent, and Olav was in the worst of humours. For the first time since they had lived together he was unfriendly to Ingunn; he constantly used a harsh tone toward her and he would not have a word said as to how he had met with his hurt.—The housefolk guessed too that he had very little joy of his wife being with child again.

When Eirik was up and out of doors once more, he talked of

nothing but his misfortune. He was unspeakably proud of his maimed hand and showed it off outside the church to all who cared to see, the first Sunday the people of Hestviken were at mass. He boasted fearfully, both of what his father had done, which seemed to him a mighty exploit, and of his own hardiness —if Eirik was to be believed, he had not let a sound out of him under the ordeal.

" 'Tis my belief that boy is a limb of the Fiend himself, the way he lies," said Olav. "It will end ill with you, Eirik, if you do not give up this evil habit."

I 2

ABOUT St. Blaise's Mass [4] they had a guest at Hestviken whom they had never thought to see here: Arnvid Finnsson came to the manor one day. Olav was not at home, and the house-folk did not expect him till after the holy-day.

Olav had a happy look that evening when he came in with his friend—Arnvid had gone out to meet him on the hill. He received the ale-bowl that Ingunn brought, drank to the other, and bade him welcome. But then he saw that Ingunn had been weeping.

Arnvid told him he had brought her heavy tidings: Tora of Berg had died in the autumn. But when Olav heard that Arnvid had already been here for some days, he wondered a little—had she wept over her sister for all that time? They had not been so very closely attached. But, after all, she was her only sister—and maybe at this time her tears flowed more readily than usual.

Ingunn bade them good-night as soon as supper was over. She took Eirik with her and went out—she would lie in the women's little house tonight—"You two would rather sleep together, I ween; you must have many things to speak of."

Olav could not help wondering again: was there any special thing that she thought they wished to speak of so privily? For otherwise she might simply have lain in the closet.

After that their talk went but sluggishly as they sat at their drink. Arnvid spoke of Tora's children—'twas a pity they were all under age. Olav asked after Arnvid's own sons. Arnvid said he

[4] February 3.

had joy of them: Magnus had Miklebö now; he was married, and Steinar was betrothed. Finn had taken vows in the convent of the preaching friars; they said he had good parts, and next year they would surely send him to Paris, to the great school there.

"You never thought of marrying again?"

Arnvid shook his head. He fixed his strange dark eyes upon his friend, smiling feebly and bashfully like a young man who speaks of his sweetheart. "I too shall be found among the friars, once Steinar's wedding is over."

"You are not one to change your mind either," said Olav with a little smile.

"Either—?" said Arnvid involuntarily.

"So you will be father and son in the same convent."

"Yes." Arnvid gave a little laugh. "If God wills, it may be so turned up and down with us that I shall obey my boy and call him father."

They sat in silence for a while. Then Arnvid spoke again:

"It is on the convent's business we are now come south, Brother Vegard and I. We would rebuild our church of stone after the fire, but Bishop Torstein has other use for his craftsmen this year; so we were to see whether we can hire stonemasons in Oslo. But Brother Vegard said that you must do him a kindness and come into the town—and bring Ingunn with you if you could—so that he might see you."

"Ingunn is not fit for any journey—you may guess that.—But he must be as old as the hills now, Brother Vegard?"

"Oh, ay—three and a half score, I believe. He is sacristan now. —Ay, 'twas that I was to say, that you must not fail to come. There was something he must needs say to you"—Arnvid looked down and spoke with a slight effort—"about that axe of yours, the barbed axe. He has found out a deal about it—that it is the same that was once at Dyfrin in Raumarike, at the time your ancestors held the manor."

"I know it," replied Olav.

"Ay, Brother Vegard has heard a whole saga about that axe, he says. In former times it was the way with it, they say, that it sang for a slaying."

Olav nodded. "That I have once heard myself," he said quietly. "That day when I was in the guest house, ready to fare northward —you know, the last time I visited you at Miklebö—"

Arnvid was silent for a while. Then he said in a low voice: "You told me that you had lost your axe on that journey?"

"You think me not such a fool as to set out through the forest with that huge devil of an axe?" Olav laughed coldly. " 'Twas a woodcutter's axe; it served me well enough, that one. But true it is, I heard Kinfetch ring—she would fain have gone with me."

Arnvid sat with his arms crossed before him, perfectly silent. Olav had got up and walked uneasily about the hall. Then he came to a sudden stop.

Aloud and as though defiantly he asked: "Was there none who wondered—was nothing rumoured, when that Teit Hallsson disappeared from Hamar so abruptly?"

"Oh—something was said about the matter, no doubt. But folk were satisfied that he must have been afraid of the Steinfinnssons."

"And you? Did you never wonder what had become of him?"

Arnvid said quietly: "It is not easy for me to answer that, Olav."

"I am not afraid to hear what you thought."

"Why do you wish me to say it?" whispered Arnvid reluctantly.

Olav was silent a good while. When he spoke, it was as though he weighed every word; he did not look at his friend meanwhile:

"I trow Ingunn has told you how it has gone with us. I thought it must be because He would that I should offer atonement to the boy for the man I put out of the world. That vagabond"—Olav gave a little laugh—"he was mad enough to imagine he would marry Ingunn—keep her and the child, he said. I *had* to put him out of the way, you can see that—"

"I can see that you thought you had to," replied Arnvid.

"Well, he struck first. It was not that I decoyed the fellow into an ambush. He came of himself, stuck to me like a burr—I was to help him, as a man buys a marriage for his leman when he would be rid of her."

Arnvid said nothing.

Olav went on, hotly: "So said this—a man of his sort—said it of Ingunn!"

Arnvid nodded. Nothing was said between them for a while. Then Arnvid spoke with hesitation:

"They found the bones of a man among the ashes, when they came up in the spring, my tenant of Sandvold; those sæters up there on Luraasen. That must have been he—"

"Oh, the devil! Was it *your* hut? That is well so far—now I can make amends to you for it."

"Oh, no, Olav, stop!" Arnvid rose abruptly and his face contracted. "What is the sense of that? So many long years ago—"

"That is so, Arnvid. And every day I have thought of it, and never have I spoken of it to any living soul until this evening.— Then he was given Christian burial?"

"Yes."

"Then I have not that to grieve over—to think of. I need not have vexed myself with that for all these years—that maybe he still lay there. I have not that sin upon me, that I left a Christian corpse unburied.—And no one asked or made search, who it might be that lay there?"

"No."

"That seems strange."

"Oh, not so strange either. The folk up there are wont to do as I say, when for once I let them know my will."

"But you should not have done that!" Olav wrung his hands hard. "It had been better for me if it had come to light then—if you had not helped me to carry out my purpose, hush the matter up. That *you* could lend your hand to such a thing—you, a God-fearing man!"

Arnvid burst out laughing all at once, laughed so that he had to sit down on the bench. Olav gave a start at the way the other took it; he said heatedly:

"That ugly habit of yours—bursting into a roar of laughter just as one is speaking of—other things—you will have to give that up. I should think, when you are a monk!"

"I suppose I must." Arnvid dried his eyes with his sleeve.

Olav spoke in violent agitation: "*You* have never known what it is to live at enmity with Christ, to stand before Him as a liar and betrayer, every time you enter His house. I have—every day for—ay, 'twill soon be eight years now. Hereabouts they believe me to be a pious man—for I give to the church and to the convent in Oslo and to the poor, as much as I am able, I go to mass as often as I have the means to come thither, and two or three times a day when I am in the town. Thou shall love the Lord thy God with all thy mind and all thy heart, we are told—methinks God must know I *do* so—I knew not that such love was within the power of man until I myself had abandoned His covenant and lost Him!"

"Why do you say this to *me*?" asked Arnvid in distress. "You ought rather to speak to your priest of such things!"

"I cannot do that. I have never made confession that I slew Teit."

As he received no reply, he said hotly: "Answer me! Can you not give me a counsel?"

"It is a great thing you lay upon me. I can give you no other counsel than that which your priest would give you.—I can give you no other counsel than that you know yourself— And that is not the counsel you wish for," he said a moment later, as the other stood silent.

"I cannot." Olav's face turned white, as though congealed. "I must think of Ingunn too—more than of myself. I cannot condemn her to be left alone, poor and joyless and broken in health, the widow of a secret murderer and caitiff."

Arnvid answered doubtfully: "But I trow it is not certain—quite certain it cannot be, that the Bishop could not find a way out—since this happened years ago—and no innocent man has suffered for the misdeed—and the dead man had done you grievous harm, and you fought together. Mayhap the Bishop will find a means of reconciling you with Christ—give you absolution, without demanding that you accuse yourself of the slaying also before human justice."

"That can scarce be very likely?"

"I know not," said Arnvid quietly.

"I cannot venture it. Too much is at stake for those whom it is my duty to protect. Then all that I have done to save her honour might as well have been undone. Think you I did not know that had I proclaimed the slaying there and then, it would have been naught but a small matter?—the man was of no account, alive or dead, and had you then backed me and witnessed she was mine, the woman he had seduced— But Ingunn would not have been equal to it—she could face so little always—and then is every mother's son in these parts to hear this of her now that she is worn out—?"

It was a little while before Arnvid could answer. "It is a question," he said in a low voice, "whether she could face the other thing better. Should it go with her this time as all the other times —that she lose her child again—"

A quiver passed over Olav's features.

"However that may be—she is not fit to go through it many times more."

"You must not speak so," whispered Olav. "Then there is Eirik," he began again, after a pause. "This promise I have made to God Himself, that Eirik should be treated as my own son."

"Think you," asked Arnvid, "that it avails you to offer God this and that—promise Him all that He has never asked of you—when you withhold from Him the only thing you yourself know that He would beg of you?"

"The only thing?—but that is *everything*, Arnvid—honour. Life, maybe. God knows I fear not so much to lose it in other ways—but to lose it as a caitiff—"

"Nevertheless, you have nothing that you have not received of Him. And He Himself submitted to the caitiff's death to atone for all our sins."

Olav closed his eyes. "Nevertheless I cannot—" he said almost inaudibly.

Arnvid rejoined: "You spoke of Eirik. Know you not, Olav, you have not the right to act in this way—to make a promise to set aside an heir—since by so doing you play your kinsmen false."

Olav frowned in anger. "Those men of Tveit—never have I seen them, and they did not deal by me as kinsmen when I was young and had sore need of their coming forward."

"They came forward after you had fled to Sweden."

"And they might just as well have stayed where they were, for all the good I had of them. Nay, then I should rather let her son take Hestviken."

"That will not make wrong right, Olav.—And neither you nor she can know whether it will tend to the boy's happiness that you two make him a gift that he has no right to receive."

"Oh, ay, I thought as much: she has been talking to you of what is in her head—that I hate her child and wish him ill. 'Tis not true," he said hotly. "I have never had aught else in mind for Eirik but his own good—'tis she who corrupts him; she trains him to be afraid of me, to lie and sneak out of my way—"

On seeing the expression in Arnvid's face he shook his head. "Nay, nay, I blame her not for that—Ingunn knows no better, poor woman. I have not changed my mind either, Arnvid. Do you remember, I promised you once that I would never fail your kinswoman? And I have never regretted it—in whatever shape my last hour may come, I shall thank God that He held my hand when I was tempted to do harm to *her*—showed me, ere it was too late, that I must protect and support her as well as I was able. Even if I had come back and found her stricken with leprosy, I could have done no less than remember that she was my dearest friend—the only friend I had in all the years I was a child and brought up among strangers."

Arnvid said calmly: "If you think, Olav, that it would make it easier for you to judge what you ought to do in order to make your peace with God, should you be unable to care for those belonging to you, I promise to be as a brother to Ingunn, to provide for her and the boy. I shall take them under my roof, if need be—"

"But you have given up Miklebö to Magnus. And you yourself will enter the convent—" Olav said it almost with a touch of scorn.

"Thereby I have not parted with my whole estate. And if I have endured the world so long, I doubt not I can endure it to my dying day, if it must be—while my near kinsfolk need me by them."

"Nay, nay," said Olav as before. "I will not have you think of the like for my sake or for the sake of any who are properly in my care."

Arnvid sat gazing into the dying embers on the hearth, feeling the presence of his friend in the gloom. "I wonder if he does not see himself that it is no small burden he has thrown upon me tonight," he thought.

Olav pulled a stool toward him with his foot and sat down by the hearth, facing his friend.

"Now I have told you much, but not that which I had it in my mind to say: I have told you that I yearn, day and night, to be reconciled with the Lord Christ—I have told you that never did our Lord seem to me so lovable beyond all measure as when I knew that He had marked me with the brand of Cain. But I marvel that I yearn so, for never have I seen Him so hard on other men as on me. *I* have wrought this one misdeed; and then I was so—incensed—that I do not now recall what were my thoughts at the time; but I did it because I judged that 'twould be even worse for Ingunn if I did it not—I would save a poor remnant of respect for her, even if it cost me a murder. And then it all came about as easily as if it had been laid out for me—*he* begged me to take him on that journey; no man was aware that we set out together. But had God or my patron or Mary Virgin directed our way to some man's house that evening and not to those deserted sæters under Luraas—you know it would have fallen out otherwise."

"I scarce think you had prayed God and the saints to watch over your journey, ere you set out?"

"I am not so sure that I did not—nay, *prayed* I had not truly. But all that Easter I had done nothing but pray—and I was so loath to kill him, all the time. But it was as though all things favoured me, so that I was driven to do it—and tempted to conceal it afterwards. And God, who knows all, He knew how this must turn out, better than I—why could not He have checked me nevertheless, without my prayers—?"

"So say we all, Olav, when we have accomplished our purpose and then see that it would have been better if we had not. But beforehand I ween you think like the rest of us, that you are the best judge of your own good."

"Ay, ay. But in all else beyond what this deed has brought in its train I have dealt uprightly with every man, to the best of my power. I have no goods in my possession that were come by unjustly, so far as I know; I have not spread ill report of man or woman, but have let all such talk fall to the ground when it reached my door, even though I knew it to be true and no lie. I have been faithful to my wife, and 'tis *not* as she thinks, that I bear the boy ill will—I have been as good to Eirik as most men are to their own sons. Tell me, Arnvid, you who understand these thinks better than I—you have been a pious man all the days of your life and have shown compassion to all—am I not right when I say that God is harder on me than on other men? I have seen more of the world than you"—Arnvid was sitting so that Olav could not see him smile at these words—"in the years when I was an outlaw, with my uncle, and afterwards, when I was the Earl's liegeman. I have seen men who loaded themselves with all the seven deadly sins, who committed such cruel deeds as I would not set my hand to, even if I knew of a surety that God had already cast me off and doomed me to hell. They were not afraid of God, and I never marked that they thought of Him with love or longing to obtain His forgiveness—and yet they lived in joy and contentment, and they had a good death, many of them, as I myself have seen.

149

"Then why can we have no peace or joy, she and I? It is as though God pursued me, wherever I may go, vouchsafing me no peace or rest, but demanding of me such impossible things as I have never seen Him demand of other men."

"How should I be able to give you answers to such questions, I, a layman?—Olav, can you not go with me to the town and speak with Brother Vegard of this?"

"Maybe I will do so," said Olav in a low voice. "But you must tell me first—can you understand why it is to be made so much harder for me than for other men?"

"You do not know everything about the other men you speak of, either. But you must be able to see that, if you feel that God pursues you, it is because He would not lose you."

"But He has so ordered it for me that I cannot turn about."

"Surely it was not God who ordered it so for you?"

"Nay, but I have not brought it about myself either—I had to do what I did, it seems to me; Ingunn's life and welfare were laid in my hands. But that which was the cause of all this, Arnvid—that the Steinfinnssons would steal from me the marriage that had been promised to my father—should I have been content with that—bowed before such injustice? I have never heard aught else but that God commands every Christian man to fight against wrong and law-breaking. I was a child in years, unlearned in the law—I knew no other way to defend my right than to take my bride myself, ere they could give her to another."

Arnvid said reluctantly: "That was the answer you gave me when I—spoke to you of your dealings with my kinswoman. Do you remember yet, Olav, that—that you did not speak the truth that time?"

Olav raised his head with a jerk, taken by surprise. He paused a moment with his reply. "No.—And I believe," he said calmly, "most men would have done the same in my place."

"That is sure."

"Do you think," asked Olav scornfully, "that God's hand has pressed so hard upon me—and upon her—because I lied that time —to you?"

"I cannot tell."

Olav gave a fretful toss of his head. "I cannot believe that it was so grievous a sin. So many a man have I heard tell worse lies—needlessly—and never did I see that God raised a finger to chastise him. So I cannot understand His justice, which deals so hardly with me!"

Arnvid whispered: "You must have petty thoughts of God if you expect His justice to be the same as man's. Not two of us outlawed children of Eve did He create alike—should He then demand the same fruits of all His creatures, to whom He has given such diverse talents?—When first I knew you, in your youth, I judged you to be most truthful, upright, and generous; there was no cruelty or deceit in you, but God had given you a heritage of brave and faithful ancestors—"

Olav rose to his feet in violent agitation. "Methinks that if it were so—. If 'tis as you say—and truly I have often shrunk from doing what other men do every day, without a care, for smaller matters— Methinks that what you call God's gifts might just as well be called a burden not to be borne, which He laid upon my back when He created me!"

Arnvid leaped up in his turn. He moved forward to the other and stood before him, almost threateningly. "So many a man may say that of the nature he was given; unless he have a faith firm as a rock in his Redeemer, he must think himself born the most unfortunate of men." He put his foot on the edge of the hearth; with his hand resting on his knee he stood bending forward and looked down at the embers. "You often wondered that I longed to turn my back upon the world—I who had riches in abundance, and more power than I cared to use—and some respect withal. Pious you say I have been, and compassionate to all— God knows if you do not deem it must be because I *love* my even Christians!"

"I believed you helped every man who sought your aid because you were—meek of heart—and pitied everyone who was in any —difficulty—"

"Pitied—oh yes. Many a time I was tempted to reproach my Creator because He had made me so that I *could* do naught else— I had to pity all, though I could love none—"

"I believed," said Olav very low, "that you—supported me and Ingunn with deed and counsel because you were our friend. Was it only for *God's* sake you held your hand over us?"

Arnvid shook his head. "It was not. I was fond of you from our childhood, and Ingunn has been dear to me since she was a little maid. Nevertheless I was often so mortally weary of all this—it came over me that I desired more than all else to be rid once for all of this suit of yours."

"You might have let me know this," said Olav stiffly. "Then I should have troubled you far less."

Again Arnvid shook his head. " 'Tis you and Ingunn who were ever my best friends. But I *am* not pious and I am not good. And often I was weary of it all—wished I could transform myself and become a hard man, if I could not be meek and let God judge mankind, not me. There was once a holy man in France, an anchorite; he had taken upon himself a work of charity for the love of God, that he would harbour folk who fared through the forest where he dwelt. One night there came a beggar who sought shelter with the anchorite—Julian was his name, I think. The stranger was full of leprosy, grievously tainted with the sickness, gross and foul of mouth—returned ill thanks for all the kindness the anchorite showed him. Then Julian undressed the beggar, washed and tended his sores and kissed them, put him to bed—but the beggar made as though he was cold and bade Julian lie close and warm him. Julian did so. But then his foulness and ugliness and evil speech slipped from the stranger as it were a disguise —and Julian saw that he had embraced Christ Himself.

"It has been my lot that, when I thought I could not bear all these folk who came to me, lied and threw the burden of their affairs on me, begged advice and acted as seemed good to themselves, but blamed me when things went wrong, greedy and envious of everyone they thought had been better helped—it was borne in upon me that they must be disguised, and that under the disguise it would one day be granted to me to see my Saviour and my Friend Himself. And indeed it was so in a way—since He said that everything ye do unto one of My little ones— But never would He throw off the disguise and appear to me in the person of any of them."

Olav had seated himself on the stool again, hiding his face in his arms.

Arnvid said in a yet lower voice: "Do you remember, Olav, what Einar Kolbeinsson said that evening—the words that goaded me so that I drew my weapon upon him?"

Olav nodded.

"You were so young at that time—I knew not whether you had guessed their meaning."

"I guessed it later."

"And afterwards, those rumours of Ingunn and me—?"

"Hallvard said something of that—when I was north to fetch the boy."

Arnvid drew a couple of deep breaths. "I am not so holy but that I took it greatly to heart, both one thing and the other. And I often thought God might have granted me my only prayer—given me leave to serve Him in such guise that I dared work deeds of compassion, as far as I was able, without folk whispering behind my back and defaming me or calling me a sanctimonious fool. Or believe the worst of me, because I took to myself neither wife nor leman after Tordis's death." He struck out with his fist and brought it down on the other hand with a crack. "Often I had a good mind to take my axe and make an end of the whole pack!"

Thereafter, during the two days Arnvid yet stayed at Hestviken, the friends were shy and taciturn with each other. It pained them both that they had said far too much that evening; now it seemed they could not talk freely of the simplest trifles.

Olav rode with Arnvid a part of the way up the fiord, but when they were halfway to the town he said he must turn back. He drew out something from the folds of his kirtle—a hard thing, wrapped in a linen cloth. Arnvid could feel that it must be the silver cup that Olav had shown him a day or two before. Olav said he was to give it to the convent at Hamar.

"But so great a gift you ought to place yourself in the hands of Brother Vegard," thought Arnvid.

Olav replied that he must be home that evening—"but it may be that I come in to Oslo one day to greet him."

Arnvid said: "You know full well, Olav, that it is vain to seek to buy your atonement with gifts, so long as you live as you do now."

"I know it—'tis not for that. But I had a mind to give to their church—many a happy hour have I had in the old Olav's Church."

So they bade each other farewell and rode their ways.

Olav did not come to Oslo. Arnvid spoke with Brother Vegard about it, saying that he was doubtless unwilling to come while Ingunn was unfit to accompany him. But she had grieved so much that she could not see the instructor of her youth while he dwelt so near, Arnvid proposed that the monk should borrow a sledge and drive south to Hestviken one day. Brother Vegard was well minded to make the journey, but he had been so unwell and full of rheum ever since he came to Oslo. By Peter's Mass [5] a hard frost set in. A few days after, the old man fell suddenly sick of a fever in the lungs and died the third night. Thereafter Arnvid had to deal single-handed with the hiring of the stonemasons, and it took up all his time, until he had to take the north road again.

Olav got Ingunn to keep her bed in the daytime when the weather turned so cold: she was scarcely able to move now, so far gone was she, and then her feet were frostbitten so that there were great open holes in the flesh. Olav tended them himself and smeared foxes' fat and swine's gall on the sores. Ever since Arnvid's departure he had been gentle and solicitous with his wife; he had quite put off the cross and unfriendly air that he had shown her during the autumn and winter.

Ingunn lay huddled under the skins, whispering a little word of humble thanks whenever Olav did anything for her. She had bowed beneath his displeasure and harsh words, silent and submissive; now she accepted his affectionate care with almost the same dumb meekness. Olav kept an eye on her privily as she lay motionless by the hour together, staring out into the room, almost without blinking. And the old, wild fear rose up in his heart, as hot as ever—it was no matter if he had neither use nor joy of her; he could not lose her.

Ingunn was glad to be allowed to creep thus into hiding. She had come to feel it as an unbearable disgrace every time she was to have a child. Even before she had her first two she had been distressed and shy, because it made her so ugly—Dalla's insults had bitten into her mind so that she never got over them. She winced when she had to appear before Olav—and when he was away from her, she felt as though she could not sustain herself without his sound health close at hand to draw strength from.

But as time went on and it proved that she could not bring into life a single one of these creatures who came and dwelt in her, one after the other, she was filled with a horror of her own body. She

[5] February 22.

154

must be marked in some mysterious way, with something as terrible as leprosy, so that she infected her unborn infants with death. Her blood and marrow were spent, her youth and charm wasted long ago by these uncanny guests who lived their hidden life beneath her heart for a while and then went out. Till she felt the first warning grip as of a claw in her back, and had to let herself be led by strange women to the little house on the east of the courtyard, give herself into their hands without daring to show a sign of the mortal dread that filled her heart. And when she had fought through it, she lay back, empty of blood and empty of everything—the child was as it were swallowed up by the night, taken back into a gloom where she had not even a name or a memory to look for. The last premature births the women had not even let her see.

And yet she sometimes thought that it was even worse with Audun. When she lost the year-old child, he had already shown in many ways that he knew her for his mother; he would not be with others than her, and he was so fond of her. But he must be so still. When they sang in the litany: *Omnes sancti Innocentes, orate pro nobis*, Audun was one of them. In purgatory she would know that Audun was one of the holy Innocents who prayed for her. And when her hour of grace arrived, perhaps our Lord Himself or His blessed Mother would say to Audun: "Run down now and meet your mother."

How it might go with her this time, she tried hard not to think.

But when the men came in at mealtimes, Olav and Eirik together, a deep, uneasy tension came to life in the sick woman's great lustreless eyes. Olav noticed how wide awake she was, watching every movement of his features, listening to every word he spoke, when he was with the boy. And he always kept a guard over himself, taking care not to show it, when he was impatient or annoyed with Eirik.

The boy was troublesome enough; Olav liked him but moderately, now that he was big enough to show his nature. Noisy, full of boasting and idle tales, he chattered more than becomes a youth; not even when the men sat over their food, tired and worn out, could Eirik keep his mouth shut. There was that Arnketil, or Anki, as they called him. Olav had had him in his service some six years, and the man was now well on in the twenties, but he had poor parts, might indeed be called almost half-witted, though he was useful for many kinds of work. He had always been Eirik's best friend. They quarrelled—half in jest—raising their voices, till Eirik flew at Anki as he sat on the bench, pushing and pulling him till he got him to join in the game; they thrust each other hither and thither about the room, laughing and screaming and shouting without a thought of the other men who sat there and wanted rest and quiet. Grossly disobedient he was too; whether his father taught him something or forbade him to do this or that, he forgot it at once.

And Olav was angry that Eirik did not show his mother more affection. He was himself aware of the unreasonableness of this: formerly he had felt a secret exasperation when he knew that mother and son clung together behind his back. But now it made him angry to see Eirik spend the whole day out of doors among the men, never going in to sit by his sick mother. Olav himself had taught the boy his prayers some years ago—when he saw that Ingunn did not seem to think it was yet time. Now he made Eirik say a Paternoster and three Aves for his mother every evening, when he had prayed for himself. The boy gabbled off his prayers while his father stood over him—Eirik rose to his feet before he had finished the last Ave; at *In nomine* he was up on the bed, hastily crossed himself, and plunged headlong beneath the skins in the northern bed, which he shared with his father. He was asleep in an instant, and when Olav had finished smearing Ingunn's feet, he found Eirik curled up in the middle of the bed, so that he had to straighten him out and push him against the wall to make room for himself.

At times Olav felt a stab of pain when Eirik sought him out with his foolish talk, boasting of his little, unhandy attempts to make himself useful among the men—"If only the boy had been so that I could have liked him." In his innocent stupidity Eirik seemed never to guess that his father was not so fond of his company as he was of his father's. But Olav had taken his resolution: he had acknowledged this child and raised him up in order to set him in the high seat here at Hestviken in succession to himself— though God knew Eirik was unpromising material for a great franklin and the head of a manor: the boy seemed to be a loose-tongued chatterer, untruthful, boasting and cowardly, lacking in hardiness, and born with little sense of seemliness and quiet good manners. But he would have to do what he could to teach Eirik good behaviour and drive the bad habits out of him—even if he had to let the discipline wait till Ingunn was stronger—so that the lad might learn to comport himself as became Eirik Olavsson of Hestviken.

Some years before, herds of deer had moved into the districts on the west side of Folden, and there were now not a few deer on Olav's land—they were to be found up in Kverndal, on the ridge of the Bull and in Olav's oak wood, which lay inland, toward the church town. The summer before, they had grown so much fodder in Hestviken that they had stacks of hay and dried leaves standing in the open. Now, in late winter, the deer came as far as the manor in the early morning to snatch what they could of the fodder. Hiding behind some timber that lay in the yard, Olav one morning shot a fine young stag of ten points. Eirik was then quite wild to go with him—he would bring down a stag too.

Olav laughed a little at the boy's chatter. The next few days the wind was off the fiord and he made Anki go out in the morning so that the deer might get scent of him and keep off the hay, and Eirik was allowed to go with them. The boy lay stiff with cold— with bow and spear by him— but when he came in he made out that he had both seen and heard the red deer.

Then one night Olav woke up and went to the outer door to see the time. It was two hours to daybreak, intensely cold and a dead calm—with the faintest breath from the east down Kverndal. In the early morning the deer would certainly come down and take tithe of the stacks. Olav dressed in the dark, but in order to choose his arrows he had to light a torch. That waked Eirik—and the end of it was that his father gave him leave to go with him, but he was not allowed a weapon.

As soon as they had crept into hiding behind the timber stacks, Olav had hard work to keep the boy quiet. Eirik forgot himself every minute and would whisper. Then he fell asleep. He had on a thick leathern jacket of his father's; Olav wrapped it well about the child, so that he should not get frostbites—it was bitterly cold just before dawn—and thought with satisfaction that now Eirik could do no harm.

Olav had a long time to wait. The eastern sky was already turning yellow above the forest when he espied the deer coming out of the thicket. Four dark spots moved against the dun-coloured ground; patches of it were clear of snow. Now and again they stopped, looked about and sniffed the air—now he could see that they were a stag, two does, and a calf.

Excitement and joy warmed his stiffened body as he rose on one knee, took his bow, and laid an arrow to the string. He held his breath. The stag came on, proud and stately—now he saw it against a snowdrift. It climbed onto an old balk of sods—stood there with feet close together: the neck and head with the antlers showed clearly against the yellow sky. Olav gave a noiseless gasp of joy—he had not met this old fellow before: a mighty beast, full-shouldered, with a great crown of antlers, fifteen or sixteen points, no less. It moved its head this way and that, spying out. It was a rather long shot, but the target was just right: Olav took his aim, and his heart laughed with joy—he felt too that Eirik was on the point of waking.

The boy started up with a shout—he too had seen those glorious horns against the sky. Olav sent his arrow after the flying deer, chanced to graze the shoulder, making the stag leap high into the air—it went on in flying leaps and the whole herd disappeared in the thicket.

Eirik received a couple of hearty cuffs on the side of the head— he took them with a little gasp, but did not cry out; he had wit enough to be ashamed of what he had done and did not cry out; besides, the thick leather cap he wore must have deadened the blows.

"Say nothing to your mother about this," said Olav, as they went back to the houses. "She need not know that you can behave yourself like an untaught puppy, old as you are."

Later in the day Olav followed the blood-tracks of the stag with his hound, found the deer, and killed it on the hillside at the top of Kverndal. And when the quarry was brought home at evening, Eirik went about boasting—it was he who had warned his father when the great stag came within range.

Olav did not care to say a word to the boy—he was afraid of losing his temper.

The seal now came in thickly on the approach of spring, and the farmers of the country round took their boats out to the edge of the ice and went seal-hunting in the south of the fiord. Olav let Eirik go with him, but the result was not very happy; the massacre of seals and the brisk life among the hunters made him wild with excitement. It was quite incredible that the boy should have so little idea of how to behave anywhere in seemly fashion. But on coming home again he had the most extraordinary tales to tell. It was not easy for Olav to listen to the boy's talk without losing patience.

St. Gregory's Day [6] brought a change of weather, southerly winds and rain—this was thought to presage a good year both on land and on sea.

On the morrow Ingunn was lying alone in the house early in the day. It was fairly dark indoors, for the smoke-vent was closed; it was raining outside.

Olav came in. He sat down on the bench, drew off his boots, struggled out of his jerkin and shirt, and opened his clothes-chest to find other garments.

"Are you asleep, Ingunn?" he asked with his back toward her. "How is it with you?" he said when she whispered in reply, no, she was not asleep.

"Oh, well. Will you ride out?"

Olav said yes, the Thing at Vidanes was summoned for today. He came up to the bed, naked to the waist, and put one foot on the step. "Must I change my hose, think you?"

Ingunn involuntarily drew her head away. "Indeed you must—they smell so ill."

"They will scarce smell sweeter, the other men who come there —we have been out seal-hunting day and night of late, all of us."

"But if you are to meet strangers from other parts—" suggested Ingunn.

"Ay, ay, as you will." He drew off his breeks and hose, stood quite naked, stretched himself and yawned.

The sight of his faultlessly shaped body hurt her, it made her own ravaged wretchedness so hopeless. That time was so impossibly long past when she had been young and lovely, when they were well matched—but Olav was yet a young man, sound and handsome. His muscles were more knotted than of old, chiefly about the shoulder-blades and upper arms; they moved freely and powerfully as he stretched himself, raising his arms and lowering them. His flesh was still white as milk.

[6] March 12.

He came back to his wife when he had put on his red woollen shirt, long hose of black leather, and linen breeks.

"Then I must wear the blue kirtle too, think you—since you will have me so tricked out?" he asked with a smile.

"Olav—?" As he bent over her, she suddenly threw her thin arms around his neck and drew him down to her, pressing her face against his cheek. Olav felt that she was trembling.

"What is it?" he whispered. She only clung to him and made no answer.

"Are you sick?" He loosed her arms from about his neck; it was so uncomfortable to stand bent double. "Would you have me stay at home today? I can ride to Rynjul and fetch Una to you—at the same time ask Torgrim to speak for me at Vidanes."

"No, no." She pressed his hand hard in hers. "No—there will be no change with me till mid-spring be past. But stay with me a little while"—it came as a faint moan. "Sit here a little while, if you have the time."

"That I may well do." He held her hand, stroking her arm. "What is it with you, Ingunn? Are you so afraid—?" he asked quietly.

"Nay. Yes. Nay, I know not that I am so afraid, but—" Olav pushed the step out of his way, sat on the edge of the bed, and patted her wasted cheek, time after time.

"I had a dream," said his wife softly. "Just before you came in."

"Was it an evil dream, then?"

The tears began to pour down her cheeks, but she wept without a sound; only her voice was more veiled and broken:

"It seemed not evil while I dreamed it—*then* it was not evil. I saw you, walking along a path in a forest; you looked happy and seemed younger than you are now; you sang as you walked. I saw you here at Hestviken too, out in the yard, and it was the same, you looked happy and well. I could see it all, but it was as though I myself was not—I was dead, I knew. Children I saw not here—not one."

"Ingunn, Ingunn, you must not lie here thinking such thoughts." He knelt down so that he could get his arm in under her shoulder. "There would be little joy for me here in our house were I to lose you, Ingunn mine."

"A joy for you I have never been—"

"You are the only friend I have." He kissed her, bending lower over his wife, so that her face was quite hidden against his breast.

"If now it is as Signe and Una say," he whispered, hesitating, "that you are to have a daughter this year— They were all sons till now. But a little maid—her maybe God would let us keep."

The sick woman sighed: "I am so weary—"

Olav whispered: "Have you never thought, Ingunn—that maybe I have paid Eirik no more than—the price of his father's slaying?"

As he received no answer, he asked her—and he could not make his voice sound quite firm: "Have you never wondered what became of—that Teit?" She clasped him closer. "I never believed that you did it."

The man felt strangely overpowered—as though he had suddenly come into a bright light and were trying to distinguish things in it. She had *known* it, all the time. But what did that mean —had she guessed what was on his mind, or had she been afraid of his blood-stained hands—?

Ingunn turned her face to his, clasped his neck, and drew his head down to her. She kissed him on the lips, with a wild gulp. "I knew it. I knew it. Yet I was afraid, sometimes—when things were at their worst with me and I almost lost heart. I could not help it— I thought, what if he were alive and came after me, avenged himself. But indeed I believed you had done it, and I could feel safe from him!"

Olav had a queer feeling—as though numb or frozen. Was *that* what she had thought?—ay, ay. Perhaps that was all she could take in, poor thing. He kissed her again, a gentle little kiss. Then he said with a laugh of embarrassment:

"You must let me go now, Ingunn—you will break my ribs against the bedpost soon."

He got up, patted her cheek once more, and crossed the room to his chest, searched among the clothes. Then he asked again:

"Are you sure, Ingunn—should you not rather I stayed at home today?"

"Nay, nay, Olav, I will not keep you."

Olav buckled on his spurs, took his sword, and threw his rain-cloak of thick, felted homespun over his shoulder. He was already at the door—when he turned and came back to her bed.

Ingunn could see that a change had come over him and he was

not as she had seen him for a long, long time—his face was still as a rock, his lips pale, his eyes veiled, unseeing. He spoke as though in his sleep:

"Will you promise me one thing? Should it go with you as—as you said—should it cost your life this time—will you give me your promise that you will *come back* to me?" He looked at her, bending slightly toward her. "You must promise me, Ingunn—if it is so that the dead may come back to the living—then you must come to me!"

"Yes."

The man bent down hastily, touching her breast with his forehead an instant.

"You are the only friend I have had," he whispered quickly and shyly.

Olav came riding home late in the evening, wet and cold, so that he could not feel his feet in the stirrups. His horse trotted wearily, splashing the snow-slush over him at every beat of the hoofs.

Clouds and fog rolled over the landscape, the earth breathed moisture—it was an evening of steaminess and mist, the whole world strangely dissolved, forest and field bare and dark in patches among the melting snow. The fiord spoke in dull surf-beats with long intervals, like a sluggish pulse, but the stream in Kverndal roared with a glut of water. A sigh went through the woods as the firs shed their snow, and water purled and gurgled everywhere in the dusk—the cold scent from the fields and the sea brought the first reminder of springtime and growth.

On the hillside by the barn a dark figure came toward him—a woman in a hooded cloak.

"Welcome home, Olav!" It was Signe Arnesdatter; she hurried to meet him as he drew nearer.

"Ay, now Ingunn is over it for this time—and she does better than we had looked for." Olav had reined in his horse, and Signe caressed its muzzle. "And the child is so big and fine—none of us has even seen so big and fair a new-born babe. So you must bear with it that 'tis not a son!"

Olav thanked her for the good news, feeling that, had he been as in his younger years, he would have leaped from his horse, embraced his kinswoman, and kissed her. He *was* relieved and he *was* glad, but as yet he did not *feel* it to the full. Then he thanked Signe again for the kindness she had shown once more to Ingunn.

It had come upon her so suddenly, said Signe, that they had not been able to take her out to the women's house. Olav would have to put up with sleeping in the closet while they had the cradle and kept watch in the great room.

But in a moment he saw Ingunn herself—her face shone snow-white, she lay on her side with one light-brown plait showing from under her cheek. Una knelt behind her in the bed, plaiting her other thick rope of hair. The other times Olav had seen her lying thus, she had been ugly, swollen and blotched in the face—but now she was unlike herself, marvellously fair, as if an un-earthly light were shed upon her white and wasted countenance. Her great dark-blue eyes glittered like starlight mirrored in a well. And the thought sank into the man that a miracle had taken place.

Signe came with a little bundle—white swaddling-bands wound crosswise about the leaf-green woollen wrapper. She laid the child in Olav's arm. "Have you ever seen so fair a maid, kins-man?"

And again it was as though he had fallen among incredible things—a girl's face, impossibly small, but perfect, the fairest! A new-born life, and it could look like that. Her eyes were open; dark they were and bottomless—and she was red and white like a brier-rose and had nose and mouth like a human being, but so small that he could not understand it.

Signe drew the swaddling-cloth aside so that the father might see that she had fine hair too. Olav cupped his hand under the delicate, round head: it lay in his palm no larger than an apple and as sweet and soft to hold.

Olav still held his little daughter in his hands—a gift, a gift she was. It softened him—so grateful beyond measure he had never been before. He laid his face against the baby's breast—her face was so pure and fine that he durst not touch it.

Una leaped to the floor, arranged Ingunn on her back, with the plaits over her bosom. They took the child from him, and he sat down on the edge of the bed by his wife. He held her hand in his for a while and took up one of her plaits; neither of them said any-thing.

Then a maid came in with food and drink for him, and after-

wards they said that he must go into the closet and lie down—
Ingunn needed sleep. Then she called to him softly.

"Olav," she whispered, "there is one thing I would beg of you,
husband"—at other times she never called him that—"will you do
what I ask of you?"

"I will do all you ask of me." He smiled as in pain, so un-
manned was he by his joy.

"Promise me that she shall not be called after my mother. Cecilia
I would have her named."

Olav nodded.

He lay awake in the darkness—against the wall Eirik was sleeping like a stone. Through the door opening he could see the reflection of the fire flickering on the logs of the wall; it rose and sank.
But the holy candle burning beside the mother and child shed a
mild and golden light.

The watching women whispered and went about their work,
clattering with the kettle and the pot-hook. Once the new-born
child began to cry—and her cries called to his heart; he listened
to her and was tender and happy. The women got on their feet;
the cradle was set rocking, and Signe sang softly.

Here he lay before her door; it seemed as natural as a dream
that he should lie and listen while they watched over her sleep.
Ingunn slept sweetly now; she had given birth to a child, and now
she was to take a long rest, which would make her young and
healthy and happy again. A child had been born here in his house,
the first one. All that had gone before had been as one endless,
unnatural sickness—an uncanny spell upon the unhappy woman.
The little lifeless deformities that the women had brought to him
that he might see them, though he was so loath to do so—the sight
of them had filled him with infinite disgust; and the poor little
abortion that had lived his brief, tormented life, until God had
pity on him and took him to Himself—in his heart he had never
been able to acknowledge that these were his children—the fruit
of his and Ingunn's bodies.

Never had he known how it felt to be a father—till now, when
he had a daughter, a treasure like this little, little—Cecilia.

1 3

CECILIA OLAVSDATTER grew and throve so that the neighbours' wives said they could see a difference in her from day to day. What fattened her none could guess, for the mother would nurse her at her own breast, and there she could hardly suck many drops of milk. But that she grew more in one month than other infants in three was the boast of Signe and Una. Now and then they poured cream into her, or let her chew at deer's marrow in a cloth.

Folk who came out to Hestviken asked to see this little maid whose fame was already abroad—she was so peerlessly fair. They let it be seen that they wished Olav and his wife well of their happiness. True, there was none who liked the Hestvik folk very well. Olav was strangely reserved, a man of few friends—folk thought it a trouble if they had to be in company with this cross-stick—but no doubt this was mostly his manner: one had to admit that in his actions he had always shown himself an upright and pious man, by no means unhelpful either. The wife was incapable and weak-minded, but indeed she wished nobody ill, poor thing. So it was a happy thing after all that at last they had gotten a child that looked as if it would grow up.

But Ingunn continued poorly for a long time—she must have suffered some hurt in her back, and she could not regain power over her legs, when at last she was up again.

One Sunday when Olav came home from church, it was such fine weather—that day summer had come. In the fair-weather breeze the leaves and green meadows gleamed with light, and every puff of air was like a warm and healthy breath from the growing grass and the new foliage and from the earth, which still had the moisture of spring within it. When he entered the house and saw Ingunn lying outstretched on the bench, he was a little uneasy; then he said that when they had broken their fast she must go out with him and look at the "good acre," the corn there was coming up so thick and fine this year again.

This was the field that lay farthest out toward the fiord under the crags; Olav had a peculiar affection for it and always chose the best and heaviest corn to sow there. He had fishes' heads and offal from the quay brought there, and it suffered less from drought

than was to be expected—for the mould was not very deep—but
it was ready for reaping before any of the other fields of Hestviken.

Olav had to carry Ingunn over the threshold, and when he had
set her down outside the door, he saw that she walked as though
she could not lift her feet—she slid them along the ground in short,
uncertain jerks, and at the slightest obstacle she nearly fell forward.
He took her by the waist and she leaned heavily against him, with
one hand on his shoulder; at every third or fourth step she had to
pause, and he noticed that she was sweating profusely and trembling with fatigue.

On arriving at the look-out rocks Olav spread his fur-lined
winter cloak, which he had brought with him, in a hollow among
the rocks. There she could lie in shelter and watch the breeze
caressing the young blades of corn as though currying them, sending flames of light down the green slope.

Sea and land were all aglitter; the summer waves ran in toward
the rocks, splashed, and trickled back with the pebbles of the
beach—the sound of the surf was a gentle murmur; but farther off
under the Bull the spray was thrown higher; the wind was going
round to the south-west now. Olav sat following with his eyes a
heavily laden trading vessel that was making her way up the fiord,
rather fast. He was lost in thought; old memories floated before
him of the time when he was an outlaw and free as a bird—knew
nothing of bearing another's burdens. Alone he had been, one man
among many others, who were never so near to him that he felt
their pressure—it was strangely far away now, after all these years
he had had the whole of Hestviken depending on him, and his
sick wife as close to him as his own flesh. He had struggled on with
her, who was always infirm and suffering; it was like fighting
with one arm hanging broken and useless. Nevertheless he did not
feel unhappy as he sat here in the midday sun—he did not think of
the old days in such a way that he wished himself away from the
present or fretted at his lot with Ingunn. He sat and took his rest—
in a kind of melancholy, but even that which oppressed him was
his infinite affection for her; it seemed too great for him to carry
it alone.

He turned to Ingunn, was going to say something about the
vessel; then he saw that she had fallen asleep. She looked like one
dead.

He felt with wonder that he was even fonder of her now than he had ever been before—just because he could see that every trace of her beauty was so utterly destroyed. No one who had not seen her in her youth could imagine that this middle-aged, faded wife had once been fair. She had been lovely, as a pure and delicate flower is lovely—now the yellow skin, flecked with brown patches, was drawn tightly over her hollow-cheeked and long-chinned face. Her tall and slender form had long lost its willowy suppleness: she was flat as a board over the narrow chest, heavy and shapeless about the waist—looked like an aged and worn-out cottar's wife who has borne many children.

The husband sat and looked at her—not daring to touch her; she must be in need of sleep. He merely took the ends of her linen coif and tucked them in, lest the wind should blow them in her face, and wrapped the cloak better about her—she looked so bloodless that he must not let her take cold.

Both Olav and the house-folk saw that she was less able to walk day by day, and about the time of St. John's Mass she could not get up from her seat without help, nor push one foot before the other without someone to support her. But still they dressed her every morning; it was Torhild who had to do this now, for Liv, Ingunn's own maid, was fit for nothing at this time.

Olav had never been able to understand Ingunn's obstinate dislike of Torhild Björnsdatter in all these years. Torhild was a woman whose match was not often to be met—loyal, capable, and strong—and however unreasonable Ingunn might be with the housekeeper, Torhild remained as patient and attentive as ever toward her sick mistress.

Equally incomprehensible did it appear to Olav that she should have taken a fancy to this Liv, who had entered her service the year before. For one thing, the girl was almost the ugliest being Olav had ever seen: at the first glance one was tempted to doubt whether she was human—undersized, hugely broad, and notably squat and bandy-legged. Her red hair was thin and straggling, her skin was a reddish grey, with freckles over her arms and hands and down to her chest, and her face was marvellously hideous, with little blinking pig's eyes, a pointed nose, and no chin—the lower part of her face slanted in and made one with the flabby flesh of her throat. Nor was she of kindly disposition—lazy and unwilling with Torhild and the dairymaid, and exceedingly stupid. But Ingunn had set her affection on this girl. When it came out that she had gone astray the autumn before, when she was given leave to go home and visit her parents at Michaelmas, her mistress besought Olav not to turn Liv out of the house. Olav had had no such thought; he knew that there was great poverty and many children in the croft from which she came, so it was better for her to stay at Hestviken. But as she was under his roof and very young —fifteen—he thought he would have to try to see justice done to the girl and questioned her about the father. But all she knew was that it was a man who had borne her company a part of the way through the forest, when she was going home at Michaelmas.

"Ay—and did he maltreat you then?" asked Olav.

"Nay, nay"—Liv beamed all over her face. He had been so merry and kind. Jon he said was his name.

"Ay, so every man is called who has no other name."

Now in any case she would soon be a fit foster-mother for Cecilia. For it would go ill if the sick mother were to nurse this big and greedy child—but hitherto Ingunn had refused to hear of Cecilia being taken from her breast.

Olav had sent for all the men and women of the country round who had a knowledge of sickness and leechcraft. None could say what ailed the mistress of Hestviken—and most of them thought it must be caused by treachery or envy. Olav knew that she had been sick in the same way sixteen or seventeen years before, when she was at Miklebö, and then Mistress Hillebjörg had said it was certain that Kolbein had caused spells or other witchcraft to be put upon her. He wondered whether this might not be true after all, and that she had never been entirely set free from the power of evil.

Then he became acquainted with a German merchant, Claus Wiephart, in Oslo, who was said to be a very learned leech—he had been a captive among the Saracens in his youth and had acquired their knowledge. Olav fetched him, and this man saw at once what ailed Ingunn.

What might have been the origin of it he was not able to say; it might be one thing or another, but most probably it came from the stars: for example, that her husband had first had knowledge of her in an hour when the position of the heavenly bodies was hostile to them, according to the stars under which they had been born. It might be a question of less than an hour—a little before or a little after, the auspices might have been particularly favourable to them. But this might have had such an effect upon her, who was the weaker, as to disturb the harmony in her body between the solid matter and the humours, so that the solid matter had shrunk and the humours had obtained the mastery—nay, she might even have had a disposition toward this disharmony in her hour of birth, but the disharmony was the especial cause of her weakness. The proof of this was that she had not been able to bear children of the male sex that were capable of surviving, beyond the first one; for man's body is by nature drier than woman's and demands from the very beginning more of the solid matter; but a daughter she had been able to bring forth alive. Even so, this child too had absorbed more solid matter than the mother's body could afford to give up; she was now, Clause Wiephart would say, in a state of decay, as it were; bones and flesh were saturated with humours—even as wood floating in the sea becomes soft and full of water.

In the first place they must see to getting her body drained of moisture, said the German. The child should by no means be taken from her breast; she must be given sudatory and diuretic medicines, she must drink very little, but take burnt and pounded bones and *terra sigillata*, and eat hard, dry food with hot spices in it.

The learned man's opinion filled Olav with fresh courage. It sounded so reasonable—and the Latin words used by the German came back to Olav from his young days. *Prima causa, harmonia, materia,* and *umidus, disparo, dispono*—these words he remembered to have heard from Asbjörn All-fat, Arnvid, and the friars at the convent, and, as far as he could judge, Claus knew them rightly. And then, even before they were grown up, he himself had noticed that Ingunn's body was strangely weak and without firmness—it made him think of green corn—surely she had always had too little of the solid matter. *Terra sigillata* must certainly be good for her—it was good for so many things, he knew.

And he had learned about the four elements of which the human body is composed, and had heard that the position of the heavenly bodies influences a man's destiny. Learned men at home did not know so much about this; Asbjörn All-fat said that Christian men have no need to inquire what is written in the stars. But the Saracens were said to have more knowledge of the stars than any other folk.

Olav was unspeakably relieved at heart. Perhaps he had been on an entirely false scent all these years—he had always believed it was he who had brought misfortune upon them both, because he dared not break out of the sin in which he lived. He *was* living in sin, there was no doubt of that, so long as he made no offer to atone for that unhappy deed, but God must know that he could not; he could not jeopardize the welfare and honour of his wife and child. In all else he had endeavoured to walk as a Christian man. And God must know even better than himself how unspeakably he longed to live at peace with Him, to be allowed to love Him with his whole heart, to bend the knee in prayer, without grieving at his own disobedience.

But what if he might now believe that all their misfortunes had a natural origin? Cecilia was the pledge that God had remitted his debt—or would give him respite till the hour of death. That the stars had been the cause of Ingunn's weakness in body and soul—

But *Prima Causa*—that was one of God's names. He knew that.

She said herself that she was better for these remedies of Claus Wiephart's. As yet she had not regained sufficient vigour to be able to move her legs, but she felt less of the pain in her back.

He came into the cook-house one evening just before Olav's Mass [7]—there was something he wished to say to Torhild Björnsdatter before he forgot it.

She was baking bread for the holy-day. The flour dust floating in the air was golden in the evening sun as he opened the door and the light filled the sooty little room. A sweet, yeasty scent came from the round loaves that lay baking on slanting stones around the glowing, heaped-up fire—Olav's mouth watered at the smell. The girl was not there.

Olav was turning to go out when Torhild appeared at the door, carrying a board so heavy that she supported it on her head with both arms. She was obliged to walk even more erect than usual, and in the warm summer evening her light clothing looked but well and suitably free; she was in her working-clothes, a short-

[7] July 29.

sleeved shift of homespun, and bare legs; she was so deft in her movements, firm and strong.

Olav took the board from her; it was of oak and very heavy. He carried it in and laid it on the trestles. Torhild followed, filled both her fists with chopped juniper from a basket, and spread it over the board. She gave off a fragrance in her rapid movements—of meal and fresh bread, of the healthy warmth of work. Olav threw his arms about the maid and pulled her roughly to him. His chin came near her shoulder—for an instant he pressed his cheek against her skin—her neck was dewy, at once cool and warm. Then he let her go and laughed to cover his confusion and shame at this foolish wantonness that had come over him so suddenly.

Torhild had turned red as blood—and the sight of her added to his embarrassment. But she said nothing and showed no sign of anger—went about quite calmly, moving the loaves that were done from the stones onto the board.

"You can lift as much as a man, Torhild," said her master. And as she did not answer, but went on with her work, he began again, more seriously: "You support our whole household—do more work than all the rest of us together."

"I do my best," muttered Torhild.

"Ay, I know not how you think—perhaps you think we might reward you better—if so, you must tell me; we shall soon be agreed—"

"Nay I am well content with what I have. I have now put out all mine own into the world, save the two youngest—and you have helped me well."

"Nay, say naught of that—" He gave her the message he had come for, and went out.

Ingunn continued to use the wise German's remedies, but after a while it was seen that the results were not entirely beneficial after all. She had violent pains in the stomach and burning of the throat from all the pepper and ginger. But she held out as long as she could, struggling to get down the dry and irritating diet, although she seemed to feel the pains even at the sight of the food. She was tortured by thirst day and night; but she bore it all with patience and made little complaint.

Then Olav had to be away from home for a few nights, and

Signe Arnesdatter came to sleep with the sick woman meanwhile. Afterwards Signe told Olav it was quite wrong that Ingunn should still have Cecilia with her at night; the mother no longer had a drop of milk in her breast, and it was hunger and temper that made the child shriek so wildly at night, keeping Ingunn and all awake. Olav had never known any other infant than Audun, and he shrieked almost continually, so the man thought it was the way of little ones. Now Liv had long nursed Cecilia in the daytime, and her own child was lately dead, and the girl was as full of milk as a fairy cow; the only natural thing was to let Liv be Cecilia's foster-mother and have the child both day and night.

But when they spoke of this to Ingunn, she was quite beside herself with grief. She begged and besought that they would not take Cecilia from her: "She is all that is left of me; I bought you this daughter at the price of lying here powerless and palsied to the waist. If you love her, Olav, have pity on me—take not Cecilia from me, the little while I have left to live. 'Twill not be long ere you be freed from this wretched life with me."

He tried to make her see reason, but she screamed, thrusting her elbows into the bolster under her, raising her shoulders and struggling, as though she would force her palsied body to rise. Olav seated himself on the edge of the bed, comforted her as well as he could, but it was in vain; and at last she had raged and wept till she was so weary that she sank into a doze, but even in her sleep she gasped and shook.

The end was that he promised she should have Cecilia in bed with her at night, but Liv was to lie on the bench near by, so that she might quiet the child when it shrieked.

When he came to say good-night to her before he went to bed, she put an arm about his neck and drew his head down.

"Be not angry, Olav. I cannot sleep but I have her with me. I have ever been afraid when I had to lie alone," she whispered; "ever since the first night you slept with me it has seemed as though I could not feel safe unless I had your arm about me. And now that will never be again."

Olav knelt down, took her under the neck, and let her head rest against his shoulder.

"Do you wish me to hold you thus until you fall asleep?" he asked.

She fell asleep almost at once. Then he arranged the pillows under her shoulders, stole quietly across the floor and crept in to Eirik in the north bed.

He kept a little charcoal lamp burning on the hearth at night— he had to get up so often, to help Ingunn and turn her. And now he had to get up and take Cecilia too, when she shrieked, and carry her to the girl—Liv never woke.

At last he must have fallen asleep and slept heavily—the child must have been shrieking a good while, so persistently as to succeed in waking Liv. In the feeble light of the little lamp he saw the maid padding about by Ingunn's bed with Cecilia in her arms. She looked so shapelessly broad and squat that he could not help thinking of tales he had heard of ogres and gnomes. Though he knew how foolish it was, it made him uncomfortable to see Cecilia in the arms of this foster-mother.

Olav came in to Ingunn about midday on the morrow—he and one of the house-carls had been bringing in the hay on pack-horses from some outlying meadows on the high ground. The nap of his short cloak was thickly beaded with drops of mist, and his boots were heavy with wet earth and withered leaves. He gave off a raw scent of autumn as he bent over Ingunn and asked her how she did.

With a little embarrassed smile he showed her what he had brought in his hand—some big watery strawberries threaded on straws—as they had used to do when they were children. The berries were soft, so that the palm of his hand was red with them.

"I found these up by the mill."

Ingunn took them, without remembering to thank him. It was these little red spots within his coarse, worn hands—and she recalled their life together from childhood, all the way till now. Twice he had reddened that hand with blood for her sake, and it was the same hard, resin-smirched boy's fist that had helped her over fences and opened to show her gifts.—Their life appeared as a tapestry to her—as one long tissue: little images of brief, hot, happy love, with long intervals between of waiting and longing and barren dreams, the time of shame and mad despair like a big dark spot, and then all these years at Hestviken—all appeared to her in an instant as though embroidered on a ground—a single fabric, a whole tapestry of the same stuff from their childhood's days until now, until the end.

True, she had always acknowledged to herself that Olav was good to her. She had known in a way that few men would have had patience with her so long, would have been equal to the task of protecting her and sustaining her all these years. She had indeed thanked him in her heart—thanked him sometimes with burning intensity. But only now did she see, as a whole, how strong his love had been.

He was standing by the cradle now. The rockers bumped and bumped against the floor, and the child gurgled and cried with delight, drumming its heels with wild persistence against the skin rug under it—the mother could just see its little pink hands waving above the side of the cradle.

"Nay, Cecilia—you will soon strangle yourself in these snares!" Olav laughed and lifted up the child in his arms. She had wriggled so violently that her clothes were quite undone, and the swaddling-band had become so tangled about her arms and legs and neck and her little body that it was a wonder she had not strangled herself with it. "Can you get this straight?" He laid the child on the bed by its mother.

"Are you weeping?" he asked, saddened. Ingunn was blinded by tears, so that she could scarcely see as she tried to free Cecilia from her bands.

"She will be just as fair-haired as the rest of us Hestvik folk," said the father; "and now you have seven curls—" he passed his hand over the child's forehead, where the hair had grown long and curly in little, pale-yellow locks. "Are you in such pain today, my Ingunn?"

" 'Tis not that. I am thinking that, though you have been good to me and faithful so long as I have known you, I have never had it in my power to reward you for your affection."

"Say not so. You have been a—gentle—" he could not find another word in her praise on the spur of the moment, though he was trying to say something to please her. "You have been a gentle and—and quiet wife. And you know how fond I am of you," he said with feeling.

"And now it will soon be a year," she whispered, distressed and shy, "that you have been as a widower—with an infirm sister to take care of—"

"Ay, ay," said her husband softly. "But if I love you— Sister, you say. Do you remember, Ingunn, the first years we lived together; we slept in the same bed, drank from the same bowl, and were as brother and sister; we knew of naught else. But then too we were happiest when we were together."

"Yes. But we were children in those days. And then I was fair—" she whispered with more passion in her voice.

"You were. But I fear I was too childish to see it. I believe in those years I never had a thought whether you were fair or not."

"And I was not a burden on you. I was healthy and strong—"

"Oh nay, Ingunn—" Olav smiled weakly and stroked her arm. "Strong you have never been, my dearest friend!"

It was a long winter for them at Hestviken.

Olav was at home all the time; he thought he could not leave her for a single night. She now suffered greatly from lying in bed, since she was so emaciated, and then she had got some hurt in her back: when she had lain awhile in one position, it felt as if a pain crept over her ribs and filled her whole chest. The only thing they could do to relieve her was to move and turn her constantly. She could take no food at all; they kept life in her by giving her gruel, broth, and milk, a mouthful at a time.

She had tried to do a little needlework as she lay in bed, but her hands became numbed whenever she held them raised a little while, so that she could neither sew nor plait. And then she lay in a doze, altogether motionless. She never spoke a word of complaint, and she thanked them gently when anyone came and turned her or arranged her pillows. Sometimes she slept a good deal in the daytime, but at night she seldom had any sleep at all.

Olav had the fire burning on the hearth all night and he had shut off the closet with a door, to make the great room warmer. The winter was not a very cold one, but all this smoke day and night was troublesome.

He watched by the sick woman night after night. Eirik lay in the bed behind his back asleep, Liv slept on the bench, and Cecilia slept in her mother's bed. Olav lay in a sort of doze, but it was never too deep for him to hear an ember shooting out of the fire, or Ingunn's almost inaudible groans—he was up and beside her in a moment. All that winter he was never out of his clothes, except every washing-day, when he went to the bath-house.

He knelt beside her bed, laid the palms of his hands under her shoulders, then under her back, and then he held her heels in the hollows of his hands for a while. In his heart he expected with a kind of morbid horror that she would get bed-sores there. It was like the last glowing ember of all he had once felt for her body— he thought he could not bear to see the skin broken and the sores eating into Ingunn's flesh while she yet lived. Never had it been so hard for him to endure the sight and smell of wounds and impurities—though he was ashamed of this weakness. But he prayed desperately to God that at least it might not come to this—he asked it as much for his own sake as for hers.

He was away tending the fire.

"Are you thirsty, Ingunn?—Shall I take you in my arms, Ingunn?"

Olav wrapped the bedclothes about her and lifted her up in his arms. He sat with her on the settle before the fire. Carefully he bent the lifeless legs, laid down pillows under her feet on the bench, supporting her hips and back on his thighs, as he laid her head to rest on his shoulder.

"Is that better?"

Sometimes she fell asleep when she lay thus in his arms. And Olav sat by the hour holding her, till he was chilled through about the shoulders, stiff in all his limbs. She woke if he made the slightest movement. Then she extricated a hand from the bedclothes and passed it over his face.

"Now I am much better. Carry me back to bed now, Olav, and go and lie down—you must be tired."

"I am become a heavy burden for you, Olav," she said one night. "But bear with me a little—'twill not last longer than this winter."

He did not deny it. He had thought the same himself. When spring came, it would take her with it. And now at last he was ready to submit to it.

But as winter drew to a close, she seemed rather to be slightly on the mend. In any case she revived sufficiently to ask how things were going on the farm and in the fishery. She listened for the cow-bells morning and evening, mentioned her cows by name, and said one day that when spring was fully come they must carry her out of doors, that she might see her cattle once more.

Cecilia was now a very pretty child, and big for her age; Ingunn had great comfort of her in the daytime, but then she had to have Liv in with her. At night she slept with her foster-mother in another house—Ingunn could no longer bear the big, heavy child in bed with her: Cecilia rolled over on her mother in her sleep, and when she was awake she stumped about the bed and fell heavily over her palsied body.

Olav had so little liking for Liv that he avoided the room while the maid was there. He knew too that she stole in a small way, and he had more than a suspicion that she was too good friends with Anki and thus taught the man to pilfer and lie— Arnketil's word had always been untrustworthy, but till now it had mostly been because he had no better wit. What they stole was no great matter, but he did not like having dishonest folk in his house. And now there was such disorder in the household in many ways—he himself was so tired every day that he could not accomplish all he ought, and downhill is an easy road.

So now he did not see much of Cecilia in the daytime. But by degrees it had come to this, that his affection for his daughter was mingled with a profound soreness—it pained him sharply when he recalled that blue, damp night of spring when he came home and found her in the cradle. The first time they laid her in his arm he had believed so surely that she betokened a turn in their fortunes, that Cecilia came into the world bringing their happiness with her.

He loved this little daughter, but his affection was, at it were, spread within him, it lay at the bottom of his heart, shy and mute. In the first days of her life her father had often stopped before her cradle and touched her with a couple of fingers, playfully and caressingly—full of quiet joy and wonder when he got her to smile. And he had lifted her up and held her to him a moment, in his clumsy, unpractised way: Cecilia, Cecilia— Now he usually stopped at a little distance when he saw her being carried from house to house; he smiled at his daughter and beckoned; she never took the smallest notice. The very fact that she was so pretty, and that he recognized in her the fair complexion of his own race, seemed only to increase the father's melancholy.

Not much was seen of Eirik now. The nine-year-old boy instinctively kept away from the grown people, whom he saw to be always heavy at heart. He found enough to do about the manor and only came into the hall to eat and sleep.

. . .

Olav had to go in to Oslo for the Holy Cross fair [8] in the spring. There he received a message asking him to go to the convent of the preaching friars.

The Prior had news for him that his friend Arnvid Finnsson had died during the winter. In the middle of last summer he had adopted the professed habit among the friars at Hamar. But by the second week of Lent he died suddenly—none could say of what. As they went to morning mass, the monk who walked beside him saw that Brother Arnvid turned pale and faltered, but on his asking in a whisper if he were sick, Arnvid shook his head. But when they knelt at *Verbum caro factum est*, his neighbour saw that Brother Arnvid was not able to rise to his feet again, and when the mass was at an end he lay in a swoon. Then they carried him into the dormitory and laid him on his couch; he moaned a little now and again, but was unconscious. In the middle of the day, however, he came to and asked in a low voice for the last office. As soon as he had received the sacraments he fell asleep, and when the monks came from vespers he was dead, so calmly that the friar who sat with him could not say when he ceased to breathe.

The Prior told him also that before Arnvid entered the convent he had disposed of a great part of his treasure to kinsmen and friends, and he had bidden his sons send these two drink-horns to Olav Audunsson. But the Arnvidssons were so unlike other men that they would never leave their home parish, and only when they went down to Hamar for their father's burial had Magnus brought the horns to the convent; and Father Bjarne had been unwilling to send these rare treasures south until he could place them in the hands of one of his own order.

Olav knew the horns well from Miklebö. They were small, but very costly: two griffin's claws mounted in silver and gilt. Olav and his friend had used them on the evenings of high festivals, when they drank mead or wine—they only held drink for one man.

The news of Arnvid's death shook Olav to the heart. He could not bear to stay in town among the other men, but sailed out to Hestviken the same evening.

There had been times when he thought of his friend and recalled their last talk together, and it pained him that he had stripped himself so bare to the other. He regretted this weakness

[8] May 3.

so, that at times he had doubtless thought it would be easier for him if he heard that Arnvid was no more.—And then he felt all at once that this was the last stroke, and now he was no longer capable of fighting against his own heart—now that he knew that not a single one shared his secret: alone he would not be able to keep it any longer.

And for the first time he saw the true nature of this friendship. It was he who had taken advantage of the other—and Arnvid had allowed him to do so. He had lied to his friend, and his friend had seen through his untruthfulness; not only the first time, but always he had told Arnvid what suited himself—even to their last meeting; and Arnvid had accepted it and held his peace. It was always he who had sought support, and Arnvid had supported him—as Arnvid had given to all, whatever was asked of him. And the reward they had given him was to scourge him—he had found such reward as awaits the man who has courage to follow Christ's example. And nevertheless Arnvid had blamed himself and thought himself an unfaithful follower, whenever he was unable to see his path clearly and whenever his heart was full of bitterness and contempt for men's baseness—as must at times befall a sinful man, when he ventures to follow where God went before.

Olav stayed at home during the spring sowing, even more silent than usual.

But one morning, when he had set his folk to work, he walked back to the houses alone.

The sunshine flooded the room through the open smoke-vent, the light fell upon the fireless hearth, upon the clay floor, and touched Ingunn's bed. Both the children were with her: Eirik lay with his dark, curly head in his mother's arm and his long legs hanging over the edge of the bed. Cecilia crawled about, climbing up the bedpost and dropping down with a thump and a little scream of joy upon the lifeless form under the clothes. The little maid had nothing on but a flame-coloured woollen shift; her skin was pink and white and her hair had grown so that it fell in bright, flaxen ringlets about her face and neck. Her bright eyes were so blue in the whites that they seemed blue all over, and this gave the charming little face a strangely wide-awake look, like that of an animal.

"Your mother cannot bear you to weigh so heavily upon her,

Eirik." Olav took Cecilia and seated himself on the edge of the bed with the girl on his knee. Once he clasped his daughter impetuously, and the child struggled—she was not used to being with her father. Olav felt how good and firm the little body was between his hands, and the silken hair had a fresh, moist scent.

As she was not allowed to get at her mother, she wriggled in her father's arms and tried to reach her brother. Eirik took her, held her under the arms, and tried to make her walk. Cecilia thrust out her round stomach, straddling with her arms and one foot, as she threw her head back and laughed up in her brother's face. Then she humped herself along with wild little kicks—laughing and shrieking: "Goy, goy, goy"; she curled up all her toes under the sole of her foot, which was quite round—as yet it had scarcely trodden the ground.

Olav swept his hand over the bed—it was strewn with half-withered flowers, such as bloom between spring and summer: wild vetch, catchflies, buttercups, and great violets. Ingunn gathered them into a bunch:

"They have long come out, I see."

Olav sat looking at the children. They were of rare beauty, the two of hers that had lived. Eirik was a big boy now, tall and slight, with his knife-belt on his slender hips. Olav could see he was handsome: his face had lost its childish roundness, it was narrow and sharp, with a slightly curved nose and a high, arched jaw; he was brown-skinned and black-haired, had golden-yellow eyes. Could his mother help thinking of whom he resembled?

"Take your sister with you, Eirik, carry her out to Liv. There is a matter your mother and I would speak of."

Ingunn raised the bunch of flowers with both hands to her face and drank in with open nostrils the acrid scent of spring.

"Now, my Ingunn," said Olav in a clear, calm voice, "you shall soon be released from lying here in torment. I have bespoken a passage for us in a vessel to Nidaros this summer, to St. Olav, so that you may recover the use of your limbs at the shrine of him, the martyr of righteousness."

"Olav, Olav, do not think of such a thing. Never could I bear the voyage—I should not come to Nidaros alive."

"Oh, but you will." The man closed his eyes, smiling painfully—his face had gone pale as death. "For now, Ingunn, now I have the courage to do it. When I come thither, to the sanctuary—I will confess my sin. Of my own free will I shall put myself in God's hands, make amends for my offence toward Him and toward the law and justice of my countrymen."

She looked at her husband in dismay; he went on with the same haggard smile:

"The thing which befell you that time at Mikleböö—when you rose from your bed and walked—that must have been a miracle! —Think you not that God can perform another miracle?"

"Nay, nay!" she cried. "Olav, what are you saying—what is this sin you speak of?"

"That I slew Teit, what else? Set fire to the hut where the body lay—and never made confession of it. I have been to confession all these years, have been shriven for all else, great and small—received *corpus Domini* like other Christian men, gone to mass and prayed and pretended, pretended—but now there is an end of it, Ingunn—I will have no more of it. Now I will put my case in the hands of my Creator, and whatsoever He will that I shall suffer, I will thank Him and bless His Name."

He saw the look of terror in her face and threw himself down by the bedside with his head in her lap.

"Ay, Ingunn. But now you shall suffer no more for my sins. If only you will *believe*, you know that you will be helped."

She put her hand under his chin and tried to raise his head. The sun was now shining full upon the bed, upon the crown of his bowed head—she saw that Olav's hair was quite grizzled. It did not show unless the sun shone straight upon it, as it was so fair in colour.

"Olav, look at me—in Jesus' name, have no such thoughts as these. Have I not sins enough myself to atone for? Do you remember"—she forced him to raise his face—"'you are not *human*,' you said to me that time—you know what I would have done with Eirik, if you had not prevented me. Should *I* cast reproach upon God for deeming I was not fit to bear children?—all that winter long I thought of nothing but of stifling the innocent life I felt quickening within me."

Olav looked at her in surprise. He had, as it were, never thought she remembered this, much less recalled it as guilt.

"I may thank God's mercy and naught else that I have not child murder on my conscience. And no sooner was I saved from that sin than I went about to do a worse one—God stretched out His hand again, when I was already halfway through the gates of hell. I perceived it long ago—I was not allowed to send myself straight to hell; every day I have lived since has been a loan, a respite given me to bethink myself and understand—

"I do not complain as I lie here—Olav, have you *once* heard me complain? *I* know well that God has chastised me, not from un-kindness—He who has twice plucked me out of the fire into which I would have thrown myself—"

Olav stared at her—a light was kindled far in behind his pupils. Unspeakably dear as she had been to him in all these years, he had never expected much more thought in her than in an animal, a tender young hind or a bird, that can love its mate and offspring, and lament its dead young—easily scared out of its wits, helplessly at the mercy of wounds and pain.—Never had he imagined he could talk to his wife as to another Christian person of that which had been growing in his soul for years.

"Oh nay, Olav!" She took his hand, drew him down and clasped his head to her bosom. He heard her heart beating violently within the narrow, wasted chest. "Say not such things, my friend! Your sin—'tis white by the side of mine! You must know that they were long for me, these years, and ofttimes heavy—but now it seems to me they were good in spite of all, since I lived with you, and you were always good!"

He raised his face. "It is true, Ingunn, that we two have had some good here in Hestviken—in that we were always friends. In sickness and in health I have had you with me always, and you have been dearest to me of all human creatures, in that I grew up away from all my kinsmen and friends, and you were the one with whom I consorted most. But then God was so kind to me, in spite of all, that He gave you to me—and I see now that it would have been difficult for me to prosper here, had I dwelt here alone with-out a single person that I had known from my youth.—You see, then, 'tis for that I can no longer bear to be God's enemy—of my own will I will no more live apart from Him. Let it cost what it may—

"I am no poor man either. There too God spared me—He gave success to many of the enterprises I undertook to better our for-tunes. I own more now than when we came together. And you know that by our marriage bond half our estate is yours, whatever may befall. You and your children will not be unprovided for."

"Speak not so, Olav. It *cannot* be so grievous a sin that you slew Teit. I have never told you before, I have never made complaint of it to any soul—but he took me by force! I could not bring myself to say it—'twas a thing I could not bear to speak of—" she sobbed aloud—"nor was I myself innocent, I had borne myself so that he must have thought I was not above such things—but I had never thought it would end as it did—and then he forced me. 'Tis true, Olav, I swear—"

"I know it." He put out his hand as though to stop her. "He said it himself. And I know that this slaying was a small matter in the beginning—had I declared it at once. But I took the wrong road at the start—and now the guilt has grown, and I see that it will go on and breed new guilt. And now I must turn about, Ingunn—else I shall become the worst of inhuman wretches. It has come to this, that I scarce dare utter three words, for I know that two of them will be untrue."

She laid her arm across her face, wailing low.

"You know," said Olav, trying to hush her, " 'tis not certain either that the Archbishop will demand that I accuse myself before the King's judges. Haply he will deem it enough that I confess my sin before God. I have heard that men have been given absolution for the gravest of sins without being forced to destroy all their kinsfolk's honour and welfare—they were made to do such penance as a pilgrimage to Jerusalem—"

"Nay, nay!" she cried out again. "You would be sent away from us—to the world's end—"

"But 'tis not impossible"—he laid his hand on her bosom to quiet her—"that I might come home to you again. And you know you would dwell here and possess Hestviken—"

"But then it would come out that Eirik is not your son!"

Olav said quietly: "I have thought of that too, Ingunn—and it held me back, so long as I had no child of my own by you. Whether you might be driven out of Hestviken with your son—by my remote heirs. But now there is Cecilia. You can adopt the boy to full inheritance in your share of the estate—and he has a rich sister beside him—"

"Olav, do you remember what you said yourself?—that you had made Eirik no more than amends for his father's death—"

"I remember. But I see now, Ingunn, that I had no right to do it—give away my daughter's inheritance as amends to the child of a stranger—"

"Cecilia—Olav, Cecilia will be a rich maid for all that; she is rich and born in honour, of noble race—she will be fair besides. She will not be among the unfortunate—if she must be content with sister's share after you—"

Olav's face was stiff and closed. "A child of such birth as Eirik's has no *right* to amends for his father."

"Nay—you have always hated—my bastard." She burst into a wild fit of weeping. "I have heard you call him that."

"Oh ay—'tis a bad name that may escape the lips of an angry man, even when he speaks to one who is true-born." He made an effort to speak calmly, but could not help showing a touch of bitterness. "But I will not deny I have regretted it—'twere better I had called the boy by another name when he vexed me."

"You hate him," said the mother.

"That is not true. I have never been too hard with Eirik. God knows, he has had less of the rod than he needs—I *cannot* do it, when you look at me as though I stabbed you with a knife if I do but speak a little harshly to him—and you spoil him yourself—"

"I! who lie here and see naught of the boy from morning to night—" she had picked up the flowers and was pulling them to pieces. "Weeks pass, and he never comes to see his mother—has no time to speak to me—as today. You came at once and drove him out."

Olav said nothing.

"But if Eirik is to suffer for my misdeeds—then it had been better he had not come living into the world—though I myself should have suffered death and perdition for it—"

"Be reasonable, Ingunn," her husband begged her gently.

"Olav, listen to me—Olav, have pity! Too dearly will you have bought my life and my health, if on this account you should wander through the world, a poor and homeless pilgrim in the lands of the black men, among wicked infidels. Or if the worst should happen—that you should be forced to stand naked and dishonoured, in danger of your life maybe, be called caitiff and murderer—for the sake of that man—you, the best among franklins, upright and gentle and bold above all—"

"Ingunn, Ingunn—that is what I am no longer. A traitor I am to God and men—"

"You are *no* traitor—it *cannot* be a mortal sin that you made away with yon man.—And you know not how it feels to have to bend beneath shame and dishonour—*I* know it, *you* have never tried what it is to be disgraced. I cannot, nay, so help me Christ and Mary, I *cannot* have this brought upon me again—even if I were granted life and the use of my limbs—and I should feel that everyone who looked upon me knew of my shame: what manner of woman you had brought home to be mistress of Hestviken— and my Eirik a base-born boy without rights or family, whom a runaway, outlandish serving-man had begotten on me—tempting me among the wool-sacks in the loft, as though I had been a loose-minded, man-mad thrall woman—"

Olav stood and looked at her, white and stiff in the face.

"Nay, were I granted life to suffer in such wise—to stand up and walk with this to face—with your little Cecilia and my bastard holding my hands—and you away from us three, all of us equally defenceless—then I should surely regret the time I lay here waiting for my back to rot away—"

She stretched out her arms to him. Olav looked away—his face was immovably stiff—but he took her hand in his.

"Then it shall be as you wish."

14

Next year, at the beginning of Lent, Torhild Björnsdatter moved home to Rundmyr. And at once it was over the whole country-side that she had to leave Hestviken so suddenly because she was to have a child by Olav Audunsson.

If such a misfortune had befallen another man, who had been as a widower for years with a sick wife living, no one would have spoken aloud of the matter, but all the best men and women of the neighbourhood would have given thoughtless youths and those who knew nothing of good manners to understand that the less there was said about it, the better. Olav knew that. But he also knew that *he* was the man—and that he was regarded almost as a sort of outcast. Not that he had ever wronged any of his neighbours, so far as he knew. And at times folk had remembered this—when they thought it over, they knew of no particular stain on his name; no ugly or dishonourable action could be laid at his door. Olav Audunsson had simply acquired the reputation of being unpopular, a most uncongenial fellow.

In the brief days of sunshine after Cecilia had come into the world—before it became clear that her birth had cost the mother the last remnant of her health—the folk of the country round had met Olav with goodwill. Now that this strange curse had been lifted that denied them living children at Hestviken, his equals had rejoiced with him, and they had thought that now perhaps the man would be more sociable, not such a kill-joy as he had been—he extinguished life and merriment around him simply by the way he sat in silence, glaring with unseeing eyes in good company.—But Olav seemed so little able to meet them halfway—he remained the most arrant cross-stick, with whom nobody could get on.

Then there came to light this matter, which was as ugly as need be. While his wife lay palsied and full of torment, broken by one childbirth after another, each harder than the last, the man had been whoring with his housekeeper under his own roof. They had known it for years, folk called to mind now—this man and that knew that Olav had often brought his servant gifts from the town, far too costly for her position. He had helped her to provide for Björn's and Gudrid's children. And all the time he had worked the land for her up at Rundmyr, whither she had now betaken herself again. It was no long way between Rundmyr and Hestviken—so they showed no great shame: folk had seen Torhild swaying about in broad daylight, broad as she was now below the belt—she carried pails between her cot and the byre, far abroad she went along the edge of the wood, chipping bark and cutting twigs.—While they were about it, folk dug up again all the talk there had been at Björn Egilsson and Gudrid.

Olav's nearest kinsfolk in the neighbourhood, Signe of Skikk-justad and Una of Rynjul, had taken his part all through and done their best to excuse their cousin. But now even they were silent and looked ill at ease if anyone did but name Olav of Hestviken.

Olav knew most of what was said of him and Torhild. When he had made his confession, Sira Hallbjörn asked if that was *all*.

And then he discovered what kind of rumours were afloat about him—that this affair between him and Torhild had been going on for years, and that some folk hinted that maybe he was also father to the child Liv Torbjörnsdatter had had a year or two ago out at Hestviken.

One of the first Sundays when he was not permitted to ride to church with other people, the weather was mild. Olav was walking about the yard. A great washtub stood there; it had thawed so much that there was water on the top of the ice. Olav chanced to bend over it and saw his own reflection in the water. The face that looked up at him from the dark depth of the vessel, blurred and somewhat indistinct, was like the face of a leper—his pallor showed like patches of rime-frost against the weatherbeaten skin, and the whites of his eyes were red with blood.—Olav was frightened at the sight of himself.

He had almost expected it to come as a relief in a way when he was forbidden to enter the church this year. In the end he had felt he could no longer endure to go to mass with his unshriven sin. But, for all that, it was worse to be shut out. He had thought that the heavy penance for his adultery would at the same time heal some of his old wound. But it only caused him to reflect that this last sin was but a consummation of the old sin.

But this was the last thing in which he had ventured to put trust in himself—that nothing on earth would be able to break down his fidelity to Ingunn.

Not a word had been spoken between them of his faithlessness. But he knew that she knew of it.

The beginning of it all was that he felt all at once that he could no longer bear the burden of Ingunn. After that day in the previous spring when he had told her that he could live no longer with a deadly sin stirring in his mind, begetting fresh sins from day to day—and she had begged him to go on enduring it, for the boy's sake and hers. And in her sick and tortured state she had the advantage—no man worth calling a man could have opposed such a living bundle of pain.

He could not humiliate himself so far as to broach the subject again. He made as though nothing had been said, helped her through the long nights as before. But now, when at last his heart had run dry of love and patience, it was far more trying. Now not a day passed but he felt how tired and worn he was from the endless watching in the air of the sick-room. And the great bitterness in his heart received constant accessions of petty bitterness every time he found himself growing sluggish and forgetful in his work, heavy and inactive of body.

One night before midsummer he had gone out toward morning. Ingunn had fallen asleep at last, and he wished for a breath of the cool night air before lying down. Olav paused before the door of the house—it was light, calm, and grey outside. The boat's crew were not expected home for some hours yet; all on the manor were asleep. Then he noticed a thin column of smoke above the roof of the cook-house. At that moment Torhild Björnsdatter appeared at its door and emptied a cooking-pot—her wet hair hung about her, dark and straggling.

Olav had always been strangely touched to see how Torhild strove to keep herself clean and tidy in spite of all she had to do. She was always first up and last in bed, and thus she found time to wash and plait her hair even in the middle of the week, and mend her clothes. Ingunn had given up all such things before they had been married four years.

Olav went across to Torhild and they spoke together for a while—instinctively whispering, as it was so still—not a sound but that of the birds beginning to wake. He had dozed a little at times, he said in answer to her questions. But now he would go in and lie down.

"Could you not come over to us and lie down in my bed?" asked the girl. "Then you would have more peace." She herself and the children lay in one of the lofts now that it was summer.

Torhild lived in the house that Olav's parents had had when they were first married. It was a little old house which stood a little way apart, in a line with the cattle-sheds, under the Horse Crag, on the east of the yard toward the valley. Olav had had it set in order, so that it was now good and weather-tight, but it was very cramped inside.

Torhild accompanied him to the house and drew out the cudgel with which she had bolted the door. The air from within smote him like a sweet breath: the floor was strewn with juniper. The room was so narrow that the bed at its end filled it from wall to wall: in the dim light its sheepskin covers shone white as snow; around it were hung wreaths of flowers to keep off flies and vermin. Torhild had made it all trim before she moved out for the summer.

She bade him sit on the edge of the bed while she pulled off his shoes. Olav felt sleep well up from this clean, fresh couch, rising about him like sweet, tepid water. He was already half off as he rolled over into the bed—was just aware that Torhild lifted his feet in and spread the coverlet over him.

When he came to himself again, he saw the evening sun shining yellow on the meadow outside the open door. Torhild stood over him with a bowl in her hands—it was fresh, warm milk. He drank and drank.

"You got some sleep?" asked Torhild; she took the empty bowl and went out.

His shoes stood before the bed; they were soft, well smeared with tallow. And a clean everyday jerkin was laid out for him—still damp across the chest where she had washed away the stains, and the tear was mended that had been there when he wore it last.

During the summer it happened more and more often that he went and lay down in Torhild's house to get a night's sleep. But each time he rested thus made it harder to go back to the nights of watching; he was fairly hungry for sleep and again sleep—he could not have had his fill of sleep for many years, he thought.

Torhild brought him his morning bread when she came to wake him. If his clothes were wet the night before, he found dry ones ready when he woke, holes and tears were mended. Olav asked her not to do this—it was Liv's work, though she seldom did it. Torhild had enough to do as it was. The girl gave a little smile and shook her head.

And then there arose in him a desire for her—to know for once in his life what it was like to hold a sound and healthy woman in his arms, one he need not be afraid of touching. But, for all that, it was as though he had never *willed* it—even that morning when he reached out and took hold of her, he had expected her to thrust him back, perhaps in anger.—But she yielded to him, without a sigh.

All through that autumn and winter he seemed to be walking at the bottom of a thick sea of mist. He could not bear himself, and sometimes he could not bear her either; but he had no force to pull himself out of the mire. When she moved back into the house with the children, it must surely come to an end, he comforted himself; but it did not.

He stayed indoors with Ingunn from early in the morning till late in the evening. He had not been away from home a night except for a week in the seal-hunting. Now that he had betrayed his wife, he remembered his bitterness toward her as a temptation of the Devil to which he had yielded. "Ingunn, my Ingunn—how could I treat you thus, while you lie here, patient and kind, helpless as a maimed animal? Was that to be the end of our friendship, that I turned traitor to you?"

Night after night Olav carried her wrapped in skins and blankets, as one carries a child, so that she might have some relief from the stress of lying in bed. The more weary and cold and sleepless it made him, the greater was the relief he got from it.

He and Torhild had scarcely exchanged a word since that fatal morning. In all these years Torhild had been almost the only person with whom Olav had much talk—as with a grown-up equal. He remembered that—remembered what he owed this Torhild, whom he had rewarded thus. He could find nothing to excuse his misdeed. She had known no man before him—all she had known was hard work for other folk's welfare—and to make no complaint if life was too hard for her. And now he durst not speak to her, checked her when she would speak—in his heart he knew full well what she had long treasured up, and why this upright and scrupulous woman who was no longer young had allowed him to possess her without resistance. He was aware of it in her silent caresses. But if she *once* forgot herself and put it into words, his shame would stifle him.—

Of Björn, her father, he also thought. Ay, had he been alive now, he would have cut him down straight.

He guessed that it would not remain hidden either. It was in the darkest days before Yule that his fear changed to certainty. And in his despair temptation came to him. It was as though the Devil, who had led him for all these years into an ever increasing slough, going before him cloaked and half disguised—had now turned about, thrown off his hood of concealment, and shown him his true face:

He knew that Torhild would do whatever he asked of her. In former years it had often happened that they had been out together in a boat alone. She would go with him again—even if she guessed what was in his mind, she would follow him, he felt that. Then something might easily happen.

And Ingunn would be spared the knowledge of this. And he would be spared the shame of being exposed to every mother's son around the fiord as the worst of wretches. If he was already in the Devil's power neck and crop—he could no longer have a soul to lose.

But no, for all that. It was Satan who held out all this to him, but he himself said no. "This crime I will not be guilty of—no matter whether you have my chair ready for me in hell. I have nothing to lose, I can well believe that—honour and hope of salvation and my happiness with Ingunn, which I had saved so far—all this I have sold. But nevertheless you will not get me to do this. I will not do Torhild more harm than I have done already. Not even for Ingunn's sake—

"Lord, have mercy! Holy Mary, pray for us! Not for me, I beg nothing for myself—but, Lord, have mercy—upon the others."

"Ay, now it is too late," he said scornfully to the Devil. "They have guessed it, my whole household has guessed it; now you may cease to mutter about it. Be quiet! You will get me, when the time comes."

An ugly silence had fallen about him. The house-folk ceased speaking when the master came near. Scarcely a whispered word was spoken at mealtimes. Olav sat in the high seat; the housekeeper brought in the food and served it out. No one could mark the slightest change in her bearing; she was about from dawn to late in the evening, industrious as ever, her back was as straight and her foot as nimble, though it was plain to all that she no longer went alone.

Ingunn turned her face to the wall when Torhild came into the room.

So much had already gone by of the new year that Lent was at hand, and yet not a word had been said between Olav and Torhild of that which awaited them. But one day he saw her go up to the storehouse loft after the morning meal. He followed. She was taking pieces of bacon out of the salt-barrel and scraping off the worst of the scum that had formed on them.

"I have been thinking, Torhild"—Olav went straight to the point—"that it is not much I can do for you; I cannot help you much. But I will do what is in my power. And therefore I thought —that farm of Auken that I bought over on the Hudrheim side five years ago—that I give you a deed of it and make it over to you. Rundmyr I can continue to work for you and your brothers and sisters, as we have done in these last years."

Torhild reflected for a moment. "Nay, it may well be better that I do not stay up there at Rundmyr—"

"It will surely be better for you if you do not have to live hereabouts. After the trouble I have brought upon you," said the man in a low voice.

"Auken—" Torhild looked at him. "That is no small gift to make to a woman of my condition, Olav."

"It was reckoned to be a three-cows' croft, and there were some good cornfields on the south side of the knoll the houses stand on. But you know that no folk have lived there for a score of years, and they who rented the land of me have not kept it in good tilth."

Torhild turned round to him and held out her hand. "Then I say thanks, Olav. I see that you wish to make good provision for me."

Olav squeezed her fingers. "I have behaved worst to you of all people," he whispered. "You had the right to expect a different reward of me—"

Torhild looked him in the eyes. "The fault is mine as much as yours, I ween, master."

He shook his head. Then he said quietly: "Will it not be too hard for you now—all the work of the house here?"

"Oh no." She smiled feebly. "But perhaps it were best that I stay here at Hestviken no longer—?"

Olav nodded stiffly. "But the houses over at Auken are in a sorry state—sunken and roofless. I shall have them repaired and put new roofs—but you cannot move in before the summer."

"Then I must stay at Rundmyr meanwhile," Torhild suggested.

"Ay, I see no other way," said Olav.

. . .

A week after, Olav left home for a few days, and when he came back, Torhild had moved home to the croft at Rundmyr. And Olav discovered that he missed her—unspeakably.

It was not that his affection for Ingunn was less or other than it had been. This was something that had grown up entirely outside it. As in a sort of mirage he had had a vision of a life very different from his own; had seen how it might be for a man to have a sound and sensible wife by his side in all things, one who took her share of their common burden and bore it with as much discretion and strength as he bore his—or even more. And to see children, sons and daughters, succeeding one another, without its breaking and slowly killing the mother to bring them into the world. It was not that he would have changed his lot for this that the vision showed him—he thought that, had he known from his first meeting with the child Ingunn what she would bring him as a dowry, he would nevertheless have reached out both hands for her.

And yet he missed Torhild painfully. She had done him more good than any other creature. And he had repaid her in the worst way.

Eirik had seen how it was with Torhild, like everyone else in the house, and he had not given it much thought. But there was this silence that spread around Torhild—and it began to dawn upon Eirik that there was something sinister behind it. It could not be merely that she had gone the way of so many other serving-maids.

This silence which spread like the soundless rings in water when a stone is thrown into it. And by degrees, without a word having been said to him, Eirik became aware that this same sinister silence surged about his father too. A vague, evil dread stirred in the boy's soul—but he could not guess what his father had to do with Torhild's being with child. For his father was married to their mother—

Sira Hallbjörn sent word to Hestviken that this year Eirik Olavsson must go to confession in Lent and receive the Easter sacrament; the boy was now in his tenth winter, he ought to have come the year before. Eirik forgot all his gloomy anxieties on the morning his father sent him off—the priest wished to have the children with him for a week to teach them. It was the first time Eirik was to ride alone right up to the church town; his father had lent him a little light sword, and behind his saddle he had a bag of gifts for the priest and provisions for himself.

The day after his return he asked Olav:

"Father—who is my godmother?"

"Tora Steinfinnsdatter, your aunt, who is dead." Olav was not sure of this, but believed he had heard it once. Eirik asked no more.

Memories that he had not thought of for years began to swarm upon the boy. Half-forgotten feelings of insecurity and bewilderment were revived.—The other children had spoken of godmothers and godfathers—Sira Hallbjörn had wished to hear on the first day how much they knew of Christian religion from their homes. His father had taught Eirik his Credo, Paternoster, Ave Maria, and Gloria Patri, but that was long ago, and now he never saw that the boy said his prayers. So Eirik did not know them well, and he had almost forgotten what they meant in Norse. Nearly all the other children were better taught—and most of them had learned something from their godmother or godfather.

Eirik remembered that while he was at Siljuaas the mother he had there pointed out a stout, splendidly clad woman one day when they were at church, saying that she was his aunt. But she had not so much as looked at him as she walked past them. He was not even sure that she was the same aunt as the one in whose house they had lodged when his father fetched him from Siljuaas. At any rate, he had never heard that she was his godmother. For the first time it occurred to him to wonder why he had been there, at Siljuaas, when he was small.—He had often heard of other children being brought up away from their parents; but it was always with kinsfolk, solitary people or old. That little maid Ingegjerd who was so pretty and wore a silver belt about her waist like a grown-up maid, only that the plates were quite small, and who knew all the penitential psalms almost right—she was with her godmother, and she ruled the whole house for the childless couple and was given everything she asked for. But at Siljuaas the cabin had been poor and narrow, and Hallveig and Torgal had had plenty of other children—and he had never heard his parents mention these folk since; so they could not be kinsfolk of theirs.

Bastard and straw-brat, he knew well enough now what those words meant, and leman too. The memory of his mother's visit, which had frightened him so much that time—now it came up again, a living riddle. Words that he had heard his mother murmur almost to herself, when she could not hide her tears—they came up; and he remembered that his mother had once borne the keys, but they had been moved to Torhild's belt even before her mistress became bedridden.—And now, since his mother had lain low, palsied and unfit for anything, his father had taken to himself Torhild in her stead, and she was already far gone with child, and Eirik guessed now that it was his father's. But if his father had been *married*, this was a sin so grievous that scarcely any man would dare commit it. But then it must be so, that his mother was only his father's leman.

But then, but then—! That a rich franklin sent away his leman and children, assigned them a little home to dwell in far from his own, while he himself took in another or married—that had happened many times in the country round, and Eirik had heard of it.

The boy's heart was gripped by the dread of it, so that he could not sit still or stay quietly in one place. His father might send them away, if he wished. And he no longer cared for any of them. It was over a year since his father had taken Eirik about with him; he no longer taught him anything, scarcely spoke to him. Nor did he take any notice of Cecilia. And his mother lay there, needing constant attention and unable to do the merest trifle of work. If his father ordered them all three to leave Hestviken, he would bring Torhild and her child hither in their stead.

He had always remarked his mother's dislike of Torhild and never thought about it. *Now* he saw— And hatred, of which hitherto he had known nothing, was born in the boy's heart. He hated Torhild Björnsdatter, his cheeks turned white and he clenched his fists if he did but think of her. He took it into his head that one night he would steal up to Rundmyr and kill her, who would force his poor sick mother and all of them out of their home—drive his knife straight into her wicked, false heart.

But his father, his father— Eirik stood as it were with two arrows in his hand, not knowing which to lay to his bow. Should he hate his father too—or love him even more than before, now that he was in danger of losing him? To Eirik, Olav had always appeared the most perfect being on earth—the man's impatience, taciturnity, and coolness had made no impression on the child; he shook them from him as the sea-bird shakes off the water, and thought only of the times when his father had treated him differently. Above all when they had been out together without other company, in the forest or on the fiord, and his father had been the all-knowing, helpful being who warmed the child and gave him a feeling of security by his quiet good humour; but even at other times Eirik had often been able to feel that his father wished him well. And then there was that time when his father had to cut off his poisoned finger, and thrust the red-hot iron into his own flesh to show his son there was nothing to be afraid of. To the boy this was such a shining deed that he did not remember it clearly—it dazzled him to think of it.

Lose his father—Eirik turned to fire and ice with pain at the thought. Then he had dreams of doing something or other—a manly deed that would bring him fame. He imagined many things, but did not quite know which to choose. But when his father's eyes were opened to the kind of son he had, when he saw that he was bringing up a lad of spirit—when Eirik had won his father's heart, then he would say to him that he claimed an honourable position for his sister and himself, and his father should not send away his mother, were she never so sick and useless and in the way. But Torhild he should drive so far abroad that he need never more fear her coming with her child to claim their place.

But even if his affection for his father was more lively than ever, his confidence and sense of security were gone; and now Eirik noticed this—that his father was not fond of him, although the man never corrected him now, scarcely paid heed to him.

Olav hardly gave Eirik a thought now, only noticed with a vague relief that the boy was quieter than before, less in the way.

Not to a living soul did Eirik so much as hint at the conflict of thoughts that possessed him.

At last, one day in the course of spring, Olav stayed behind when the household went out after the morning meal—and then he said it:

" 'Tis likely you have heard—Torhild has a son—" he spoke in a low voice, which sounded husky.

"I heard it—" With a painful effort she turned her head so far as to see a glimpse of her husband as he sat leaning back in the high seat. His face was white and patched with red, his eyes swollen and bloodshot. She guessed he had been weeping.

She had not seen him thus in all these years, not when Audun died, not when she herself received the last sacraments, that time the women expected her to bleed to death. Only once before had she seen Olav weep.

"What is it like?" whispered his wife—"Torhild's child?"

"Fair and shapely, they say."

"Have you not—*seen*—your son?"

Olav shook his head. "I have not seen Torhild—not since she left us."

"But surely you will *see* it—?"

"I can do no more than I have done—for her. I cannot amend the boy's lot. And so—"

Olav got up and crossed the room—was going out.

Ingunn called to him: "What name has she given him?"

"Björn." Ingunn saw that his tears were about to overcome him again.

"That was the name of your mother's father."

"She can have had no thought of that. 'Twas her father's name, you know."

Olav made as though he would bend over his wife, but then he turned abruptly and went out.

She said no more to him till supper-time. From Liv she had heard that he had gone straight off to the smithy in the morning, and no one in the place had seen the master all day. He looked as if he had wept most of the time.

Then came the night. Olav and Ingunn were left alone in the house—with Eirik, who was asleep against the wall in his father's bed. The man tended the sick woman as he did all the other nights. Several times his wife saw that he was near bursting into tears again. And not a word did she dare to say—to him, who had now gotten a son, and who could never lead in his own son to sit beside him in the high seat in his ancestral manor. But what of Eirik —when she herself was no more—?

Withal Ingunn had an obscure feeling that it was not only sorrow over his son that had so shattered Olav.

The man himself was not thinking so much of his child. He wept chiefly over himself—it was as though he saw the last remnant of his honour and his pride lying crushed before his feet.

Not till after Olav's Mass had Olav Audunsson finished repairing the houses at Auken so far that Torhild Björnsdatter could move thither with her belongings. His house-carls were to carry her and her goods across the fiord. Olav himself had gone off south to Saltviken the day she was to move.

Ingunn lay listening—she had had both doors thrown open to the yard. She heard the coming of the pack-horses, the hoof-beats on the rock. Then the cow-bell, the tripping of little hoofs—the children, Rannveig and Kaare, ran about, driving and keeping together their flock of sheep and goats.

Liv stood at the outer door, sniffing and making game of the procession. "Torhild takes the lower path along the creek," announced the maid, buzzing with excitement. "To bring her whoreson among the houses here—that's more than even she has a mind to."

"Hush, Liv!" whispered Ingunn, breathing rapidly. "Run down to her—bid her—ask if she will—tell her I would so fain have a sight of her child."

A moment later Eirik dashed in hurriedly. His narrow, swarthy face was burning—his yellow eyes sparkled with indignation:

"Mother! Now she is coming hither! Shall I drive her off? We must not let the filthy hell-sow drag her bastard in here!"

"Eirik, Eirik!" His mother called to him in a wail, stretching out her thin, yellow hand. "For God's mercy's sake, say not such ugly words. 'Tis a sin to scoff at a poor creature and call her bad names."

He was so tall now, her boy, slender as a reed and slight of build. Angrily he tossed his shapely head with its black curls.

"It is I who sent for her," whispered Ingunn.

The boy frowned and turned on his heel; then he went and flung himself down on the edge of the north bed, sat there staring with an angry, scornful smile as Torhild entered.

The girl came forward with bent head—she had bound up her hair under a coarse, tight-drawn coif—but her back was as straight as ever. She carried a bundle in her arms, wrapped in a kerchief with a red and white border. It was strange to see that she bore herself with all her old dignity and calm, even as she appeared before Olav's wife, humble and sorrowful.

The women greeted each other, and Ingunn remarked that Torhild would have good weather for the passage across. Torhild agreed.

"I had so great a mind to see your boy," whispered Ingunn shyly. "You must do me the kindness to let me see him. You must lay him down here before me; you know I cannot raise myself," she said as Torhild held out the bundle. Then the girl laid the child down on the bed before the mistress.

With trembling hands Ingunn undid the kerchief that was wrapped about it. The boy was awake—he lay staring, at nothing in particular, with big blue eyes; a little smile, as it were a reflection of a light none but himself could see, hovered about the toothless, milky mouth. A fine, fair down curled from under the border of his cap.

"He is big?" asked Ingunn—"for his age—three months, is it not?"

"He will be three months by Laurence Mass." [9]

"And fair he is. He is like my Cecilia, methinks?"

Torhild stood silent, looking down at her child. There was no great change to be seen in the housekeeper—though in some way she had grown younger and fairer. It was not only that her figure seemed yet more shapely: she was broad-shouldered and had always been high-bosomed, with a chest as deep and broad as a man's. But now her full, firm breast looked as if it would burst her kirtle, and this made her seem slighter in the waist. But it was not that alone—her grey, bold-featured face had softened as it were and become younger.

"He has no look of knowing what hunger is, this fellow," said Ingunn.

"Nay—I thank God," replied Torhild quietly; "he knows not what it is—and with His help he shall never know it either, so long as I am alive."

"You may be sure Olav will see to it that the boy shall never lack aught, even if you be taken from him," said Ingunn in a low voice.

"That I know full surely."

Torhild threw the cloth over her child again and lifted him in her arms. Ingunn held out her hand in farewell—Torhild bent deeply over it and kissed it.

Then Ingunn burst out—she could not keep back the words:

"So in the end you got your old desire fulfilled, Torhild!"

Torhild replied calmly and with a mournful air: "I tell you, Ingunn—as truly as I hope in Christ and Mary Virgin for mercy for myself and this my child—I do not believe, mistress, that I ever

[9] August 10.

desired to deceive you—and he, your husband, never desired it, as you must know—but it came about nevertheless—"

Ingunn said bitterly: "Nevertheless I have seen it, years before I lost my health, what thoughts you had of Olav—you liked him better than all beside—and that has been so for more than three years or four—"

"Ay, from the time I knew him first I have liked him best of all."

She bowed stiffly and went out.

Eirik started up, spat after the woman, and swore.

His mother called to him, in a hushed and frightened voice. "Eirik mine, be not so sinful—never say those ugly words of any mother's child," she begged him, bursting into tears and trying to draw the boy to her. But he wrested himself from her and dashed out of the door.

15

NEVERTHELESS it overtook Olav as something quite unexpected when the end came.

The winter following the misfortune with Torhild Björnsdatter passed like the two that preceded it. Everyone marvelled that life still clung to Ingunn Steinfinnsdatter—it was more than two years since she had been able to take dry food. She had bed-sores now, and in spite of all Olav's efforts they grew worse. She herself felt little of the sores, except those under her shoulders; they sometimes burned like fire. She always had to have linen cloths under her, and although Olav smeared the places where the skin was broken thickly with grease, the linen often clung fast to the sores, and then it was pitiful to see her torments. But she complained wonderfully little.

One morning Olav had carried her over to his own bed, and while Liv spread clean skins and linen on hers, he tended her back; he had laid her on her side. He was dizzy with fatigue and sickened by the bad smell there was now in the room. Suddenly he bent over his wife and cautiously touched with his lips the moist, open sores on her thin shoulder-blades; he had recalled something he had heard—of holy men who kissed the sores before they bound up the lepers whom they tended. But then this was the other way about: it was he who was the leper, though he seemed clean and sound outside—and she must indeed be washed clean now, who had borne the torments of all these years meekly and without complaint.

He accused her of *nothing* now.

Ingunn guessed it must be hard for Olav to be shut out of the church. And one night, when her husband had fasted on bread and water during the day, so that he was quite worn out when he had to watch by her, she whispered, as she drew him down to her:

"I *will* not complain, Olav—but why *could* I not be suffered to die, when Cecilia was born? Then you would not have fallen into this sin with Torhild—"

"Speak not so." But he could not tell her that was not what had brought about the misfortune. It was that he had been embittered against her, and then he had grown careless and weary of himself, had longed for rest from all that weighed upon him. Now he no longer gave her any blame for it—she had known no better. He had known for close on thirty years that Ingunn had little wit, and God had laid it upon him to judge and answer both for himself and for her. Simple she was—and unspeakably dear to him. He put no blame on any but himself. *Mea culpa, mea culpa*—and the fault of no one else.

All things went regularly at Hestviken now, both with the farming and the fishery. If the master could not take part himself —but he had to be with her. He always consoled himself with the thought: "It cannot possibly go on much longer." But at the same time he could not imagine it would be today, or tomorrow, or the next day. The end must indeed come soon, but there was still a little time.

Easter fell early that year, so that the Oslo fair was held in the week before St. Blaise's Day. Olav had to go into town: he had some goods lying in the hands of Claus Wiephart—had entered into a kind of trading partnership with the German, but he did not trust that fellow farther than he could see him, nor had he cared to lodge with Claus on his recent visits; it came too dear. Hitherto he had excused himself by saying that he would lie in the guest-house of the preaching friars, since from his youth up he had been a friend of that order. But this year he could not very well be in the convent, since he was banned from taking part in the mass. So this time he had put up at the Great Hostelry.

On the evening of the last day of the fair he sat in the great room of the hostelry munching the provisions he had brought and washing them down with their indifferent ale, when Anki came in and asked for Master Olav of Hestviken.

"Here am I. Is there any news from home, Arnketil, or what brings you hither?"

"God help you, master. Ingunn lies at the point of death—she was given extreme unction as I left home."

She had had a fit of colic, but no worse than often before, and she had coughed violently for some nights. But when she collapsed that morning they did not guess that she was dying—until old Tore came in to dinner. As soon as he saw the state the woman was in, he went out, saddled his horse, and rode for the priest. Sira Hallbjörn was again away from home—ay, now his parishioners would complain to the Bishop on his next visitation—but one of these barefoot friars of his occupied the parsonage and was called his vicar. Even before the monk began his ministrations to the dying woman, he told the house-folk that they must send for the master in all haste—it was uncertain at the best whether he could reach home in time to say farewell to his wife.

There had been no cold worth talking about that winter; beyond the islands the fiord had been open, so that Olav had come by boat. But then here had been a few nights' frost, followed by a strong southerly wind, and now it was freezing again—Anki had been able to row as far as Sigvaldasteinar, but there he had had to take to the land and borrow a horse. And now it was likely that the fiord was full of ice a long way out; it was hard to say how Olav would reach home quickest. No doubt he would have to ride round inland. Claus would be able to find him a horse.

People had collected about Olav Audunsson and his man; they stood listening and offering advice. Some young, well-dressed squires in long, coloured kirtles and cloaks also came up; they had been sitting farther up the hall, laughing rather noisily as they drank German mum and threw dice. Now one of them spoke to Olav—he was a tall, fair lad with silky, flaxen hair, which he wore long upon his shoulders according to the latest foreign fashion. Olav knew him by sight: he was one of the sons of the knight of Skog and was in company with his brother; the others were doubtless pages from the King's palace.

"It means much to you to reach home quickly, I can guess. You can borrow a horse of me—I have a well-paced horse out in the friars' paddocks—if you will go thither with me?"

Olav protested that this was too much—but the young man was off already, settled his gaming debts and drank up his ale while he took his sword and cloak. Then Olav gave Arnketil orders about his baggage and threw his cloak about him.

The snow crunched under their feet as they came outside. The sky was clear and the hills were still green; the first stars were coming out. " 'Twill be villainously cold tonight," said Olav's companion. They struck out eastward through the alleys toward Gjeitabru.

Olav asked the other about the road—he was totally unacquainted with the districts lying east of the town toward Skeidissokn, had never come to Oslo overland. The young man answered that he could ride across the whole of the Botnfiord, the ice was safe enough—well, it was unsafe too, in some places, "but I can ride over with you."

Olav said that was far too much and he would find his way sure enough; but his companion, Lavrans Björgulfsson was his name, made off at once: "I have my horse standing in Steinbjörn's yard; if you will wait for me in the church—I shall not be long—" He turned and went back to the town.

The Franciscans' church was not yet dedicated and the friars said mass in a house within the garth; but the church was roofed, Olav had heard, and they preached there in the evenings during Lent. Not before Easter would his first year of penance be ended, but he was free to enter this edifice, which had not yet become the house of God.

For all that, he had a queer feeling as he crossed the bridge and took the trampled path over a field, where the snow shone grey in the falling darkness, toward the church, whose black gable-end was outlined against the blue, star-set gloom.

It was colder inside than out. From habit he bent the knee as he came in, forgetting that the holy sacrament had not yet been brought into this house. From the farther end of the dark nave his eye was met by the blaze of a great number of little tapers—they were burning at the foot of a great crucifix that stood against the grey stone wall. Beside it the chancel arch yawned before a pitch-dark empty space.

A little farther down the nave a solitary candle was burning by a lectern; before the book a monk stood reading, clad in the order's brown garb of poverty. He was standing on an inverted tool-chest, and about him were assembled a score of men and women in thick winter clothes—some stood and some had drawn up beams and overturned vessels to sit upon. Their breath showed like white smoke in the light of the candle.

The very incompleteness and desolation of the place caught at him like a hand clutching at his anxious heart. The openings for windows in the wall were boarded up; the scaffolding still stood at the western end of the nave, and he made out boxes and mortar-vats and boards and ends of beams as his eyes grew accustomed to the darkness. But most desolate of all was the black chasm of the choir—and above this image of the world, without form and void, rose the great crucifix with the glittering assemblage of candles at its foot.

It was not like any crucifix he had seen before. At every step he took forward, an immense pain and dread rose within him at the sight of this image of Christ—it *was* no image, it seemed alive— God Himself in mortal agony, bleeding from His scourging as though every wound men have inflicted upon one another had stricken His flesh. The body was bent forward at the loins, as though contorted with pain; the head had fallen forward, with closed eyes over which streamed the blood from the crown of thorns, down into the half-open, sighing mouth.

Beneath the crucifix stood Mary and John the Evangelist. The Mother held her thin hands clasped, one above the other, against her bosom, as she looked up—mournfully as though she raised the sorrows of all races and all ages to her Son, praying for help. Saint John looked down; his face was contracted with brooding upon this mystery.

The monk read—Olav had known the words since he was a child: *O vos omnes, qui transitis per viam, attendite, et videte, si est dolor sicut dolor meus.*[1]

The monk closed the book and began to speak. Olav did not hear a word—he only saw the image on the cross before him: *et videte, si est dolor sicut dolor meus.*

Ingunn lay at home, in the agony of death, if she were not dead

[1] Lamentations, i, 12.

already. It did not seem real to him, but he knew now that this sorrow of his was also as a bleeding wound upon that crucified body. Every sin he had committed, every wound he had inflicted on himself or others, was one of the stripes his hand had laid upon his God. As he stood here, feeling that his own heart's blood must run black and sluggish in his veins with sorrow, he knew that his own life, full of sin and sorrow, had been one more drop in the cup God drained in Gethsemane. And another sentence he had learned in his childhood came back to him: he had believed it was a command, but now it sounded like a prayer from the lips of a sorrowing friend: *Vade, et amplius jam noli peccare—*[2]

Then it was as though his eyes lost their power of sight, and his blood rushed back to his heart, so that he grew outwardly cold as a dead man. All this was as it were within him: his own soul was as this house, destined for a church, but empty, without God; darkness and disorder reigned within, but the only sparks of light that burned and sent out warmth were gathered about the image of the rejected Lord, Christ crucified, bearing the burden and the suffering of his sin and his despair.—*Vade, et amplius jam noli peccare.*

My Lord and my God! Yea, Lord, I come—I come, for I love Thee. I love Thee, and I acknowledge: *Tibi soli peccavi, et malum coram te feci*—against Thee alone have I sinned, and done evil in Thy sight.—He had said these words a thousand times, and only now did he know that this was the truth that held all other truths in itself as in a cup.

My God and my all!—

Then someone touched him on the shoulder—he gave a start: it was Lavrans Björgulfsson; the horses were standing in the garth. This was the shorter way—the young man went in front, up through the church, into the choir. Now that Olav's eyes were used to the darkness he could make out the altar—the naked stone, as yet undedicated and unadorned, a cold, dead heart. There was a little door on the south of the choir:

"Look how you go—the steps are not finished—" Lavrans jumped down into the snow. Out in the yard stood two of the friars. One held the horses, the other carried a lantern. Lavrans must have told them how things stood, for one of them came up

[2] St. John, viii, 11.

to Olav—it was one of those who had been with Sira Hallbjörn, and he had come out to Hestviken once. Olav knew the monk's face, but did not remember his name.

"Patiently and meekly she bore it all, your wife. Ay, and now it is Brother Stefan who is with her—ay, we shall remember her in our prayers here too tonight."

The north wind was at their backs as they rode over the ice—long stretches of it were like steel, swept of the little snow that had fallen lately. The moon would not rise till toward morning; the night was black and strewn with stars.

"We shall have to ride up to Skog," said Olav's guide, "and get fur cloaks on."

It was a great manor, Olav saw—many great houses stretching away in the darkness. Young Lavrans sprang from the saddle, unhindered by the long folds of his mantle, stretched his tall, supple frame, and went across and opened the door of one of the houses. Then he stood by his horse, caressing and talking to it, till a man came out with a lantern—the light seemed to hover over the snow.

"You must dismount, Olav, and come in with me." He took the lantern from his man and showed the way across the courtyard. "We live where we have been since we were married—my stepmother and Aasmund, my brother, have the great house, as in father's time—" he seemed to take it for granted that everyone knew all about the great people of Skog.

"Is your father dead?" asked Olav for the sake of saying something.

"Ay, 'tis a year and half since—"

"You are young though—to be master of this great manor."

"I? not so young either—I am three and twenty winters old." He opened a door. They did not seem to bar their houses here at Skog. Through an anteroom they entered a little hall, warm and tidy. Lavrans lighted a thick tallow candle that stood near a curtained bed, threw the pine torch on the hearth, and spoke to someone within the bed. He handed in some woman's clothes behind the curtain.

A moment after, a young woman stepped out, lightly clad, with a red cloak over her long, blue shift—she was tucking locks of jet-black hair under the coif she had flung around her narrow, large-eyed face. While she busied herself, with easy, youthful briskness, her husband lay half-hidden within the bed. There were sounds of a little child behind the curtains, and the young father laughed aloud:

"Nay, Haavard—will you pull your father's nose off? Leave go now. Or maybe you want to feel if 'tis frozen off me—" The hidden youngster choked with laughter.

The mistress had brought in food from the closet and offered her guest a foaming bowl of ale. Olav thanked her, but shook his head—he could no more eat and drink now than if he had been dead. Lavrans shook off the child he was playing with, came up, and took some food standing.

"You must give me a drink of water then, Ragnfrid.—My wife and I have made a vow to drink naught but water in Lent, except we be in company with guests or on a journey"; he gave an affectionate look at the foaming bowl of ale. With a little crooked smile Olav accepted the draught of welcome, took a taste of it, and passed the bowl to the master of the house, who now did justice to his guest—the young man did not seem minded to say good-bye to the slight intoxication that had been on him when they left Oslo. It had been passing off as they rode along, but now he made up for it, generously.

The single draught he had taken worked upon Olav so that he felt awakened from his ecstasy. Gone was the strange sense that all he saw and felt was a shadow, but that he himself had been taken away this night by God from the paths of men, brought before His face alone in a desolate spot—for now He willed that this His creature should understand at last.—And he heard all sounds from the visible world outside as he heard the voice of the fiord under the crags at home in Hestviken, sensed them without hearing. Voices reached him as though they were speaking outside a closed hall, where he was alone with the Voice which adjured and complained, full of love and sorrow: *O vos omnes, qui transitis per viam, attendite, et videte, si est dolor sicut dolor meus!*

But now the door of the closed room was thrown open, the Voice was silent—and he sat in a strange house with total strangers, the night was far spent, and he was to find his way through country that was quite unknown to him ere he reached home. And there death awaited him, and the choice that, as he now saw, he had made more and more difficult for himself every day and every year he had put it off. But now he *must* choose—he knew that, as he sat here feeling dazed and frozen, roused out of his strange visionary state: after that vision or whatever it might have been, he could not go on drowsily hoping that one day God would choose for him—*force* him.

So many a time had he allowed himself to be driven out of his road, upon false tracks that he had no desire to follow. Long ago he had acknowledged the truth of Bishop Torfinn's words: the man who is bent upon doing his own will shall surely see the day when he finds he has done that which he never willed. But he perceived that this kind of will was but a random shot, an arrow sent at a venture.—He still had his own inmost will, however, and it was as a sword. When he was called to Christianity, he had been given this free will, as the chieftain gives his man a sword when he makes him a knight. If he had shot away all his other weapons, marred them by ill use—this right to choose whether he would follow God or forsake Him remained a trusty blade, and his Lord would never strike it out of his hand. Though his faith and honour as a Christian were now stained like the misused sword of a traitor knight, God had not taken it from him; he might bear it still in the company of our Lord's enemies, or restore it kneeling to that Lord, who yet was ready to raise him to His bosom, greet him with the kiss of peace, and give him back his sword, cleansed and blessed.

Olav felt a vehement desire to be left alone with these thoughts —though he did not forget that this young Lavrans had shown himself very kindly, and he knew it might be difficult for him to reach home that night without the other's help. But the young folk troubled and disturbed him by their constant services. The wife knelt before him and would help him change his boots—she had brought out foot-clouts of thick homespun and big fur boots stuffed with straw. The scent of her skin and hair was wafted to him, warm and healthy—it made him shrink within himself, as though to ward it off. The young mother breathed a fragrance of all the things in life from which he had been led away step by step, until tonight he saw that he was parted from them as completely as though he had already taken a monk's vows.

The husband came in with his arms full of fur clothing and set about finding something that would fit his guest. Olav was queerly abashed to see how much too large for him the other's clothes were—he was quite lost in them when he got them on. Olav's broad shoulders gave him a look of bulk, and the other seemed so slight; but he was doubtless more substantial than he looked, and he was tall besides. And in the pride of his grief Olav felt mortified that he should appear a lesser man than Lavrans Björgulfsson in everything, stature and worship and power—this tall, fair-skinned boy who breathed this air of home with wife and child, who was master of this rich knightly manor, helpful, kind, and well content. He had a long face with handsome, powerful features, but his cheeks were still smooth and of a childlike roundness; life had not marked his young and healthy skin with a single scratch—was never likely to do so either: he looked as though destined to take his course through the world without ever meeting sorrow.

Olav protested that he could well find his own way through the forest in Skeidissokn, and Lavrans must not think of riding from home so late at night for his sake in this cold. But his host was quick to reply that, as it had not snowed properly for so long, the forest was full of old trails; a man must be well acquainted with the paths by Gerdarud to find the shortest way. And as for a night out of doors—nay, he made nothing of that.

Outside in the courtyard a groom held two fresh horses, fine, active animals. An excellent horseman was this young squire, and he had the best of horses. Olav was secretly vexed that he had to be given a hand in mounting—it was these boots that were far too big.

The road lay through forest most of the time, and the thin coating of snow was frozen hard and broken in every direction by old, worn tracks of ski-runners, horsemen, and sledges—and the moon could not be expected for an hour yet. Olav guessed that he might have strayed far and wide ere he had found his way out of these woods alone.

At last they came through some small coppices and saw Skeidis church ahead of them on the level. The moon, rather less than full, had just risen and hung low above the hills in the north-east. In the slanting, uncertain moonbeams the plain was raked with shadows, for the snow had been blown into drifts with bare patches of glimmering crust between; all at once Olav recalled the night when he fled to Sweden—more than twenty years ago. It must have been the waning moon that reminded him—then too he had had to wait for moonrise and had started at about this time of night, he remembered now.

He told his guide that from here he was well acquainted with the roads southward, thanking Lavrans for his help and promising to send the horse north again at the first opportunity.

"Ay, ay—God help you, Master Olav—may you find it better at home than you look for.—Farewell!"

Olav remained halted until the sound of the other's horse had died away in the night. Then he turned into the road that bore south and west. It was fairly level here, and the road was well worn and good for long stretches; he could ride fast. It was not far now from farm to farm.

The moon rose higher, quenching the smaller stars, and its greenish light began to flood the firmament and spread over the white fields and the grey forest; the shadows shrank and grew small.

Once the crowing of a cock rang out through the moonlight; it was answered from farms far away, and Olav became aware how still the night was. Not a dog barked in any of the farms, no animal called, there was not a sound but that of his own horse's hoofs, as he rode in solitude.

And again it was as though he were rapt away to another world. All life and all warmth had sunk down, lay in the bonds of frost and sleep like the swallows at the bottom of a lake in wintertime. Alone he journeyed through a realm of death, over which the cold and the moonlight threw a vast, echoing vault, but from the depths the Voice resounded within him, incessantly:

O vos omnes, qui transitis per viam, attendite, et videte, si est dolor sicut dolor meus!

Bow down, bow down, yield himself and lay his life in those pierced hands as a vanquished man yields his sword into the hands of the victorious knight. In this last year, since he had turned adulterer, he had always refused to think of God's mercy—it would be unmanly and dishonourable to look for it now. So long had he feared and fled from the justice of men—should he pray for mercy *now*, when his case had grown so old that perhaps he would be spared paying the full price of it among men? Something told him that, having evaded men's justice, he must be honest enough not to try to elude the judgment of God.

But tonight, as he journeyed under the winter moon like one who has been snatched out of time and life, on the very shore of eternity, he saw the truth of what he had been told in childhood: that the sin above all sins is to despair of God's mercy. To deny that heart which the lance has pierced the chance of forgiving. In the cold, dazzling light he saw that this was the pang he had himself experienced, so far as a man's heart can mirror the heart of God—as a puddle in the mire of the road may hold the image of *one* star, broken and quivering, among the myriads clustered in the firmament.—That evening many, many years ago, in his youth, when he had arrived at Berg and heard from Arnvid's lips how she had tried to drown herself, fly from his forgiveness and his love and his burning desire to raise her up and bear her to a safe place.

He saw Arnvid's face tonight, as his friend admonished him: you accepted all I was able to give you, you did not break our friendship, therefore you were my best friend. He remembered Torhild—he had not seen her since the day he had had to drive her out of his house, because she bore a child under her heart, and it was his, the married man's. He had never seen his son—could not make good the disgrace, either to the boy or to his mother. But Torhild had gone without a bitter word, without a complaint of her lot. He guessed that Torhild was so fond of him that she saw it was the last kindness she could do him, to go away uncomplaining—and that it had been her chief consolation in misfortune that she could yet do him a good deed.

Even for poor sinners it was the worst of all when one's friend in distress refused to accept help. In spite of his being sunk in sin and sorrow, God had let him have his happiness in peace: he had been allowed to give to Ingunn, and never had it been said to him that now the measure was full. Again it was words from his childhood's teaching that arose, illumined so that he understood their meaning to the full: *Quia apud te propitiatio est: et propter legem tuam sustinui te, Domine.*[3]

The strange horse began to tire under him; he halted in a field and let it recover its wind. The steam rose from its sides like silvery smoke under the moon, which now shone from the height

[3] Psalm cxxx. *De profundis.*

of heaven. They were covered with rime, both he and his horse
—Olav woke up and looked about him. Behind him, under the
brow of the wood, lay a farm he did not recognize; before him
he saw a great white surface bordered by high rushes, glittering
with rime and rustling feebly in the breeze—a lake. No, he did
not know where he was. He must have gone much too far inland
to the eastward.

The moon had sunk low in the south-west and had lost its
power, the sky began to grow light, blue with a touch of orange
on the land side, when at last Olav came out of a wood and knew
where he was—he had reached some small farms in the south of
the parish. The shortest way home to Hestviken was over the
Horse Crag. Stiff, frozen, and deadly tired he stood stretching
himself and yawning—he had dismounted to lead the poor horse
over the height. Silently he caressed the strange animal, taking its
muzzle in his hand. Its coat was covered with rime and frozen
foam.—It was now full daylight.

Arrived at the top of the ridge, he stopped for a moment and
listened—an unwonted stillness penetrated him through all his
senses: the last frost had silenced the fiord. The ice lay as far as
he could see up and down, rough and greyish white. The southern
wind at the beginning of the week had broken up the first sheet
of ice and driven the floes inshore; the last night's cold had bound
them all together. A thin mist rose from the ground, covering
everything with a downy greyness, and the air was tinged pink
by the sun, which was rising behind the fog.

The monk came into the doorway to meet him, when his horse
was heard in the yard. "God be praised that you are here in time!"

Then he stood by her bed. She lay in a doze, with her narrow
yellow hands crossed upon her sunken bosom—looking like a
corpse but that her pupils just moved under the filmy eyelids.
With a sharp stab of pain the husband felt that soon she would lie
here no more. For more than three years he had gone in and out
while she lay stretched here in bed, racked with pain, unable to
move more than her head and hands.—Lord Jesus Christ, had it
been worth *so* much to him, merely to have her here alive!

The monk talked and talked—what a happy thing it was that
at last she was to be released from her sufferings, after the way

she had been lying of late, with the flesh of her back raw and bloody; Patient and pious—ay, he, Brother Stevne, had prayed as he was about to administer extreme unction: "God grant we may all be as well prepared to meet death, when the hour comes, as Mistress Ingunn."—As soon as she had received the sacrament she had sunk into a doze—she had lain as she lay now for twenty hours, and like enough she would not come to herself again; it seemed she would be allowed to die without a struggle.

Then he began to question Olav about his journey home—his mouth was never still—but now they must see that the master had something to keep him alive!

The serving-maid brought in ale, bread, and a dish of steaming, freshly boiled salt ling. Olav turned sick at the nauseous, washy smell that rose from the fish and set himself against it, but the monk affectionately laid a dirty, frost-bitten hand on his shoulder and forced him. Olav felt repelled by this Brother Stefan—his frock smelt so foully, and his face had the look of a water-rat with its long, pointed nose that seemed to have no bone in it.

At the first mouthful of food he was almost sick—his throat hurt him and his mouth filled with water. But when he had got down a bite or two, he found he was famishing. While he was eating he stared, without knowing it, at Eirik, who was busy with something in his place on the bench. When the boy noticed his father looking at him, he came up and showed what he was doing —he was so eager about it that he forgot his shyness of Olav: he had kept two pairs of shells from the walnuts his father had brought home from the town the year before, and now he had found good use for them. He was collecting the wax that dripped from the candle by his mother's deathbed and filling the walnut-shells with it; one was for Cecilia and one for himself. Brother Stefan was at once interested in the boy's occupation; he pulled off the lump of wax that had run down the candle and discussed with Eirik how they should prevent the shells bursting apart afterwards.

Olav was overpowered by fatigue when he had eaten his fill. He sat with his neck leaning against the logs of the wall, the pulses throbbed in his throat and about his ears, and his eyes would not keep together when he tried to fix them upon anything—he saw the flame of the holy candle double. Now and then his eyelids closed altogether—images and thoughts whirled within him as a

mist rolls and drifts along—but when he took a hold of himself
and opened his eyes again, they were all forgotten. He felt numbed
and empty, and the memory of the last night and all he had gone
through in it was as far off as the memory of an old dream.—This
untiring Brother Stevne came and pestered him again, wanting
him to lie down awhile in the north bed—he would be sure to wake
him if there was any change in his wife. Olav shook his head
crossly and stayed where he was. Thus the hours wore on till
midday.

He had slept and dozed by turns when he saw that Brother
Stefan was busy beside the dying woman. Kneeling, he held a
crucifix before Ingunn's face in one hand, while with the other he
beckoned eagerly to Olav.

Olav was there in an instant. Ingunn lay with eyes wide open;
but he could not tell whether she *saw* anything—whether she
recognized either the crucifix in the priest's hand or himself bending over her. For a moment something like an expression came into
the great, dark-blue eyes; they seemed to be seeking. Olav bent
lower over his wife, the monk held the crucifix close to her face—
but the feeble, fluttering disquiet was still there.

Then the husband got up, took Eirik by the hand, and led him
forward to his mother's bed. The monk had begun to say the
litany for the dying.

"Are you looking for Eirik, Ingunn? Here he is!"

He had put his arm about the boy's shoulder and stood holding
him close. Eirik came up to his shoulder now. Olav could not see
whether Ingunn knew them.

Then he knelt down, still with his arm around the child. Eirik
was sobbing, low and painfully, as he knelt side by side with his
father and said the responses.

"*Kyrie, eleison.*"

"*Christie, eleison,*" whispered the man and the boy.

"*Kyrie, eleison.—Sancta Maria—*"

"*Ora pro ea—*" The two kept their eyes on the dying woman.
The man was watching for a sign that she knew him. The boy
looked at his mother, in dismay and wonder, as the tears streamed
down his cheeks and he sniffled between the responses—"*ora pro
ea, orate pro ea—*"

"*Omnes sancti Discipuli Domini—*"

"*Orate pro ea.*"

Ingunn sighed, moaning softly. Olav bent forward—no word came from her white lips. The three continued the prayer for the dying.

"*Per nativitatem tuam—*"

"*Libera ei, Domine.*"

"*Per crucem et passionem tuam—*"

"*Libera ei, Domine.*"

She closed her eyes again; her hands slipped from each other, down to her sides. The monk crossed them again over her bosom, as he prayed:

"*Per adventum Spiritus sancti Paracliti—*"

"*Libera ei, Domine.*"

—Ingunn, Ingunn, wake up again, only for a moment—so that I may see you know me—

"*Peccatores,*" recited the monk, and the father and son replied:

"*Te rogamus, audi nos.*"

She still breathed, and her eyelids quivered very slightly.

"*Kyrie, eleison.*"

Olav remained on his knees by the bedside, holding Eirik to him, even after they had reached the end of the prayer. Inwardly he was beseeching: "Let her wake up, only for a little instant—so that we may bid each other farewell." Although every night of these three years had been like entering the valley of death with her, he felt he could not part from her yet. Not till they had given each other one last greeting before she went out of the door.

Eirik had laid his face on the edge of the bed; he was weeping in an agony of grief.

Suddenly the dying woman opened her lips—Olav thought he heard her whisper his name. Quickly he bent over her. She muttered something he could not distinguish; then more clearly: "—not go forth—'tis uncertain—out yonder—Olav—do not—"

He could not guess her meaning—whether she spoke in a dream or what. Almost without knowing it, he put his arm around Eirik, stood up, and raised the boy to his feet.

"You must not weep so loudly," he whispered as he led his son to his seat on the bench.

Eirik looked up at him in despair—the child's face was all swollen with weeping.

"Father," he whispered, "Father—you will not send us away from Hestviken, will you—because our mother is dead?"

"Send away whom?" Olav asked absently.

"Us. Me and Cecilia—"

"No, surely—" Olav broke off, held his breath. The children —they had never entered his mind when he was thinking of all the rest last night. It took him by surprise—but he would not think of this now, would thrust it from him. As though asleep he sat down on the bench a little way from Eirik.

He was not fit to contend with it now. But the children—he had not thought of that.

The day wore on to nones. And little by little the inmates of the house tired of watching and waiting for the last sigh. Liv had been in once or twice with Cecilia, but as the mother lay in a doze and the child was noisy and restless, the maid had to take her out again. The last time Eirik went with her—Olav heard their voices outside.

He had seated himself on the step by the bed. Brother Stefan was dozing at the table with his book of hours open before him. The house-folk came in quietly, knelt down and softly said a prayer, paused awhile, and quietly went out again. Olav dropped off—he did not sleep, but it was as though his head were full of grey wool instead of brains, so tired and spent was he with the strain.

Once, when again he looked at Ingunn, he saw that her eyelids had half-opened, and underneath he had a glimpse of her eyes, sightless.

In the first weeks after Ingunn's death Olav could not have said when he had slept. For slept he must have at times, since there was still life in him. Toward morning he felt as if the grey fog rolled within his head, leading his thoughts astray and deranging them. Then the fog settled, grey and dense, but never so that he escaped feeling the pressure of his burden even in his light morning doze, while his thoughts were busied with the same things deep down within him, and he was aware of every sound in the room and out of doors. He longed to be given real sleep for once—to sink into perfect darkness and forgetfulness. But as far as he was aware, it never happened that he enjoyed a deep sleep.

It was the thought of the children that kept him awake.

He knew that that night as he rode home to Ingunn's deathbed, he had formed a resolution. He had answered yea to God. "I will come, because Thou art my God and my All; I will fall at Thy feet, because I know that Thou longest to raise me up to Thee—"

But the children—it seemed as though both God and himself had forgotten them. Until Eirik asked—he would not send them away from Hestviken, haply?

He could not guess how the boy had come to think of such a thing. It could not have come about in any natural way.

And then he recalled Ingunn's last words, pondered over them: "—Do it not, Olav. Not go forth—'tis uncertain out yonder—"

Perhaps she had only spoken in a dream—dreaming that he was about to venture on to unsafe ice. But it might also be that, as she lay with her soul scarce in her body, she had learned what had befallen him that night. That both she and Eirik had had knowledge of it—and both had pleaded with him.

The children had none but himself to look to. Hallvard Steinfinnsson far away in the north at Frettastein was their nearest kinsman. And he could imagine how Hallvard would take it if he now came forward and accused himself of a secret murder twelve years old. His children would not be given a very cordial reception at their uncle's. And no doubt it would be revealed who Eirik was.

For that too he would be forced to confess, that he had tried to push forward a bastard heir, cheat his nearest kinsmen of the family manor in favour of a stranger.

If he carried out what he had resolved that night, he could see only one way of dealing with the children: Cecilia he would have to offer as an oblation to the sisterhood at Nonneseter, with her mother's inheritance, and Eirik to the Church or to the preaching friars.

The man shuddered to his very soul—was *that* the meaning? Was his race to die out with him because he had struck the crown from his own head by a dastard's deed? He *was* to be a childless man, because it is an ill thing that a dastard carry on the race? And those children he had begotten while he lived in rebellious outlawry might not carry on the line on which he had brought misfortune. A son he had, a single one, whom he could never adopt into his kin. And his only daughter was to be lost to the world behind the gates of a convent.

Eirik— At times he thought he was sorry for the boy. It would be hard for him to send the young lad back to the state of life from which he had once been willing to raise Ingunn's son, born in secret. Now and then he had thought he was fond of the boy too, in spite of all.

It was chiefly at night, when Eirik slept with him on the inside of the bed, that he thought, no, he could scarcely have the heart to thrust the child back into the lot to which he had been born.

At other times, when he heard the boy roistering among the house-carls, laughing as if he had already forgotten his grief at his mother's death, it seemed to Olav that Eirik was now the chief of his burdens; it was the boy above all who stood in the way, made it difficult for him to break through all that kept him from winning peace and relief for the sickness of his soul.

He noticed that he was drifting farther and farther away from the resolution he had made on the night before Ingunn's death. But he did not know whether he was being drawn back into the old slough against his will, or whether he had taken flight of himself, because after all he dared not come forward, when it came to the point.

One night Olav got up and went across to the house where Liv, the maid, lay with his daughter. With great trouble he succeeded in shaking her awake.

The girl lay huddled under the bedclothes, blinking with her little screwed-up pig's eyes, at once afraid and expectant, at the master who stood by her bed with a candle in his hand. Under his shaggy, unkempt, grizzling hair his face was furrowed and pale as ashes, the firm edge of his chin lost in a fog of stubble; he had nothing on but his linen beneath the long, black cloak, and his feet were thrust bare into his shoes.

Olav looked down at her and guessed that the maid must think he had come to let her share the fate of Torhild Björnsdatter without more ado—she had already moved as though to make room for him by her side. He gave a short, harsh laugh.

"Cecilia," he said—"I was dreaming so of her. There is nothing wrong with Cecilia?"

The girl turned aside the coverlet so that he could see the child. She lay asleep in the bend of her foster-mother's arm, with her little pink face well buried, half concealed by her own shining, silky curls.

Thε Snake Pit

Without more words Olav put down the candle, bent over, and lifted up his daughter. He wrapped her well in the folds of his cloak, blew out the light, and went out with his child.

Coming into the great room, he dropped his cloak on the floor, kicked off his shoes, and crept into bed with his daughter, who was still fast asleep against his chest.

At first all he felt was that sleep was just as far from him as before. But it was good to hold this tiny young creature in his arms. Her baby hair was soft as silk under his chin, with a sweet, fresh smell of sleep, and her little breath played over his chest and throat, warm and dewy. Silky of skin, her body was firm and plump and strong; the little knees that bored their way into her father's body were quite round. Olav allowed himself the luxury of loving his child as a miser indulges himself by taking out his hoard and handling it.

But by degrees the little maid acted like a hot stone. The warmth of the sleeping infant penetrated the father, soothed the throbbing, aching unrest in his heart; it flowed through his whole body and resolved its strain into a sweet, soft tiredness. He felt slumber settling down upon him, a blessing worth he knew not what. With his chin buried in Cecilia's soft, curly hair he sank into a deep sleep.

He was awakened by her howling wildly and furiously. The little maid was sitting up, half on his chest, roaring, as she rubbed her eyes with two small fists. On the inside of the bed Eirik sat up in surprise. Then he leaned over his father's chest, coaxing and trying to quiet his little sister.

Olav did not know what time of night it might be—the smoke-vent was closed; the little charcoal lamp standing on the edge of the hearth was still burning—it must be very early.

When her father took hold of the little one, she raged more violently than ever, hitting about with her little round fists and shrieking at the top of her voice. Then she swung round, threw herself upon her father, and tried to bite him, but could not get a proper hold of his thin cheek. Eirik was laughing boisterously.

Then she took to nipping Olav's worn eyelids between two of her nails—she pulled them out and pinched them, and this gave her so much amusement that she kept quiet—stopped screaming for a while as she punished her father all she could. After that she looked helplessly about her.

"Liv—where Liv?" she wailed loudly. "Bringlum!" she said in a tone of command.

That was her name for food, Eirik interpreted. Olav got out of bed, went into the closet, and returned with a thick slice of the best cheese, a bannock, and a cup of half-frozen milk.

While he revived the fire on the hearth, holding the cup of milk he was going to warm, Cecilia sat up, stared angrily at the strange man with her deep-blue kitten's eyes, and threw bits of bread at him. She gobbled up the slice of cheese till nothing was left but the crust. "Bringlum," she said as she threw the last of the cheese on the floor.

Olav went to fetch more food for his daughter. She ate all she was given, and when there was no more, she screamed again that she wanted to go to Liv.

When the milk was warm enough, Olav gave it to his daughter. She drank it to the last drop and then would not let go the cup, but hammered on the edge of the bed with it. It was a fine cup, made from a root, very delicately turned, so Olav took it from her. Cecilia caught hold of his hair with both hands and pulled it; then she got her claws into his face and scratched all down her father's cheeks with her sharp little nails. She clawed him to her heart's content—Eirik tumbled all over the bed in fits of laughter. He knew his sister better than her father did and could witness that Cecilia was the most spiteful little monster: "She has drawn blood from you, Father!"

Olav fetched more food, all the dainties he could find, but Cecilia seemed satisfied now; she refused all he offered her. She scarcely seemed to have the makings of a nun, this daughter of his.

Finally he had to let Eirik take the ill-tempered brat and carry her back to her foster-mother.

Then one night Olav awoke in black darkness—the charcoal lamp had gone out. He had slept—for the first time since Ingunn died he had had a deep, sound sleep. His gratitude made him strangely gentle and meek, for he felt born anew and healed of a long sickness, so good was it to wake without feeling tired.

He closed his eyes again, for the darkness was so dense that it seemed to press against them.—Then it dawned upon him that he had dreamed too, while he slept. He tried to put together the fragments of his dream—he had dreamed of Ingunn the whole time, and of sunshine—the glow of it still lingered in him.

He had dreamed that he and she were standing together in the little glen where the beck ran, due north of the houses at Frettastein. The ground still looked pale and bare with the withered, flattened grass of the year before, but here and there along the bank of the stream some glossy leaves, reddish brown and dark green, shot up among the dead grass. They were just by the white rock that filled the whole bed of the stream, so that the water swept over it and round the sides in a little cataract, swirling and gurgling in the pool below. They stood watching the bits of bark that floated round in the whirlpool. She was dressed in her old red gown—they were not yet grown up, he thought.

Throughout the whole dream he seemed to have been walking with Ingunn by the side of their beck. Olav thought they stood together under a great fir in the middle of the steep scree; this was farther down, where the stream ran at the bottom of a narrow ravine; great fallen rocks choked up the little river-bed, and on the rough slopes on both sides grew monk's-hood, lilies of the valley, and wild raspberries so thick that one could not see where to plant one's foot among the stones which gave way and rattled down. She was afraid of something, put out both hands to him with a little moan—and he felt oppressed himself. Above their heads he saw the narrow strip of sky over the glen—the clouds were gathering and threatening thunder.

Once they had been right down on the beach, where the stream runs out into Lake Mjösen. He saw the curve of the bay, strewed with sharp, dark-grey rocks under the cliff. The lake was dark and flecked with foam farther out. Ingunn and he had come there to borrow a boat, it seemed.

It must have been that journey long ago to Hamar that came back to him, he thought—his memories were confused and transposed, as they always are in dreams. But his dream had held the sweetness of their fresh young days, so that the savour of it still lingered in his mind.

In another way it was as though he had gone through his whole life with Ingunn again in his dream.

However that might be, he must have slept a whole night to have dreamed all this. It must soon be morning.

He stole out of bed in the darkness, found some clothes and put them on. He would go out and see how far the night was spent.

As he stepped out on the stone before the door, he saw the back of the Horse with its mane of trees at the highest point—it stood out black against the starry sky. Between the houses the yard was dark, but there was a faint light on the edge of the crags that closed the view toward the fiord, like moonlight on ice. Olav wondered—could it be possible?—the moon set before midnight now. But over the forest along Kverndal there was a faint uncertain glimmer of low, slanting moonbeams.

He could hardly believe it—that he had been so mistaken in the time. Hesitating, he slowly made his way westward through the yard and to the lookout rock. It was glazed and slippery to climb.

The half-moon touched the tree-tops on the other side—yellow at its setting. Under the dim, oblique beams the whole surface of the frozen earth was made rugged by the faint light and the pale shadows that scored it. The glazed surface of the rock beneath him still gleamed dimly. He saw that he had not slept more than three hours.

Again that light of the moon lying low over the brow of a hill made Olav think of the far-off night when he fled the country, an outlawed man. The sudden memory plunged him into an endless, weary despondency.

He thought upon his dream—it was so infinitely long since they had walked together along the beck, by the hillside path, down to the village. She was dead, it was only three weeks since—but so long ago.

He felt a clutching at his throat; the tears collected under his smarting eyelids as he stood gazing into the distance, where the moon was now but as a spark behind the forest. He wished he could have wept his fill now—he had not wept when she died, nor since. But the two or three times he had wept since he grew up, he had not been able to stop—furiously as he had striven to master himself, the fits of weeping had come again and again without its being in his power to hinder them. But tonight, when he wished he could weep on out here alone, without a soul to see him, it came to nothing but this strangling pain in his throat and a few solitary tears that flowed at long intervals and turned cold as ice as they slowly ran down his face.

When spring came—he thought he would go away somewhere

when spring came, the idea had just struck him. He could not face the summer at Hestviken.

The moon was quite gone, the light faded away over the distant forest. Olav turned and went back to the house.

As he was about to lie down he felt in the darkness that Eirik had stretched himself across the bed, taking up all the room between the wall and the outer board. All at once a disinclination to take hold of the boy came over him—whether it was that he shrank from disturbing his rest or felt he could not have him as a bedfellow tonight.

The south bed stood empty, since the bedclothes had been carried out and the straw burned on which she had died.

Olav went to the door of the closet and pushed it open—he was met by an icy air and a peculiar stale and frozen smell of cheese and salt fish; they kept food in the closet in winter and shut it up to make the outer room warmer; but the bed was always made up, in case they might have guests to lodge for the night.

Olav stood for a moment with his hand on the old doorpost. His fingers felt the carving that covered its surface—the snakes wreathed about the figure of Gunnar.

Then he went in—butting against tubs and barrels, till he found the bed. He crept into it and lay down—closed his eyes upon the darkness and gave himself up to face the night and sleeplessness.

Printed in the United States
by Baker & Taylor Publisher Services